THE LEGEND OF COLGAN TOOMEY

Dear Reader,
I personally placed this book in a Little Free Library in Dallas, Texas. I hope you enjoy it. Please contact me by any of the methods listed on the About the Author page and let me know what you think.

Peace, Love, & Pandas,
Dargan Ware

DARGAN WARE

The Legend of Colgan Toomey
By Dargan Ware

Interior Design: The Author's Mentor www.theauthorsmentor.com
Cover Graphic Design: Elizabeth E. Little, Hyliian.deviantart.com
Cover photos © 123rf.com, Denys Bilytskyi (path), Serezniy (man)

ISBN-13: 9781096681151
Also available in eBook

PUBLISHED IN THE UNITED STATES OF AMERICA

DEDICATION

This book is dedicated to my father, the late Christopher Watson Ware. I'm sure it's not perfect or brilliant or amazingly literary, but the only regret that I will ever have about this book is that he will never get to read it. I came dangerously close to never finishing it for that very reason. He would not have wanted that. So, this is for you, Dad.

TABLE OF CONTENTS

PROLOGUE

July 18, 1983, Kellyville, Alabama

To an Athlete Dying Young
By A.E. Housman

The time you won your town the race
We chaired you through the market-place;
Man and boy stood cheering by,
And home we brought you shoulder-high.

Today, the road all runners come,
Shoulder-high we bring you home,
And set you at your threshold down,
Townsman of a stiller town.

Smart lad, to slip betimes away
From fields where glory does not stay,
And early though the laurel grows
It withers quicker than the rose.

Eyes the shady night has shut
Cannot see the record cut,
And silence sounds no worse than cheers
After earth has stopped the ears.

Now you will not swell the rout
Of lads that wore their honours out,
Runners whom renown outran
And the name died before the man.

So set, before its echoes fade,
The fleet foot on the sill of shade,
And hold to the low lintel up
The still-defended challenge-cup.

And round that early-laurelled head
Will flock to gaze the strengthless dead,
And find unwithered on its curls
The garland briefer than a girl's.

I heard those words before they became a cliché. Before ESPN trotted them out every time some pro athlete did too much coke and blew up his heart, like it was a national tragedy that we'd never get to see him dunk a basketball again. I heard them in response to a real tragedy.

When I heard them, I was sitting on a makeshift stage along the side line at Panther stadium. It was south Alabama in July and, in the local lingo, it was hotter than two rats making whoopee in a wool sock. Especially since I was dressed in a suit for about the third time in my life. There was no way around it though; the stadium was the only place in town big enough for Colgan's funeral, and the only place he would have wanted it.

Coach Brooks read the poem without breaking up, but then he stood there bawling like a baby. I had never seen that man bat an eye or pause half a second in a speech (and he gave some doozy locker room pep talks), but that day it took him at least ten minutes before he started talking again. Everyone in the stadium, which was everyone who lived in Kellyville, Alabama plus a couple thousand, bawled right along with him.

Coach finally regained his composure and started talking about how Colgan was the best player he had ever coached – quick, decisive, always knew where everyone on the field was, and lethally fast on a straight sprint – the epitome of a perfect option quarterback.

He talked about the state semifinal game against Cherokee County our junior year. We got behind early because Colgan fumbled twice. Coach Brooks paused and looked around the stadium. "Then I made quite possibly the dumbest decision I ever made in my thirty plus years of coaching football. I benched Toomey. We played even for the rest of the first half and fell further behind in the third quarter; three plays into the fourth, the backup quarterback broke his leg." He looked at Matt Haynes, that backup quarterback, who had recently been hired as an assistant coach, sitting in the front row of the stands with his wife and baby. "With all due respect to Coach Haynes, that injury was the best thing that ever happened to us."

Colgan came back into the game with just over ten minutes left and Cherokee County leading Kellyville 35-10. The first play, Coach Brooks called a pitch to the running back. Colgan turned out from under center, faked the pitch, and went 60 yards around the other end for a touchdown. Coach Brooks wanted to bench him again, but we didn't have another quarterback on the roster. The benching had awakened something – Colgan stopped playing by the book and just let himself go. In that fourth quarter, Colgan ran for almost 200 yards and three touchdowns, and threw for two more. The legend of Colgan Toomey was born.

We scored to take the lead at 45-42 with less than a minute left, and we never trailed again during Colgan's high school career. In the state championship the next week, Colgan scored all seven of our touchdowns and made the front page of the *Birmingham News* sports section. The next season we went 14-0 and repeated as state champions, and it seemed like every college coach in the country found his way to Kellyville, Alabama.

Coach wanted us to know, though, that Colgan wasn't just the best football player he ever knew, he was also the best student and the best person. He ran down a list of accomplishments: Eagle Scout, perfect SAT score, National Merit finalist, graduating summa cum laude from the University of Texas, getting into one of the best medical schools in the country.

Then he started talking about charity work and how even though it made no sense at all that Colgan was dead, it made perfect sense that he died trying to help people, serving on a Doctors Without Borders mission in Guatemala during the summer after his first year of medical school.

I zoned out because I had heard it all before – hell, I wrote most of it in the obituary I sent to the damn newspaper. After coach finished, Principal Alexander got up and started talking about the same shit. I looked at the eulogy I had written, balled it up, and let it drop to the stage floor. There had to be something I could say to show that Colgan's life was more than his god-damned resumé.

Everything they were saying was all about how Colgan was different from everyone else, how he was better than all the other students at everything he touched. Colgan wouldn't have wanted to hear it. Besides, what made him special wasn't that he was different -- it was that he was just like me and Matt and a bunch of other rural Alabama kids, but somehow, he managed to be a saint and a scholar and all the rest, too.

My turn was coming up and I had no idea what I was going to say. How could I show that Colgan was a real person? He wasn't some damn robot that divided his time into perfect thirds of studying biology, running wind sprints, and feeding homeless people.

My hands were shaking as I stepped up to the microphone. "Colgan Toomey is my best friend. He's been my best friend since I remember having friends, since before kindergarten, since before I could say his name. Contrary to the apparent beliefs of the adults in his life, Colgan wasn't perfect. I remember when we were in sixth grade, Colgan's aunt Maureen came to visit from Chicago. Aunt Maureen came for four days or so and brought two cartons of cigarettes with her."

"I swear I never saw this woman when she wasn't smoking a cigarette. Anyway, I was staying over at Colgan's one night while she was there. After everyone else in the house had gone to bed, Colgan snuck into the guest room and grabbed a pack. We went out behind the well house on his property and each smoked two or three cigarettes that night. I don't think either one of us inhaled. People always say the first cig made them sick as a dog, but that didn't happen to us. What's funny is that neither one of us ever became regular smokers, but every time Aunt Maureen came to town, Colgan would grab a couple packs and maybe once a week I'd come over and have a smoke with him. I don't think our parents ever found out."

Part of me couldn't believe that I was standing here talking about this. Or that I was pretending to be completely oblivious to the fact that my mother (not to mention Maureen Toomey) was almost certainly in the audience somewhere. I just kept going, saying whatever came into my head and not worrying about what anyone in this town thought; they may have worshipped Colgan, but they didn't know him.

"In tenth grade, Colgan and I convinced his dad and my mom that there was a Scholar's Bowl tournament in Birmingham on the first day of deer season, and we had to be at school at 5:30 a.m. My mom was sleepy enough that she didn't pay any attention to the fact that nobody else was in the parking lot when she dropped us off. We had hidden our hunting gear in my Uncle Jud's boat and taken it the afternoon before and tied it up in the Tombigbee River in the woods behind the school. From there it was a short trip down the river to the National Wildlife Refuge and some pretty good hunting grounds. I don't think either one of us had any clue what we would do if we actually bagged a deer that day, but that particular problem did not arise."

Thoughts tumbled out as soon as they popped into my head now. "You know, the first three or four years of school we kept trying to set up his dad and my mom. It would be like a kids' movie; we wanted to be brothers, and we thought if we just kept setting up situations where our parents ran into each other, they would just automatically fall in love. Colgan used to set up the craziest schemes and get so mad when they didn't work."

"I remember when Mr. Toomey told him why it never worked. Well, he never let on that he knew we were trying to set him up, but he must have realized it. Colgan's dad came to him right after he decided to go to Texas instead of Bama; said he was proud of him for all the effort he put into the decision and that he made it on his own without listening to peer pressure. He said that he hoped Colgan always followed his own heart that way."

"Then he told Colgan that he had made a big decision of his own. Mr. Toomey had made the decision to enter the Church some years earlier, but it was time for Colgan to know. Colgan had long known the story of how his parents met. He was fond of telling it. He would set the tone like so: In 1961, a young man named Michael Toomey was studying to be a priest at Notre Dame. The youngest of seven children of Irish immigrants, South Bend was as far as he had ever been from his childhood neighborhood on the South Side of Chicago. But then he came South with the Freedom Riders, and he never made it back from Alabama . . . .

"You know what, this is probably a story that Brother Michael should tell."

I paused and scanned the crowd. Half of them were sitting there with their mouths open. Murmurs were beginning to roll through the bleachers. I didn't look behind me to see what Coach Brooks and the principal were doing.

"My point is just that when his dad told him he was joining the Church after Colgan started college, Colgan got pissed. He said his dad was abandoning him as soon as he was legally allowed to. He ranted at his Dad every day for a month. Mr. Toomey never got cross, never raised his voice, never even really argued with him. He just said that Colgan would understand someday."

"See, Colgan's dad was the one that was a saint. Colgan had so many more sides to him. He was a normal kid, he did the same things the rest of us did. He skipped class. He snuck out at night to see his girlfriend. He tried marijuana. He fought with his dad. But the amazing thing was that he managed to do all those things, make all the adults like him, attract every football coach from here to Canada, get perfect test scores, and still, of all the kids I've ever known, he's the only one who never, ever, not once that I saw, did anything cruel to another child."

My tears were flowing now. "It didn't matter to him if you were his go-to wide receiver or the guy at the end of the bench, he treated you exactly the same. Colgan wouldn't want the people who run this damn town up here talking about how wonderful he was, or what he accomplished. I think he'd like it better if everyone here just told the person next to him one thing he did to make them happy."

With that I put down the microphone and walked across the stage to Colgan's dad. I told him that what Colgan did that made me happier than anything in all the years of our long friendship was call me from Texas in my dorm room in Tuscaloosa every Sunday afternoon. I don't think I'd ever have made it through the first two years of college without his encouragement.

I turned from Michael Toomey and looked into the stands. A few people seemed to be taking what I said to heart and whispering to people next to them. Others were staring at me in shock. The next week in the *Kellyville Gazette*, a scathing letter to the editor accused me of speaking ill of the dead. The writer wondered if I was drunk and why Coach Brooks didn't throw me off the stage. I always wondered how many people in town shared that opinion.

CHAPTER 1

THE MONK

Ten years later, the day of Colgan's funeral was still permanently seared into my brain. Of all the people watching that day, there was one whose opinion I never doubted—Michael Toomey. As I headed up U.S. 72 into the southeast Tennessee hills to see him, I understood why Brother Michael had retreated from the world. The man had suffered more loss than any one person should ever have to deal with.

That story that I almost told at the funeral? Even though I said it was one that Brother Michael should tell, I have never actually heard him tell it. Colgan was the one that was always so proud of how his parents met. I could still hear him telling the story in that overly dramatic movie narrator voice.

Michael Toomey's parents left Donegal, in the northwest of Ireland, during the Troubles, the Irish Civil War that raged right after World War I and led to the splitting up of the country. They arrived in Chicago in 1920—here Colgan's voice would go all mysterious as he mentioned the possibility of shadowy connections to the Irish gangs that ran Chicago before Capone. I had a feeling he just added that part in, though Michael did once mention an Uncle Kevin who had run afoul of the law and ended up a long-term guest of the state of Illinois.

These thoughts almost made me miss the turnoff to the monastery. It was a narrow asphalt track with hemlocks hanging over each side, and the curves got sharper and sharper as it climbed away from the highway. I could almost see the religious significance as I rounded the last curve; the sunlight on the hilltop looked like a glowing halo at the end of the long tree tunnel.

The morning sunlight bathed the slender wooden chapel that thrust out from the squat stone monastery like a hand extended in greeting.

As soon as I emerged from the tree line, I could see Brother Michael standing on the steps of the chapel. A jet-black Benedictine habit covered him from head to toe, but he had pulled back the hood to reveal a set of shaggy red curls that had turned to silver on top but remained both as thick and as unruly as they had ever been. It made for a striking picture.

I had been coming here every year, twice a year, since Colgan's funeral. I always came up on the anniversary of the funeral and again on Colgan's birthday three days after Christmas. One year the snow was so bad that I pulled over halfway up the mountain and walked the rest of the way. Every other time I've gotten to the monastery by five minutes after nine. I knew Brother Michael would stand outside to greet me, and I didn't want to keep him waiting.

"Welcome, Peter! It's good to see you, my friend." Brother Michael's voice boomed out as soon as I got out of my car. I think he's the only person that's ever used my full first name since Colgan and I were seniors in high school.

I greeted him in return as I began climbing the stairs. At the top, I was enveloped in a bear hug that always felt like it was going to crush my spine. From a distance, one might think that Brother Michael fit the medieval stereotype of the fat jolly monk, but there was little fat on his six-foot-five frame. He had played basketball his first two years at Notre Dame, but then left the team to focus on his studies.

Brother Michael finally released me, then turned and gestured for me to walk in front of him. His long strides nonetheless quickly pulled ahead as we approached the tall wooden doors of the main chapel, and we each pulled open a door and entered the sacred space side by side. Our routine was well-established and never varied. We each lit a candle and carried it to the altar, where we knelt side by side.

It occurred to me that day that I had never been in a Catholic Church when Michael Toomey was not there. My mother was raised Church of Christ, which was about as far from Catholic as you could get in the spectrum of Christianity that exists in a small southern town. She took me to church sometimes, but I'd gone more often with Colgan and his dad. I never did convert though, probably just to spare Mama's feelings. Now the only time I went to church at all was when I visited her. She probably would rather see me convert. I glanced over at the man praying next to me and wondered at how he had come to epitomize an entire religion for me.

After we prayed, Brother Michael and I went on our customary walk around the monastery grounds. I was normally the primary subject of discussion on these walks – Michael just wanted to know how I was doing. Over the years, I'd shared virtually everything with him, job triumphs and stresses, dreams for the future, marriage, divorce. He always seemed to listen with an open mind, though I'm sure there were times I was being an awful sinner or a complete moron or both.

But today, I wanted to hear him talk about himself, something he never did. I wanted him to tell the story that Colgan had told so many times. He hemmed and hawed and said it was so long ago he hardly remembered, but I made it clear that I didn't believe him. Finally, we were standing by a bench under a huge sycamore tree. He sighed as he plopped down his large frame. "What do you want to know, exactly?"

"Colgan said you had never been South of Chicago until you came down here with the Freedom Riders."

He laughed, and then said, "Sit down, this may take awhile."

"Technically Notre Dame is a little south, as well as being east, of Chicago, but basically Colgan was right. There were groups of Freedom Riders who went before my group . . . . I don't remember now exactly when they started. But toward the end of the spring semester of my junior year, around May, I remember hearing about it. That was 1961, if I'm remembering right.

"I know Colgan told you I was at Notre Dame studying to be a priest, the way the youngest son of a big Irish family is supposed to do. I don't know whether my first interest in the priesthood was real, or whether it was just because they expected it of me, but I had started planning to go to school at Notre Dame and become a priest before I ever got out of elementary school. I never really thought about doing anything else.

"Anyhow, like I said, I had paid some attention to the Civil Rights movement and everything that was going on in the South, but I didn't follow it especially closely. My junior year I was in a class on the Church's modern relationship with other Christians and the ways priests could work together with other denominations or religions and not violate our principles. Today we might call it "Interfaith Outreach." My friends and I called it "how to talk to Prods," which was our word for Protestants. It was basically a fluff class, an easy A.

"Throughout the semester, this class featured several guest speakers. One of them was a Presbyterian minister who happened to be a chaplain at Yale University. His name was William Sloane Coffin, and he later became pretty famous as an anti-war activist. These guest lectures were usually pretty dry stuff, but Coffin was different—he was a little fella, but he was a firecracker.

“He came into class in a regular suit, even though I’m pretty sure Presbyterians wear vestments. I guess it was because he was a university chaplain and not a regular parish priest. Anyway, the primary reason I remember that suit is that five minutes into his talk he had stripped off his jacket and thrown it onto an empty desk. The look on Father Farris’s face was priceless. In fact, that look had started almost as soon as Coffin started talking. I’m not sure what our esteemed mentor expected, but the visitor began by saying ‘I don’t give a darn what Catholics believe. In fact, I’m not all that concerned about what Presbyterians believe either. I’m sure there are differences, and maybe they’re fascinating to people who think they know how many angels can dance on a pinhead. But what I care about is what you’re doing—what anyone who claims to be Christian should be doing. I want to put aside petty differences in theology, not to come to some sort of grand unifying bargain and all sit around and sing together. No! I want to put all those differences aside to get something done. A lot of somethings, actually. And you guys about to be going out to the parish level are the ones who have to help me do them.’

“I don’t think anyone in the room was exactly sure what we would help him do at that moment, but we were ready to get after it. To make a fairly long speech short, Coffin basically said Christians of all stripes had a duty to get involved in the Civil Rights Movement. He told stories about church leaders down south being beaten or killed for allowing Negroes (as we called our darker-skinned brethren then) to worship together with whites.

“He eventually got around to the freedom rides and told us about how a brave group of black and white individuals were about to head south on a bus together. They had been trained to relish non-violence, to take threats, and perhaps very real beatings, from those they encountered without fighting back. They knew they would be arrested. They knew they could be killed. I immediately wanted to join them.

“Apparently, though, the project had been going for some time and they had the group they wanted for the Freedom Ride. I talked to Rev. Coffin after class. I have no idea if there was a plan then for multiple rides, but he said there were a million other things that needed doing and I was surely smart enough to find them. Nonetheless, he took the address and phone number of my dorm room and said he’d contact me when other opportunities were available.

"I'll admit that I wasn't the world's best activist. I went around for about three weeks looking for organizations doing that kind of work around Notre Dame, and I even joined a couple of them. Then the semester got busier and finals started closing in, and I basically forgot about it.

"The first freedom rides happened right after the semester ended. I was supposed to stay in South Bend all summer and take classes. We got a week off between spring semester and the beginning of summer school. Since I didn't have any more finals to worry about, I got interested in Civil Rights again, and I spent that whole week in the library when the newspapers from around the country came in, reading everything I could find about what was going on in Alabama and Mississippi. Both the courage that the riders had not to fight back and the hatred and anger that they apparently provoked by doing nothing but sitting beside one another on a bus amazed me. I couldn't fathom the kind of person who would care so much about whether two complete strangers sat next to each other.

"Well, it wasn't too far into that summer that Reverend Coffin called me and said he was getting together another group of Freedom Riders. Now, at this point, two or three groups had already gone out. Coffin organized this new group in Chicago, and I went back and stayed at home while they trained us on absolute nonviolence and how to deal with the hatred that would be directed toward us as riders.

"The bus ride started in Charlotte, North Carolina and was scheduled to end in Mobile, Alabama. Policemen took us off the bus in Greenville, South Carolina, and again in Augusta, Georgia. They searched us all, hoping to be able to charge us with something other than violating segregation laws. No weapons or drugs were found, of course, and they put us back on the bus according to how they wanted us to sit. We moved again as soon as the bus got going.

"The next few stops were in smaller southern towns. Nothing happened at Milledgeville; we didn't get off the bus or see anyone protesting us. At Macon, there was a crowd outside, so the driver just kept going, because there was nobody on the bus but us. I may have slept through a stop or two, but it was after midnight by the time we reached Albany, Georgia. No one was there on account of the late hour, and they finally let us get off the bus, stretch our legs and get some food."

Brother Michael found it appropriate to do something similar at this juncture of the story, rising from the bench and slowly unfolding his long legs. Our walk took us into the woods on the grounds, and by the time he spoke again, I had begun to fear that I would not hear the rest of his story.

"I remember I had struck up a quick friendship with a young black man named Paul Conley from Baltimore, Maryland. Like me, Conley was studying for a career in the clergy, though he was a Baptist studying at Palmer Theological Seminary in Philadelphia. I am certain that, during the course of our trip, we discussed matters of some theological importance, but what I remember of our conversation centered on the relative merits of his Baltimore Colts and my Chicago Bears.

"At Albany we got candy bars and cigarettes out of the vending machines and enjoyed the relative coolness (actually it was still pretty damn hot) of the breezy night. We chatted and ate and smoked and then eventually got back on the bus. So far, our experience had been relatively enjoyable, and perhaps our tension had lessened somewhat. I'm sure all of us would have told you that danger was still both possible and likely, but we couldn't have known how close it really was.

"The next stop after Albany was in Dothan, Alabama. It was about two hours before sunrise, and I'm sure the driver was tired. I don't know if the group at Dothan had heard what happened at Macon, but the driver later said he never saw them until he had pulled off the highway and into the bus station parking lot.

"As soon as we stopped though, they materialized out of the darkness. There were probably twenty-five or so, not that many more than the fifteen of us. But we weren't about to fight back. Some of them had nightsticks and baseball bats. At first I assumed they just wanted to scare us, maybe give us a couple broken bones to remember them by.

"I have no idea whether anyone called the cops, or whether the cops watched, or whether the people beating us were the local cops. I know that they came on the bus, each grabbed one of us by the arm, and force-marched us out into the night. They then told us to lie face down in the parking lot.

"Paul was beside me. I knew this was going to be bad when he raised his head to look at our terrorizers and received a smashing, possibly killing blow from a baseball bat. The man who had swung it then put his knee in Paul's back and lifted his shoulders slamming his bloody face into the gravel of the parking lot over and over again.

"I could see all this to my left as someone was kicking me in the ribs from the right side, not too hard really, just kind of demonstrating his dominance over me. We were taught to be still, to take it, to try not to even scream out. Paul did that perfectly, but I couldn't. When his assailant let go of Paul's shoulders, my reaction, God help me, was involuntary. I reached out and touched my friend's face, subconsciously wanting to know if he was dead or alive. I have often wondered whether it was my actions that sealed his fate. Because when he twitched and grunted in response to my touch, the big man with the baseball bat stood over him again. "Haven't had enough yet, nigger?" he said, and brought down a blow that crushed Paul's skull.

"I screamed then, and, of course, they turned their attention to me. Perhaps that's what I wanted, but if so, I'd have done it before they killed Paul. I guess they thought they might actually get in trouble if they killed a white kid, so even though I pissed them off, they kept the baseball bats below the shoulders.

"They ran off when the sun came up. I was hurting, and I thought my left leg and a couple ribs might be broken, but I thought I was doing okay, all things considered. And really I was. Two men lost their lives that night, both young, strong black men who had their whole lives ahead of them, but were willing to lay them on the line to prove that they were real people, real Americans, just as good as you and me. The fact that I survived, and they didn't, made me that much more convinced of the righteousness of their cause, but it made me sad too, of course. I knew that I was no better than they, far from it probably, and it was the same prejudice and unfairness they fought that allowed me to live. How could I ever be glad that I had lived, knowing that? How could I find enjoyment or pleasure in life again? I won't say that I thought through all of that while I was lying in the gravel that morning, but I would end up having quite a bit of time in the hospital to lie by myself and think. With the help of Colgan's mother, and then Colgan, and even you, Peter, I learned to enjoy life again

"I don't know how long we lay in that parking lot before the ambulances showed up. I was more banged up than I initially thought and was fading in and out of consciousness. Nathan Morelstein, one of three Northside Chicago Jewish kids who had joined our ride, was the only one of the fourteen of us who was able to stand up. I assume he got the medics there. Someone gave me a shot and the next thing I remember I was waking up in the hospital with an angel hovering over me."

I could see a tear forming in Brother Michael's eye. His voice had been catching for a few minutes now. I reached out and put my hand on his arm, and he stopped and looked up. Our walk in the woods had come almost back to the building. Brother Michael had stopped walking just as the bells began pealing for lunch. None of the monks ever wore a watch, but something tells me he wasn't the only one that could do that. I marveled at his sense of time because I needed something to pull me out of the emotions of his story.

Brother Michael looked up at the building. "Ah yes, time for lunch. I fear we may have to take up the rest of this story at a later date."

CHAPTER 2

THE ANGEL

Before Colgan was born and I was diagnosed with breast cancer, Michael was much fonder of telling that story about waking up to the angel standing over him. I assume he's always believed it was me. I never had the heart to tell him it couldn't have been. I was just a candy striper, a volunteer, seventeen years old. I was never allowed in what they called the critical area (hospitals call it ICU now) where he was when he woke up. It must have been a real nurse.

But the way Michael told the story was so sweet that I had to let him believe it. Maybe he had to believe that it was an angel he was falling for, to be able to accept that God wanted him to change the course of his life and not become a priest. Or maybe we were just two sinful souls, and I tempted him away from the priesthood, but he was all too eager to fall with me.

Michael Toomey was the only man I ever loved. I don't have anything to compare it with, so I guess I shouldn't say that our love was more special than the crushes the other girls developed for patients or doctors or orderlies that summer. But it certainly felt special to me.

The first time I met Michael was when he was assigned to a regular room. At least some of the freedom riders' bags had been pulled aside at the bus station and saved for them. One of the bags had Michael's name on it, and I was instructed to take it to him.

I walked into the room, and he leaned up on one elbow and said, "Hey, you!" like he knew exactly who I was. He looked me right in the face with the deepest green eyes I'd ever seen, and I just stopped and turned to mush right there. I have no idea how long it took me to speak, but I finally said "Hello, Mr. Toomey."

"You can call me Michael, hon," he said, in an accent that seemed as foreign to me as if he'd been speaking Gaelic. Maybe it came from the concrete jungle of the south side of Chicago, but when I heard it, I saw the green hills and stone walls of my great-grandmother's stories about Ireland. I just stood there and waited for him to talk again.

He was just as content to sit there and look at me I think, but finally he said, "what's your name, sweetheart?"

"Sarah Anne Sullivan, sir."

He laughed. I wasn't sure why he laughed right then, but I knew immediately that I was willing to do just about anything to hear that laugh as often as possible.

The next day I came in an hour early and just sat in his room and talked about everything that had ever happened in my life. I think they probably did some kind of confession practice or something in priest school that taught him to listen so well. We could talk about literally anything, and he always seemed genuinely and intensely interested in everything I said. By midsummer we were talking that way two or three hours a day.

I was sure that Michael would be going back to Notre Dame at the end of the summer until the morning he was discharged from the hospital. I don't even know whether he made the decision before that day. When he was leaving, I'm pretty sure the taxi driver thought he would be taking him to the bus station until he got in and asked him for a reasonably priced hotel. Right before that he had given me a note. It said simply, "I think I am in love with you. I would like to take you to dinner Friday night. I will contact the hospital with the phone number of the hotel where I am staying."

I had felt like I was in love with him for weeks, and I thought I had let him know it, so I was a little taken aback by the note at first. But that was Michael's way. He wasn't particularly poetic or romantic, but he was honest and straightforward and, unlike a lot of guys, he actually was capable of describing his feelings in most situations. He also never took anything for granted, never assumed my feelings. He let me make up my own mind, even though he should have known I would follow him on anything.

My heart did flips when, about an hour later, I was paged over the intercom to come to the front desk. The woman said I had a message. It was simple, straightforward, Michael again. It just had a phone number, followed by "call me when you can."

My father forbade me from going on a date with him. I was instructed to call Michael up and tell him that I would not be seeing him again, and, God forgive me, I did, with my father standing right beside me.

Michael answered the phone and I started crying. I said, "I won't be able to see you again, Michael." He didn't seem to miss a beat; "You don't really believe that Sarah Anne, and neither do I. But I understand you have to tell me. Have a good night and know that I love you."

Then he hung up. I was bawling like a baby and he hung up on me. I remember wondering what the hell he meant. Of course I believed it. I was seventeen years old. How could I defy my father in this or anything else? My dad was on the city council; he was on the board at the bank. He probably could have run the life of any kid at my high school, much less his own daughter. What was Michael - hell what was *love* - against that?

But Michael had sounded so assured. How could he be so certain that he would see me again? Part of me said it was just because he didn't know my Dad (though I had told him all the details of my life). But there was something in his voice that made me believe him. Maybe it was just naiveté and young love, but I knew there was something special about that man.

Michael had hung up the phone with me and immediately looked up my father's address. He dressed in his best suit and tie and walked the twelve blocks from the hotel, despite the fact that he still wore braces on both legs. He arrived at our door about 45 minutes after the call. I was lying in my room feeling sorry for myself when I heard the doorbell ring. I couldn't imagine who it would be, but I cracked my bedroom door to listen to my dad answer it.

"Can I help you?" said Dad, barely cracking the door.

The voice behind the door literally made me fall to the floor. "Mr. Sullivan, my name is Michael Toomey, and I am here to apologize. I will not ask to speak to your daughter, nor do I have any right to, but I hope you will do me the kindness of allowing me to speak to you in private. I need some advice, sir."

To my utter shock, my dad opened the door the rest of the way. He stood there for a few moments looking Michael up and down and then finally said, "By all means, come in."

Dad conducted Michael into his study and the two of them were in there for at least an hour. I never did get the full story of what happened in that room. Michael came out first, with Dad following him. They stopped in the foyer and shook hands, and my love went out into the night. I opened my door and tried to talk to Dad, but he just said, "Good night, Sarah Anne. Go to bed."

The next day was Thursday. I tried to ask my Dad again about Michael, but he just told me to have a good day volunteering at the hospital as he hurried off to the bank. I spent all day alternating between depression and hope, between going over every conversation I'd ever had with Michael and trying not to think about him at all.

By the time I got home I was so emotionally exhausted that I went to my room to lie down. But when my father came home from the bank that evening, Michael was with him. My jaw almost hit the floor when I opened my door and saw him in the foyer. I quickly shut the door and ran to fix my hair. I stood there staring at my disheveled face in the mirror, my heart pounding so hard I could barely lift the brush above my shoulders.

My mother knocked on the door and stated in her sing-song voice: "Sarah Anne, darling, your father's home and supper is ready." She didn't even mention Michael. "C-coming mother," I stammered, trying to catch my breath. I was in such shock that I don't think I ever did remember to fuss at Michael for coming over unannounced.

Apparently, my father had decided that if Michael was going to have dinner with me, he was going to be there. The conversation that night was the most adult that my seventeen-year-old self had ever heard. I knew that my dad was considered a "racial liberal" by the standards of Dothan, Alabama. In my mind and experience, that meant that black folks should be allowed to vote and shouldn't get beaten up by the cops. I never dreamed that this man of law and order would find something to admire in open acts of defiance like those of the Freedom Riders. But if Michael had told him his story the night before, it had definitely impressed Dad, and they continued to talk about race and politics at dinner.

I got a few minutes on the porch with Michael as he was leaving. I asked him what he told my Dad, and he just laughed. "I just figured someone who could create a creature as lovely as you was deserving of my respect, and I treated him as such. I told him all about why I came down here, and told him that I know it sounded crazy, but I felt like God was calling me to stay down here and face the people that did this to me and bring them to understanding."

I buried my face in his chest so he couldn't see my tears. I thought about how silly I had always been, thinking about how my dream guy looked or danced or something. Instead of a heart-throb, God had sent me a saint. Michael was here to show me what I was supposed to focus on, to be someone I could make a truly important life with. At that moment, I honestly thought anything in the world was possible.

Michael kissed me on the forehead and said he would see me the next evening. I floated back up the stairs, or maybe slid right up the bannister like Mary Poppins. Lots of people experience that first moment, but I don't think I ever came down from that high. Maybe I'm looking back with rose-colored glasses, but I just don't remember ever doubting Michael. Maybe I was a little naïve, and maybe anybody else in the world would have let me down, but Michael Toomey never did.

But it was my Dad's response that really surprised the heck out of me. For him to tolerate Michael was my wildest dream. I never even let myself think he would actually like Michael, but he honestly seemed to love him as much as I did. Dad had always done just about anything for his family, and, overnight, that included Michael. But before, it had always been on Dad's terms. Michael not only expanded that world but seemed to change the way Dad looked at it.

At dinner Friday night, Dad announced that we would all be going to Troy on Saturday afternoon to look at the college. Michael said that he needed to find a place to transfer to from Notre Dame and Troy seemed like the obvious choice. I was in such a happy haze over the fact that Michael would really be staying that I didn't even stop to think about what these plans meant for me.

The hospital was more than just a convenient place to volunteer. I had always been fascinated by the human body and dreamed of studying medicine and nursing. My dad had never taken an interest in these particular dreams or listened to plans I tried to make about what I would do after high school.

I thought I had hardly mentioned this to Michael either, but when we went to Troy, he insisted that we start at the Nursing School. Although the University wasn't officially open, Daddy had arranged for someone from the recruiting office to give us a campus tour. I remember being mesmerized by the medical posters, models, and charts in the nursing classrooms. I could have stayed in there all day.

All the plans about school for me changed when Colgan came along of course, but I never regretted it. I got a few months to enjoy something I had dreamed of, and then I moved on to a higher calling.

The rest of that summer was a complete whirlwind. In a month and a half, we got ourselves enrolled (or transferred), planned a wedding, and even snuck in a four-day honeymoon to Chicago. I have only ever told a couple of people this story – and I'm not sure either of them believed it. It was too much of a fairy tale. Ridiculous, crazy love that not only swept over us but lifted my whole family like a tidal wave. Yes, it was crazy, but I still feel it now; I was one of the lucky ones who experienced heaven early, a glimpse of the perfect love that God holds out for everyone, and somehow teaches to a precious few like Michael to share with the rest of creation.

CHAPTER 3

THE BEST FRIEND

I realize that in telling you about Colgan and his dad, I haven't said much at all about me. My name is Peter Judson Campbell, but I've gone by PJ my whole life, most of which has been spent in Alabama.

Some would say I've also been disabled my whole life, though I see what people who have real problems go through and I laugh at anyone who thinks I'm disabled. One of my legs is just shorter than the other, that's all. It apparently all happened in the womb, something about the way the ligaments developed in my right ankle. Sure, it kept me from playing football or other sports, but it's never hindered any basic life function.

I was born in Mobile, but I don't remember living there. When I was 9 months old, my father went to the store for some beer and never came back. At least that's the way my mom tells it. She also says that she's glad he left, so I'm pretty sure she had an inkling the honeymoon stage was over.

After he left, Dad apparently got a job working on freighter ships sailing out of Mobile. Before I was old enough to remember anything about it, he got swept overboard in a gale and was lost at sea. Some kind of federal maritime insurance program sent me a little bit of money every month after that. There were months when that was the only way Mom and I got by, so I was always thankful to my Dad for signing up for it.

My mother had grown up in Kellyville, so we left Mobile and headed inland before I even got to go to the beach. I can remember living in my grandmother's two-story house on Main Street, but just in bits and pieces. I was three when she sold the house to move to a retirement village in Florida. I don't know how much she sold it for, but it's still one of the nicest homes in town.

Granny gave Mom a month's notice and enough of the sales proceeds for about three months' rent then hit the road. Mom never said a cross word about her, though. Mom tried and tried to save up the money to go down to Winter Haven and see her, but by the time we did, I was in third grade, and Granny didn't know who we were anymore.

Mom's brother Judson came back to Kellyville a couple years later, after his wife left him for his law partner. He built a house down by the river, and we assumed he sat in there and counted his money while he was drinking himself to death. Uncle Jud did let us use his boat occasionally, though, and his presence made me ever-thankful that Mom never tried to get anyone to call me Jud.

I didn't know it until years later, but the rental house we moved into had actually been Colgan's from birth until about two. After Colgan's mom died, Michael Toomey couldn't bear to live there anymore, so he bought a house a couple blocks over and rented out the other one. I have no idea what he charged my mother for rent, but I would bet a lot more than a month's rent that it wasn't anywhere near market value.

Looking back on it, I'm not sure Colgan and I were really that far off when we tried to set up his Dad and my mom. I think Michael really cared about her as a person; he just knew he had been called to the church, and he wasn't going to get sidetracked again. He's also always been the closest thing I had to a dad. Even before Colgan and I started going to school, I think I spent more time in Colgan's house than I did in my own.

Michael Toomey was one of those people that everyone in town knew at some level and no one would speak ill of, but few people ever got really close to him. He had his son's intelligence and goodness, and much of his talent, but he lacked the easy charm and charisma that Colgan had in spades. Everybody respected Michael Toomey, but few loved him. Colgan was a ball of physical and intellectual energy who instantly charged up everyone who came into contact with him. Michael was, and to some extent still is, a brilliant but distant star whose light takes time to cross space and reach into another's life.

As we grew up, I wondered if Colgan's brilliance would grow more distant over time, and maybe it would have if he had lived. Or maybe Michael had just been hurt too much to fully open up to anyone. Maybe he felt some guilt that he had abandoned the Church to which he had pledged himself, and maybe he was angry because he thought God had punished him for it by taking away the love of his life.

Still, he was hardly a bitter or stern man. Sometimes he was even jovial—but his joy always seemed to be derived from his son's happiness, or sometimes mine. It was never fully internal. Like his son, I never saw him be intentionally mean to anyone. I don't think he was capable of active unkindness.

It happened years before Colgan and I were fully conscious of what was going on, but there was a time when Michael Toomey was almost certainly the only man in Kellyville that both black and white citizens would speak to. Unlike in many southern towns, the big argument in our town wasn't about school desegregation. That happened before we moved there, and, for Alabama, I'd always thought it wasn't particularly contentious, possibly because everyone knew the town really couldn't afford to run two schools and separate but equal was hurting both races. In later years, I realized I was probably extremely naïve to think that there wasn't a lot of pain and suffering that accompanied the integration of Kellyville's public schools. It just wasn't something I knew anything about.

Instead, Kellyville's public racial crucible was located where almost everything in Kellyville got its start: the paper mill. Michael worked as a manager there, and often found himself the liaison between the mostly black work force and the lily-white upper management.

On a hot August Thursday in about 1970, an African-American maintenance man named Thomas Day was killed after getting his arm stuck in a pinch point between two giant rollers on some kind of paper-stretching machine. The black workers blamed management. They said that maintenance men got in trouble if they turned off the machine to clear jams, but that it was extremely unsafe to try to clear them while it was still running, especially in the heat of summer when every surface in the plant was slicker than snot with sweat.

The management paid Tom's wife $100.00 to make sure he got a proper Christian burial, and they expected everything to go on as before. But Tom Day wasn't just another Negro plant hand. He might have been the most famous man in Kellyville at the time, despite the fact that most white residents hadn't heard of him.

In some ways, Tom's life was a bit like Colgan's might have been if he had lived out his athletic dreams and eventually come back to Kellyville. Tom was the best student and best athlete they'd seen at the Negro school and had played every sport there was to play there. Like Colgan, he played football, but baseball was his true love. They said nobody in the state touched his fastball for two seasons when he was in high school. He was pitching for the Birmingham Black Barons before he even turned eighteen, and from then until he was traded to the Kansas City Monarchs, he was their most popular player.

Tom had a unique pitching style. He threw the ball to the plate just like he threw it to first from shortstop, which had been his first position. No windup at all. Just put the ball up by his ear and let it fly on arm strength alone. His stuff was still just as good as anybody out there, majors or Negro leagues.

Then one day he blew out his shoulder and lost all idea of what to do with his life. He spent ten years in KC drunk and feeling sorry for himself, but eventually, as these stories go, the prodigal son returned to the little Southern town. For another five years, he was pissed the town didn't kill the fatted calf for him. When he started at the plant, he was still drunk half the time and only kept his job because all the other workers covered for their childhood hero.

But one night, Tom had his come to Jesus moment. He said it happened out on Highway 18, south of town. He was coming back from the beach, half-lit as always. For the rest of his life he swore up and down that there was a man in a white robe standing in the middle of the road as he came around a curve. He swerved into the ditch and slammed into a tree. Everyone who saw the car couldn't believe he lived. But Tom walked away without a scratch. And he never touched another drop of booze.

It didn't take long after that before he was preaching at the Kellyville AME Church once a month. Then a few years after that, maybe two or three years before he was killed, the Church burned down. They said it got struck by lightning, but there were some who had their doubts. Anyway, Tom used the rest of his savings and some help from friends from his baseball days to pay for the rebuilding of the Church.

So by the time he died, Thomas Day was not only the most famous but easily the most popular man in the black community of Kellyville. When the paper company just expected everything to go on as normal, they were sorely mistaken. Tom had died on a Thursday afternoon, and his funeral was on Sunday. Monday morning, everyone showed up as usual, but a group had written a petition to management asking for certain safety controls. No extra money, no better conditions, just safety.

Unfortunately for the paper company, the manager to whom they presented the petition wasn't Michael Toomey. His name was Ray Watson and he took the petition, laughed at the man who gave it to him, and balled it up and threw it at him. The next day, none of the black workers showed up. The day after that they set up a picket line.

I'm pretty sure that if there had been enough people in Kellyville to replace the striking workers, the company would have just fired everyone. As it was, they sent out notices that everyone was expected to be there the next day and that people in certain departments would eventually be replaced and fired if they didn't show up. The company threatened to shut down the plant and basically kill the town if those workers didn't come in.

The attempt to divide the workers backfired in a hurry. The next day, the entire workforce showed up, but they weren't there to work. Not a single black worker was willing to cross the picket line, and they weren't about to let any of the whites into the plant without a fight. The paper company tried to get the Kellyville PD to force their way through, but Chief Morgan was way too smart to take on 200 strikers with his seven-man force.

The next step for management was to ask the governor for the National Guard. It took two days, but they showed up and formed a perimeter around the plant. This meant that there were basically two lines of armed men on opposite sides of Highway 18. Violence seemed inevitable. Some in town even relished the idea of it.

Michael Toomey was the operations manager at the plant, essentially third in command in the management structure. He later told me that he held his tongue when the Plant Manger asked for the National Guard, because he knew that the order came directly from the corporate headquarters in Atlanta. I remember him telling Colgan and me about it years later.

"Paul Henson, the plant manager, wasn't a bad man, and he wasn't even particularly against the rights of black folks, but he was a company man through and through. He was exactly the kind of man the corporate leaders wanted running the plant, because he genuinely believed that what was good for Georgia Pacific was good for everyone that worked there. His myopic obsession with making sure the plant hit its production targets and such was part of what led to Tom Day's death in the first place, but even the loss of life and the workers' reaction to it couldn't shake his focus."

Because he was convinced that talking to the other members of management would be fruitless, Michael chose to go directly to the black workers. He went to the AME church the day after the National Guard arrived, and met with the preacher, Preston Miller. Brother Miller had himself retired from the plant, and he understood the concerns of the workers. He laid out their specific safety demands while Michael took notes, but he also told Michael that probably the most important thing he could do was listen. He appreciated Michael listening to him, but that wasn't enough;

the regular workers had to feel like someone was listening to them. There was already a meeting scheduled for the next night, and it would mean a lot if Michael would be there.

Michael knew that there was a pretty good chance he could lose his job if he went to the meeting, but he later told me that he never had a second thought about it. After Mr. Henson had left for the night, he wrote up a chart that showed Paul how much the plant was losing in the strike, but he couldn't leave it at that, so he also wrote an impassioned note telling him about everything that had happened in Dothan several years earlier. Michael said he knew that nobody he worked with at Georgia Pacific was like the people who beat him up that night, and he didn't want the company to be known for that sort of thing.

Michael left his explanation on Paul's desk and headed to the AME church. He took Reverend Miller's advice and spent most of his time there listening. The maintenance men got up and told their stories in turn. When they had finished, Michael got up and said, "Do you guys (he never did quite pick up y'all) still have that list of requests?"

When it was produced, he said "Looks reasonable to me. What should we add to it?" He then spent another hour helping them come up with ideas to improve the plant. Occasionally he would gently guide them away from proposals that were truly unworkable or prohibitively expensive, but for the most part he worked together with them to craft good solutions. He said he learned more about how the plant actually worked that night than he had in his first five years there.

Anyone but Michael Toomey would have come off as a meddling Yankee do-gooder to both the black plant hands and the white management. They probably would have gotten fired for their trouble, too. I've heard people on both sides of town say they still don't know how he did it. Everyone just assumed that the best possible outcome was a long, tense standoff that bankrupted a third of the folks in town and nearly ran off the biggest employer in the county. The more likely scenario was that violence would erupt in a day or two, and Kellyville would go down in history as worse than Selma, Montgomery, and Birmingham.

Somehow Michael made both sides agree to things they didn't really want to do, and they came out of it still pretty darn resentful of each other but seeing Michael Toomey as some kind of messiah. The whole thing was over 24 hours after Michael went to the meeting at the church. Four years later, when Paul Henson retired, they offered Michael his job. I wish I could have seen the look on that company man from Atlanta's face when his up-

and-coming star executive told him he couldn't take the promotion because he planned on becoming a monk when his kid went to college.

I guess I still haven't told you much about me, with all the focus on Michael Toomey. But he was more than just the father I never had. He was a larger-than-life honest-to-goodness home town hero. I can't talk about him without sounding like a Hallmark card or a hagiography. Hell, I can't even *think* about my own childhood without him and Colgan taking the center roles. Even my mom was just a supporting player; they were the stars.

CHAPTER 4

THE BEAR

I was the head coach at the University of Alabama for about 25 years, I reckon, starting in 1958. During that whole time, I'd have to say that Colgan Toomey was the best in-state player I didn't sign. If I could change that, I would, even though he blew out his knee at Texas, and we ended up winning two national championships with the players we actually did get around the same time. I'd change it not because of the football player he was, but because of the kind of kid he was and the way his recruitment happened.

I think it was sometime right after the end of the regular season in '76 or '77. A couple of my assistants came in chirping about some kid from one of the little paper-mill towns south of Tuscaloosa. They said he scored like five touchdowns in a quarter in a small-school playoff game. I think Dee Powell was about to cream himself right there in my office; he talked about this kid like he was the second coming of Christ himself, or at least the best option quarterback the world had ever seen.

"Guys, you're telling me about one damn game. This kid's from Podunk high. We already got that Shealy boy coming from a real high school. He's a damn good option QB himself unless you guys were lying to me last week."

Powell didn't miss a beat. "Shealy's good no doubt. This kid's a damn sight better."

"It's single A competition, Dee. You could play quarterback for some of these teams. [Dee Powell had been an offensive guard for me at Texas A&M.] Listen, does this kid play both ways?"

My brilliant staff all looked at each other. Some grad assistant finally piped up. “He’s a safety. He’s actually intercepted more balls than he’s thrown interceptions.”

“Glad to see someone was paying attention. If you guys are so all-fire sure that he’s got Bama talent, offer him at safety. I don’t think we have to worry about anybody else finding their way down to Jellytown or wherever the hell you said he is.”

“Kellyville” said that same grad student. Paying attention is one thing, but some people just can’t keep their mouth shut. No matter, though, that kid didn’t coach long before he started working at some new all-sports-all-the-time network and getting paid to run his mouth.

I know that, sometimes, my staff was afraid to tell me I was wrong. I hated that shit, so they would never admit it to me, but I knew it was true. I don’t know if this was one of those times or not. It really is hard to translate one amazing game at a small high school into knowing someone will succeed in college, but even before the next season started, I began to realize Colgan Toomey was something special.

The new coach at Arkansas, fella named Holtz, called me in May and asked if I’d have lunch with him in Tuscaloosa one afternoon. This kinda thing was more common in the old days, but coaches still get together for friendly chats sometimes. I had a bit of a soft spot for Arkansas since I was born in the state, and I hoped this new guy would do well there, so I agreed to the lunch.

Holtz was friendly enough, though he went off on all sorts of random political and cultural tangents that I really didn’t give a shit about. At least he didn’t lecture me about having a couple bourbon and cokes with lunch, though he seemed to want to.

Eventually in this long and random discussion, I asked him what the hell he was doing in Tuscaloosa. He said he was on his way down to Kellyville to see a prospect. I wracked my brain trying to remember where I had heard of Kellyville, I knew it was in there somewhere. Luckily, Holtz wasn’t exactly a great poker player. When I nodded and acted like I knew exactly why he was going there, he said “That Toomey kid is something else, isn’t he? I mean I realize you’ll probably end up getting him, but I had to at least throw my hat in the ring.”

I kept up the chit-chat, but I was slowly putting it together that I had been wrong about this kid, or at least about the fact that other coaches would be unlikely to find him.

After lunch I stormed back to the office and called up the grad student who thought he knew everything about Toomey. It turned out there was a damn good reason other coaches were finding out about Toomey, and it was the same reason my staff had found out about him. They didn't tell me (and I'll be honest, I didn't ask) where they got the film of superkid scoring five touchdowns in a quarter.

When I told the grad student I wanted to see the film we had of the wunderkind from Kellyville, he lit up like a Christmas tree. He scuttled off down the hall and came back with four 8-millimeter reels. It turned out that Toomey had some friend who thought he was gonna be the next Alfred Hitchcock. The kid had filmed and edited that game into a surprisingly professional highlight reel, complete with soundtrack. He had been doing the same thing while Toomey worked out all summer, sending reels all over the country.

The grad student wanted to show me the amazing five-touchdown quarter, but I preferred to start with one of the workout reels. Let's see how serious this kid is – he can't control his high school competition, but he could control his workout.

Ten minutes after I put the film on, I was ready to pick my jaw up off the floor and drive to Kellyville myself. I also wanted to kill my staff. Nobody told me the kid was 6 foot 6, for one thing. On top of that, he had to be about 220, maybe bigger. You just don't see a kid that size move with the fluid grace that Toomey had. I had joked about Dee Powell playing quarterback for some of these little schools, but this kid might have been bigger than Dee was when he got to Texas A&M, and, unlike Dee, he was the fastest kid on the field most of the time.

He had a group of ten or twelve kids practicing with him on the tape. There wasn't but maybe one other of them who looked like a real college prospect, but all of them were black, and most of them were pretty fast. Toomey was faster than any of them, both on a dead sprint and cutting around obstacles. You just don't see a kid that size move like that. (Yeah, I know I said that before.)

The kid was a freak of nature – at one point on the tape, he did nine non-stop one-handed pullups and then dropped straight to push-ups with the same arm. He did passing drills and ran option plays, but it was the sheer display of physical prowess that had me gaping.

Before I went to see Toomey, the last time I did a first visit myself was about my second or third year at Bama. That was only because the whole staff happened to be out of town and there was a defensive tackle at

Tuscaloosa County High that I wanted to take a look at. I don't remember whether he turned out to be any good or even whether he came to Bama or not, but I made first visits fairly often back then. This was different. If I was gonna drive three hours to the middle of nowhere to see this kid, then by God I was going to get him.

I called up the high school coach at Kellyville, and once he got over the fact that after ten years of coaching he had finally had Bama call about one of his players, he said, "Well, I imagine you'll be wanting to talk to P.J."

I almost asked who P.J. was, but it didn't really matter – the coach knew I wanted to set up a visit with Toomey, and I supposed P.J. would take care of that. Coach Brooks gave me the number and thanked me a little too much for calling him.

I expected P.J. to be either an assistant coach or a secretary. When I called the number, a woman who turned out to be P.J.'s mom answered and said that he was "over at Colgan's." It turned out he was our budding film-maker; apparently, he was running his friend's recruiting process as well. I left my number and told her that Coach Bryant from Alabama called. She let out a little gasp and said, "Oh yes sir I will tell him." I wondered what P.J.'s reaction would be when he heard – he'd probably wonder what the hell took me so long.

P.J. didn't call me back before I left that afternoon, and I started to get antsy. But honestly, I told myself, what the hell was I thinking? This was just one kid, and he lived in my backyard. He needed me more than I needed him, and if his buddy didn't call me back, the momma would. I still didn't sleep good that night.

P.J. didn't call until about 3:30 the next afternoon. Of course, he didn't, it was less than a month after the college semester ended, he was probably still in school all day. That bit of logic didn't cross my mind as I stewed in my office and snapped at my staff all day. When the call got transferred to me, I picked it up on the first ring, which almost never happened.

P.J. was all business. "Coach," he said, "Colgan's lived in Alabama his whole life. He's always been a Crimson Tide fan. He wants to show you what he can do. We have a couple of options." I wanted to chuckle, but I let him keep going.

"This Saturday we have Coach Bowden from Florida State, Coach Devine from Notre Dame and a couple of assistants from Oklahoma and Georgia Tech. They're all coming to our high school stadium at 10 o'clock. You're welcome to come down and join them. But, because we do feel a connection to Bama, we'd like to invite you to come down the following Monday and let Colgan do a special workout just for you, and of course anybody you want to bring down from Tuscaloosa."

Well, I could hardly turn down an offer like that, so I agreed to meet P.J. and Colgan at Kellyville's stadium on Monday morning. I called in the grad student and told him he was driving me to Kellyville. I said we'd be going down Sunday night and spending the night and meeting the Toomey kid Monday. I decided not to take anyone else on the staff.

I remember the look on the kid's face that Friday afternoon. After calling everyone he could find in the general area, he had determined that the nearest hotel of any kind was the Highway 43 Motor Lodge, thirty-four miles away in Thomasville. He had been warned against staying there, however, and thus recommended the Holiday Inn in Waynesboro, Mississippi, which was about 40 miles away.

"You mean we have to go into *Mississippi* to get a decent hotel room near this place?"

"It appears so, sir," he stammered.

I laughed out loud. "Well, okay then. We'll go to Mississippi."

In my years of recruiting and coaching young men, I met a lot of extraordinary kids. Both P.J. Campbell and Colgan Toomey are near the top of that list. When we arrived at Kellyville's stadium about ten minutes before ten, the two of them were standing out front at the head of two lines of high school football players ready to run whatever drills we wanted to see. I have no idea how long they had been standing there.

Colgan stepped forward and introduced himself, then P.J., then each of the kids that was there working out with him. Here he was basically at the center of the world, with every college football coach in the country coming to see him. Most of the kids I met, which usually happened after they had already committed to come play for me, were so excited they were virtually tripping over themselves. Not only was Toomey perfectly calm and collected, but he was more interested in making sure his friends were properly introduced than in showing off himself. Yet, he was also showing me that he was the unquestioned leader of this group. I could see it in the eyes of each kid I shook hands with. They would go to war for Colgan Toomey with no questions asked.

I let Toomey run through some drills for me, though I had seen all I needed to know I wanted this kid to be my quarterback for the next four years. I let the grad student teach the group a couple of plays, and honestly had a little fun trying to coach up the other kids to play a little touch defense against them. There were probably NCAA rules against all this stuff, but it wasn't enforced very much back then.

After a couple of hours, I called everyone in for a huddle and thanked them for coming out and showing me what they could do. I told them they were all clearly good kids and I'd have them all on my team at Bama if I could.

We then asked Colgan and P.J. if there was someplace nearby to have lunch. P.J. laughed and said, "My Mom runs the best diner in town, and she's expecting us." I assume the place was also the only diner in town. P.J. gave us directions and said he and Colgan would change clothes and meet us. The grad student and I watched them walk away side by side, the six-foot-six athletic specimen and the chubby crippled kid. He made a good point when he said, "If we want Toomey, we should make P.J. our film manager." Even though we didn't end up getting Toomey, P.J. Campbell actually was our film manager for five years, and he did a hell of a job of it.

We had lunch with the kids, which Colgan insisted he pay for. (I jokingly said I didn't know if there was an NCAA rule against the recruit buying me lunch.) We talked for a few minutes about the upcoming football season, and what he might like to major in when he got to Tuscaloosa. We even scheduled a visit for him and his dad and P.J. to come up to Tuscaloosa and watch us play Georgia the next season. Even though Colgan told me he wasn't going to make any decisions yet and he wanted to take as many visits as he could, I left Kellyville feeling pretty good about landing my quarterback.

During the summer, we got a couple more workout tapes from P.J., and in July I sent my offensive coordinator down to get a first-hand look. By all accounts, Colgan was still excited about the chance to come to Bama the following year (though not half as excited as Coach Moore was when he got back.)

The next season, our first conference game in Tuscaloosa was the first weekend in October against Georgia. For most teams it was either the fourth or fifth week of the season, so I knew Toomey was going on some visits before he came to see us. Still, I wasn't particularly worried, and, more importantly, I had games to focus on.

Toomey came up for his visit on the Friday before the Georgia game. I expected him to commit by the end of the game the next day. He and his father, along with P.J. and his mother, had dinner with the team that evening. The last time I saw him he was leaving for a "campus tour" with a couple of boosters. One of them was a guy named Cal Davis (actually his very official name was E. Calhoun Davis IV, but who's counting), who had a hell of a lot more money than sense.

I don't know exactly what Cal did or what he said to Colgan, but I'm pretty sure he was the reason I never saw that kid again. I cussed Cal for all he was worth the next time I saw him. Colgan was supposed to be at the stadium when we arrived for the pre-game meal. When I walked in, though, I ran into our favorite grad student instead. He had an envelope in his hand. I went to stuff it in my pocket, but he said, "you might want to read that Coach."

I stared at him. "I don't know what you're up to, but we have a football game in two hours. I don't have time to deal with bullshit."

"That envelope has nothing to do with me. Colgan Toomey left it for you."

"What the hell, isn't he supposed to be here?"

"I don't know if he's coming back, sir, I didn't open it."

Clearly something was wrong. I slipped out into the hall and walked down to the bathroom. I opened Colgan's letter and read it quickly.

Dear Coach Bryant,

I regret to inform you that I am removing the University of Alabama from my list of potential schools. I respect you very much and I believe that you run a clean and honorable football program. However, offers were made to me last night that I not only cannot accept, but also that made me feel that I cannot attend the University of Alabama. I do not want anyone to think that there was even a possibility that I chose a school based on personal or financial gain. Because that possibility has been raised, I must choose a different school. I firmly believe that your intentions in recruiting me have been sincere and honorable. I know you may be upset that I will not attend your school, but I do have a favor to ask you. My respect for you will not be diminished if you allow P.J. Campbell to attend Alabama and work with the athletic department as a film guy and trainer.

Thank you,
Colgan M. Toomey

Reading that was a punch in the gut, but I had to respect the kid. I wrote him back a letter and told him I understood, and that I would take on P.J. as our film guy because he was good at it and he deserved it. I wasn't doing him a favor any more than he was doing me one.

I was proved right, because P.J. was a pretty awesome film guy and an asset to our team the whole time he was here. But every time I saw him, it reminded me of what might have been – half of me wanted to cry and the other half wanted to punch E. Calhoun Davis IV in the face.

CHAPTER 5

THE RECRUITER

My name's Edward Dawkins, but most people call me Dixie, 'cause I was born in Alabama and moved up to Philadelphia in junior high. I guess they called me that to make fun of my accent, but I figured it was a better name than Edward, so I just stuck with it. I think it has served me well in recruiting; the kids always remember Coach Dixie.

It helps to have a Super Bowl ring, of course, even if you didn't have anything to do with earning it. Hell, I'd probably never have gotten into college coaching at all if I hadn't been drafted into the league, even though I got on the field maybe twice in three years. I was an education major at Penn State and was ready to head off to some little podunk Pennsylvania town and be a mediocre history teacher and, if I was lucky, a slightly better than average high school football coach.

Then, late in the sixteenth round of the 1973 NFL draft (there were actually seventeen rounds back then), the Pittsburgh Steelers decided they needed a backup fullback. I guess they figured a fairly hard-working kid from the school right down the road would be good enough, and a sixteenth-round pick wasn't worth much. Hey, I may not have any official NFL stats, but I can honestly tell people I blocked for Franco Harris and Terry Bradshaw. (I also let Terry get sacked one time when Alan Page flat ran over me, but I don't tell people that, and sacks allowed wasn't kept as a stat back then.)

After we won the 1975 Super Bowl, I figured there was no way in heck my career could possibly get any better, so it was time to retire on a high note. Also, that was the game when Page ran over me, and when it still hurt a week later, I figured I was done. So, I went back to Penn State for a year as a grad assistant.

While I was there, I worked closely with a fella named Dan Hershberger, who was the assistant recruiting coordinator. As it often works in the insane nepotism of the coaching fraternity, Dan was close friends with David Harris, who was the offensive coordinator at the University of Wyoming. At the end of the 1976 season, David thought he was in line to become head coach there, and he wanted Dan as his recruiting coordinator.

Dan said that if he was going to Wyoming, he wanted to take me, and I said sure. We flew to Cheyenne to meet Dave, and he and I hit it off. Dave was from Mississippi, and, like me, he'd been out of the South for awhile. After the "interview" part was over, the real interview began. We went through about a case of Coors and traded stories about everything under the sun 'til about midnight.

Well, it's kinda funny how it all worked out because Dave didn't get the Wyoming job, and Dan Hershberger stayed at Penn State. But after Wyoming had chosen someone else, Dave's old boss, Fred Akers, who had moved on to Texas, offered him a gig as quarterback coach. In turn, Dave hired me as a recruiter and weightlifting coach. We weren't called "strength and conditioning" coaches yet.

I flew down to Austin on a Monday morning in March of 1977 and signed my paperwork that afternoon. Colgan Toomey was the first recruit I saw on film. My plane left for Mobile at noon the next day. Everybody in the country wanted this kid, and I could see why. He looked like a man among boys, and maybe that's what he was in the small school games he was playing out in the middle of nowhere in Alabama. I could tell though, that the guy had something that was both really rare and absolutely uncoachable – he always knew where everyone was on the field. The instincts on this kid just blew me away. And I played college ball in a backfield with Franco Harris and Lydell Mitchell. It was one thing to be the fastest kid on the field. But it didn't seem to matter what angle you took on this guy; he always knew where you were gonna be and made sure he was somewhere else. He might have had one of the five or ten best arms in the country that year too, though he didn't have to use it much. To this day, I've never seen anything like his high school films. He looked like a combination of Fran Tarkenton and Gale Sayers.

The Longhorns were late getting into the game though, and nobody really had any expectation that Toomey would pick Texas. I think that included most of the members of our staff. Why else would they have sent a guy with one year of experience as a grad assistant and no recruiting chops to try to land him? The only reason anyone could have had was that I was born in rural southern Alabama. As I landed in Mobile, I was pretty sure Coach Akers, whom I had spoken to on the phone but was yet to meet in person, was placing way too much faith in that fact.

My initial experience in Mobile didn't reassure me that I had a chance in this business. Recruiting was a much more seat-of-the-pants operation then. We knew that Colgan also played basketball and that basketball games were on Tuesday and Friday nights. It was Tuesday. The plan was to get a rental car in Mobile and be in Kellyville by halftime that night. Maybe I could get a chance to talk to Toomey after the game. I was armed with a school credit card and the instruction to do whatever I could think of to get Toomey to come out to Austin for a visit as soon as possible.

The plan went awry before I even set foot in Alabama. The plane was delayed for about an hour because thunderstorms kept us from landing. I got the rental car without a hitch, but I made it about five miles before it started having alternator problems. I pulled into this rather seedy looking motel on Airport Boulevard in Mobile called the Alabama Palms and called the rental place. They assured me they'd send someone right over with a different car.

In keeping with the general direction of my luck that day, I had decided I'd better check into the hotel by the time they finally brought me a car. At that point, there was no way I could make it to Kellyville before the basketball game ended, so I just decided to wake up with the sun and head north. I didn't bother reporting this change of plans to anyone in Austin.

I remember looking at the map the next morning and thinking it would be a miracle if I found this God-forsaken place without getting totally lost in a swamp somewhere. Also, without a sporting event going on, what was I gonna do when I got there? Just waltz into the school and ask them to pull Toomey out of class? Probably not the best plan. I tried to think of a better one while I was winding through the cypress swamps on highway 43.

My luck changed for the better when I got to Kellyville, though. I pulled into this little place called the Panther Drive-in, even though it wasn't really a drive-in at all, just a regular sit- down restaurant. There were maybe ten or fifteen folks inside, one cook and one waitress, who also did a lot of the cooking, as it turned out. She was a slightly chubby, bouncy blonde with a perpetual smile and the practiced grace of someone who had been flitting around that dining room for a long, long time.

Her years of service had apparently also taught her to recognize everyone who had ever been in the restaurant before. As she glided over to my table, she said, "Hey stranger, can I get you a cup of coffee?" I nodded, and she spun on her heels and gave a little wiggle of her ass as she headed to the counter.

Now I would love to tell you that Colgan Toomey went to Texas because I hooked up with his best friend's mama. That'd be a hell of a story, wouldn't it? Angie Campbell was pretty darn cute, too. We didn't quite make it that far, though there might have been a chance, if I'd really tried. We had a quick connection, and since I really didn't have much of a plan to get at Colgan, I figured I'd try and learn something about the town from this friendly waitress.

Like most of the football coaches around the country, I knew that Colgan had a friend named P.J. Campbell that had been making his films and basically running his recruitment. I had been drinking coffee in there for 45 minutes before I figured out I was flirting with P.J.'s mother. Once I did though, I had an easy in. She invited me to dinner that night and assured me Colgan would be there.

The only hint that Colgan had given anyone about his recruitment was that Alabama was out of the picture and he wasn't going to tell anyone why. Auburn had a new coach who had gone 3-8 in his first season, so out-of-state teams felt like they had a shot. Other regional powers were in flux, though a lot of folks thought the new coach at Tennessee, Johnny Majors, who had made his way home to the Volunteers fresh off a national championship at the University of Pittsburgh, had a pretty good shot at Toomey. Others were betting on Coach Dickey at Florida, coming off four straight bowl games. Bobby Bowden had just gotten to Florida State and was making small waves, but he certainly hadn't yet built the Seminoles into what they would soon become.

But Texas? Sure, we had a pretty good tradition, especially with option quarterbacks. Darrell Royal won three national championships running the wishbone offense like a machine. But he had retired, and the new guy had been a head coach only two years, in the backwoods of Wyoming, no less. No one gave us a prayer.

What the hell was Dixie Dawkins gonna do to change that? I really didn't have a clue. My job was to convince Toomey to come out to Austin and hope either my bosses had a better idea than me, or he fell in love with the place. A place I didn't know shit about, since I hadn't even unpacked my stuff there yet. I'd heard great things about the town, but I hardly even knew how to describe it.

At dinner that night, it quickly became obvious that Colgan was both a heck of a lot smarter than me and far different from your average high school football player. He talked about what they were doing in his advanced biology class and wanted to know my thoughts on evolution. When I didn't have a decent answer, he replied with a thorough explanation of the theory. Then he switched gears and said when he visited Austin (news to me that he was coming, woohoo!), he wanted to make sure he met the parish priest and had a chance for a good long talk.

Next, he asked me who I voted for in the presidential election the previous fall and why. He seemed to enjoy pushing adults to the brink of uncomfortable and then reeling them back in with that magical southern-Irish charm. It's a good thing Chicago Irishmen and Alabama women don't reproduce very often; the resulting tribe would take over the world.

Don't get me wrong; I liked Colgan, I really did. I certainly didn't see anything that would make me question the idea that we wanted him more than any other player in the country. But there were small misgivings, because the kid I saw in front of me could do anything he wanted with his life, and he was clearly interested in a lot more than football. That's great, in general. But it's not what you want out of your quarterback. You want a kid who lives and breathes every aspect of the game, who saw every day as just another opportunity to play football.

As we finished eating, Colgan said he had a surprise for us. When he got home from school and heard there was going to be what he called a "recruiting dinner" that night, he had spent the next two hours whipping up a batch of crème brûlée. He even apologized to us for not having a torch to serve it in the traditional French manner.

The crème brûlée was amazing, a little slice of caramel heaven. My stomach sank as the dessert arrived in it, however, because I was pretty sure that this was not a kid who, relieved of the boredom and strictures of small-town life, was going to devote the vast majority of his energy to playing football. Landing him could still make my career though, so I wasn't about to clue my bosses in on any reservations I might have.

CHAPTER 6

THE SHERIFF

My name is Jim Burruss, and I retired last year after 25 years as Sheriff of Zavala County, Texas. That's right down on the border, just up the Rio Grande from Laredo. A lot of folks try and cross the border in Zavala County, and frankly, we're never gonna have the manpower to stop 'em all. Some of them are just decent folks looking for a better life, and some of them are running drugs for the cartels, but most are in-between, not good or bad, just people made desperate by hard times. They'll steal and trespass and fight if they have to, and, fairly often, they have to. But most of the time, it doesn't escalate to murder.

Anyhoo, I'm here to tell you about a man I never met. For years, I never even knew his name, though I heard whispers about "Colo" or "El Colo Loco." Hell, one time I even heard a fella we busted running cocaine call him "El Diablo Blanco" or "The White Devil." The name stuck.

I never was quite sure whether I wanted to catch DB, as we began calling him in the department, but I knew that I at least wanted to meet him, to try to see what made him tick. It became an obsession. I needed to know whether he was just some sicko killing for sport and focusing on people who wouldn't be missed ... or if he had some higher purpose. I'm not condoning his actions either way, but I honestly wondered if it would make a difference which one he was when I finally found him.

Before that, before we had ever heard of the white devil, there was just a single body, found by a rancher at dawn on a Saturday morning. It was around 1995 or 96, April or May when the afternoons were already hotter than hell, but the mornings were still tolerable.

The rancher was a Zavala County lifer named George Corley. One of these fellas who somehow eke out a halfway decent herd on a few hundred acres of chaparral. He called me at home about 6:30 that morning. "Sheriff," he said, "you need to get your ass out here and see this." I think I mumbled something about not taking orders from the citizenry prior to 8 a.m.

George was one of those people who spoke seriously when he spoke at all and almost never raised his voice. When he wanted to emphasize something, he just spoke even more slowly than usual. "Sher-riff," he drawled, "A . . . man . . . has been . . . murdered ... on my land... I suggest... you ... come out here."

I knew better than to ask right then just how he knew the man was murdered. When I got out to George's ranch 45 minutes later, it took me awhile to believe it. The body was down in this long narrow wash -- a perfect place for running people across the border because it was low enough that you couldn't see down inside it from a distance, and there was intermittent water at the bottom. George told me he checked it fairly regularly and there were often footprints or bits of trash that showed border jumpers had been through there.

He'd never seen any of them though, and never really thought it was much of a problem 'til that morning. George pointed out the body leaning up against a rock as we picked our way down the ravine. As we got closer, I took a basic catalogue of what I was looking at. He was short, maybe five foot six or so, but muscularly built, a Hispanic man with black hair and brown eyes. He wore a beat-up cowboy hat but a fairly nice leather vest.

I remember these details like it was yesterday. The scene burned in my mind, in part, because it had so clearly been staged after death. From a distance, he could have been taking a nap leaned up against that rock. The victim's hat had been pulled down low over his eyes and his head leaned down toward his chest. Until I got right up to him I couldn't tell that his throat had been slit. The vest had to have been put on after he died, because it covered up a lot of blood on his shirt.

I knelt down beside him and saw that a knife still protruded from the man's lower back. It was a nice knife too, with a curved, possibly mother-of-pearl, hilt and a serrated portion along the blade. The stab in the back seemed to have happened after death. I guessed that the same knife was used to cut the throat, but there was no way to be sure without pulling it out.

The knives left in the back would become a signature of El Diablo Blanco. No other weapons were ever used; no guns, despite our county being overrun with them. Sometimes the knives were just kitchen utensils, a couple were medical, maybe even surgical knives, and once it was a dagger with what appeared to be a ruby in the hilt. Oftentimes, the knife belonged to the victim. That first Saturday morning, when I saw the knife in his back, I had no way of knowing whether it belonged to the dead man.

The man who did this was a study in contradictions. You don't slit someone's throat without some measure of stealth, but if the knife was his, he left a very obvious clue for us. If it wasn't his, the victim must have known something was up when his knife was taken. Then our killer put this vest on him to cover up the blood, but left the dang knife sticking out of his back. Then he left the dead guy propped up against a rock in a wash that was a common path for border jumpers. I was pretty sure that George Corley and I were not the intended audience.

We didn't identify that first body for over three months. By that time, we had four more bodies, and we had figured out that they were all coyotes -- guys who smuggled Mexicans (more often Guatemalans and Salvadorans, actually) over the border in return for the immigrants' life savings. Most of them had ties to drug runners, but this was before the big Mexican cartels were fully organized.

The coyotes' bodies were usually propped up against a rock or a tree, and like I said, they almost always had a knife in their back. Every time the scene was staged similarly; a vest or a jacket, one time a serape, was used to make the blood impossible to see from a distance. The bodies were usually out in the scrubland, near a creekbank or in a wash, in places where other coyotes would see them.

The first one we identified was number 4. His name was Gregorio Cortazar. One of the deputies recognized him immediately because he had spent half of his adult life in the Zavala County jail. I got an inkling of the kind of victims we were dealing with when we got to Cortazar's house. This fellow who had never had any job other than small-time thug had a brand new souped up Dodge Ram pickup truck in the driveway.

Ol' Greg's Mom and girlfriend identified number 1 and number 3 as well. (They were real cooperative after we found about four ounces of pot in their house.) That's when we learned that all of the victims were coyotes. The three that our new lady friends knew worked for a guy on the other side of the border named Rodrigo Martinez.

After number four, we had a little lull. I don't know if the coyotes got smart and took more muscle with them or what. This was also in the dead of summer; fewer people chance the border crossing when it's 110 outside. Maybe ol' DB also didn't particularly like traipsing around the scrubland in that kind of weather.

Around mid-September, we busted a coke-smuggling ring and got our first lead on the killer. The guy who told us about El Diablo Blanco was a truck driver from Michigan named Ronald Martin. He owed a gang in Laredo a bunch of money, so they roped him into trying to transport their "product" to Detroit. The backroads of Zavala County were good for that, except that we all knew that anytime we saw an 18-wheeler, the driver had a damn good reason for avoiding the border station on I-35.

Martin told us that there was somebody who had all the Mexicans spooked. He said they told him the fella looked like a white guy and had red hair, but he spoke perfect Spanish. One gang member told Martin the guy was Salvadoran, but another said that he was American. They called him El Colo or El Diablo Blanco. Martin wasn't sure exactly what El Colo meant, but later we figured out it probably came from the colon; they were basically calling him a sack of shit. They said he was trying to kill all the coyotes and that it all had something to do with a girl. We started asking every small-time thug in town about El Colo. Sometimes they would go white as a sheet and start muttering to themselves, but they never had any real information.

The seventh body was an exception. It was set up at a picnic table at a rest area along U.S. 57 at the north end of the county, a good thirty miles from the border. This time the bloody shirt was covered by an Armani jacket worth several months of my salary. He was the one with the jeweled dagger in his back.

The fancy profiler sent down by the Texas Rangers took one look at the body and decided that the killer was motivated by robbery. Surely a person dressed like that had a nice car and a bunch of other property that must have been taken by the killer. I walked him around to the other side of the picnic table. "Other property like that fancy sword in his back?"

The Ranger just glared at me. He persisted with the robbery theory for about a week as he studied the files of the previous victims. He then changed his mind and decided that the killer must be either working for, or the leader of, some sort of criminal enterprise, probably a drug cartel. Not necessarily a bad theory, but then he said that the killer was trying to send a message to us (the cops) that he was in charge in this county.

My second in command, Blake Griggs, chuckled at that. "So that's why he only kills folks that we would want to arrest anyhow, right?" The Ranger was not amused. He called headquarters and told them that we weren't interested in catching this killer and that the Rangers needed to take over the case. I got on the line with the grand poobah from Austin and told him that was fine and dandy with me.

The Rangers kept us off the case for just over a week near the end of September. Three new bodies were found during that time, although one had been killed considerably earlier, around late June or early July according to the crime lab. Two of them, including the one that had been rotting awhile, fit the original pattern -- they were out in the scrubland leaning up against rocks with their throats slit.

The third body, though, was found right at the edge of Crystal Springs—that's our county seat. A widow named Susan Hopkins told us she found him leaning against a tree, fifty feet directly behind her back door. This body was white, rather than Hispanic, and young, early 20's at the latest. Apparently old DB hadn't quite gotten the jump on him like the rest because the blood wasn't covered up and his throat wasn't slit. Instead he had multiple stab wounds to his chest, and the knife was stuck between his ribs on the right side. Hopkins identified the knife, a four-inch cutting knife from her kitchen, but there was no sign of forced entry at her back door.

We eventually got an ID on the body (he was from up around Houston) but we never did get a satisfactory answer on why the killing at Hopkins' place was so different. Griggs had a theory though: despite being over sixty, ol' Susie was a bit of a hellcat; it's possible she caught the guy breaking in and set up the scene herself, trying her best to copy what she'd heard about the serial killer. I bet if we'd ever said that to the Rangers, they'd have decided Susie Hopkins was the serial killer and put a 24-hour surveillance on her.

About two weeks after the Hopkins killing, we got a lead on the rest stop body. When we finally figured out who the Armani-wearing fella was, it lent some credence to the idea that the killer worked for a drug cartel and we were caught in a turf war. The Rangers showed pictures of the guy and his fancy dagger to every law enforcement agency between Dallas and Mexico City.

I don't know if anyone would have recognized the guy, but that damn ruby-hilted mini sword would be hard to forget.

Turns out the body belonged to one Israel Martinez, brother of Rodrigo Martinez, the nefarious employer of Gregorio Cortazar and several of our early victims. It sure looked like someone was trying to put the Martinez gang out of business. The Rangers had all kinds of theories, mostly centering on groups from other parts of Mexico trying to take over the border crossing trade. In some ways, it made sense -- drug gangs were getting more and more powerful in Mexico at the time, and were beginning to coalesce into the major cartels that would terrorize that country in the 2000's.

But the cartel theory never squared with the bits of information we picked up from the small-time hoods who filled our jail and the occasional border-jumper we caught. Their stories were never detailed, but they were consistent. Someone was after the Martinez gang alright, but it wasn't another smuggling ring. This guy worked alone. And everyone we talked to, including guys who worked for other gangs, was scared shitless of El Diablo Blanco.

It was also clear from their stories that the criminal underclass on the other side of the border didn't have a clue who this guy was. We knew he was considered "blanco," but that term could mean Mexicans of European-Spanish descent as well as white Americans. One guy told me that DB was as white as I was but didn't know if he was American. Apparently, our killer also had some connection to El Salvador.

Some of the people we talked to spoke of a woman named Maribel. The Rangers, who tried to funnel everything into their cartel turf war theory, decided that Maribel was the leader of the killer's gang. They had every damn cop in Mexico trying to find a drug boss named Maribel. I was pretty sure they'd never find one. First of all, Mexican gangs are about the most patriarchal, misogynistic organizations on the planet. I really doubt there's ever been one run by a woman. Second, I had a strong hunch Maribel was dead, or at least severely harmed in some way. DB wasn't trying to win turf, he wanted revenge.

About two weeks before Thanksgiving, just as our group of three Rangers was starting to get real antsy about wrapping up the case and making it home for the holidays, we had a thunderstorm the likes of which doesn't come to South Texas very often. It rained all day and all night, nearly nine inches according to the Laredo TV station, and every ditch and arroyo within fifty miles of the border roared like mad and dumped its contents into the Rio Grande.

The day after the storm, we found four bodies. The next day, three more were found downriver in Dimmit and Webb Counties. At least five of the seven were definitively our guy. Two still had knives stuck in their back, and all five of them had a vest or jacket covering up the blood. The sixth body was a woman who was completely naked and looked like she had drowned, no visible wounds or anything. The final body (well, about half a body, really) had been rotting awhile after being torn to hell by wild dogs, so there wasn't much flesh left. No way to know if the dogs got to him before or after death, so we couldn't say for sure whether that one was courtesy of DB or not.

With all these bodies floating into town, we suddenly had a national story, and the world went into full-blown crisis mode. We had half the darn Texas Rangers force down here walking around in the desert looking for more bodies. They expected us all to work eighteen hours a day, but there really wasn't a damn thing to do but traipse blindly around the countryside and hope you run into the guy.

About two weeks after the storm, when everybody was tired as hell and, of course, no new progress had been made, I got a call one morning from the Sheriff over in Webb County. He told me they had picked up a prostitute who knew who my serial killer was. I wanted to tell him that everyone seemed to have an identity for him, but nobody really knew who he was, but I realized that sounded ridiculous. Besides it wouldn't hurt to go talk to the girl.

The Sheriff was a fella named Williams; I never got to know him much because he got beat in the next election and moved up to Amarillo or thereabouts. He said I could come over right then if I wanted and talk to the girl, whose name was Alicia Gonzales. (I guess a Maribel would have been too much to hope for.)

The Laredo police had picked up Ms. Gonzales after midnight in the parking lot of a truck stop, where an officer observed her knocking on windows and offering her charms. There was also a crack pipe and a couple of rocks in her purse, and, when they brought her into the interrogation room, it was clear she was coming down hard. I almost decided there wasn't any point in talking to her, but hey, it got me away from the damn Rangers for a little while.

"Good morning Ms. Gonzalez," I said as cheerfully as I could muster. I expected either a wisecrack like "what's so good about it" or a dismissive grunt. Instead she leaned forward, suddenly focused her eyes to stare at me, and said "I know who your killer is. You're not going to catch him."

"So does that mean you're not going to tell me who he is?" I asked.

"You already know his name."

"I've heard him called El Colo Loco and El Diablo Blanco. Neither of those are the kind of thing you see on a birth certificate very often."

She let herself smile for half a second. "Colo is his name. It's not a nickname."

"What kind of parent names their kid after a sack of shit?"

"He's not Mexican. You gringos think Spanish slang is the same everywhere."

"Ok, fine, he's not Mexican. I've heard people say he is Salvadoran. Is that true? They always say he is white."

"He chose to become Salvadoran. He deserves that name more than most. He fought in our civil war. I am sure he has seen and done many bad things, but what he has done here may begin to atone for those sins."

"You seem like you know him pretty well. Who is Maribel?"

The name visibly shook her, and she took a deep, ragged breath. "That is a story that will not pass my lips. Today, Maribel is an angel. That's all I will say." She made the sign of the cross. It was a little unnerving coming from someone you know is a crack whore.

I thought for a moment. "But Colo gets revenge for her, no?"

She shook her head. "I'm not going to talk about her. Colo does what must be done. The federales, the gringo cops, nobody else does it. I don't know if they can't or they just don't. But Colo is not going to be doing your dirty work anymore."

"Are you saying he's done killing people? How do you know?"

"I just know. He is ready to move on."

"How do you know Colo anyway? Is he a client of yours?"

She looked indignant. "Absolutely not," she said. "He would not do such a thing. He brings me food sometimes. He tries to get me to stop doing what I do, you know. He tries to help me; he talks to Saint Romero for me."

I had never heard of a Saint Romero, but I'm not Catholic, so I figured it was just my ignorance. It was clear she had a reverence for this Colo character, so I really doubted I would get any good leads from her.

"You said Colo was ready to move on. Is he leaving town? Is he from here in Laredo?"

"He usually stay on the other side, in Los Artistas. He's not there anymore though. He's already left. He said he was going home, but he wouldn't tell anyone where that is."

"I thought you said he was Salvadoran?"

"NO, I said he chose to become Salvadoran. He came from somewhere else. I have no idea where."

I tried to tease out anything else about where Colo might be going or when he left, but there was some information she either didn't have or wasn't giving. I told Griggs the whole story when I got back to Crystal Springs, and he chewed on a straw for a minute before he looked up and said, "I believe her," and went outside for a smoke.

I wasn't sure if I believed her or not, but I did think she believed her own story. I'll never know how much of it was true, but she was right about one thing. We never found any more bodies. El Colo Loco, El Diablo Blanco, whatever you wanted to call him; he had moved on, just like she said.

CHAPTER 7

THE TEACHER

A lot of people, perhaps especially people who spend their lives in small towns, have a somewhat distorted view of the world. This is probably true in a lot of ways, but the sense in which I mean it is that people believe that the best they've seen of something is at least among the best there is. Everyone thinks the best cook they know could be a world class chef, or the best player on their church softball team could have made the majors with a couple of breaks. There's somebody singing in your church choir or neighborhood karaoke bar just waiting to be discovered and record number one hits. Your girlfriend's poetry should be anthologized with Tennyson or Plath.

For the most part, everyone is wrong. The range of expertise or skill within your own personal experience almost never reflects the entire range of humanity. Most people never meet someone that is truly world-class at anything, and that's fine. There are lots of levels of "really good" that enrich people's lives. The lady that runs the Panther Drive-In, Angie Campbell, almost certainly couldn't be Julia Child even if given the opportunity, but that doesn't mean she doesn't make the best Denver omelet I've ever tasted. I'm content with it being the best one I ever will taste. The fact that there's someone out there who could make a better one, or make something that made me forget Denver omelets ever existed, simply isn't relevant to my life.

Colgan Toomey is the one exception to that rule that it has been my pleasure to know.

I will freely admit to being one of Colgan's hagiographers that hot July day in 1983. Yes, I described him as a saint, and yes, I listed a bunch of his many accomplishments. I'm not saying P.J. was wrong in the way he felt about his friend, and I certainly don't think he did anything morally wrong in his unorthodox but heartfelt eulogy. But Colgan really was different than all the other kids I saw come through Kellyville High. For thirty-seven years I taught every single student who made it to tenth grade. I taught many of them again in twelfth. I could have retired the year before Colgan was in my senior English class. I taught another twelve years, but I never saw another student like Colgan. I honestly believe I could have taught another forty years and not had another student like Colgan.

Maybe I am engaging in the type of thinking I have described in others. Quite possibly the best student in my experience, no matter how far ahead of all the others I've known, might be nothing more than a little above average in another setting. But I honestly believe Colgan was different. He could have competed with the best students in any school in the world.

I know I taught in small-town Alabama. Unlike some, I realize the limitations of that. I never thought I would end up in a place like Kellyville. I grew up in Atlanta and was the salutatorian of Emory University's preparatory school. The valedictorian went to Harvard. I got a full scholarship to the University of Virginia, where I was an English major. I then got master's degrees in English and Education at Vanderbilt. Literature was Colgan's third or fourth favorite subject, after biology and history and probably Spanish (though his love of Spanish came in part from being drawn into the magical worlds of Jorge Luis Borges and Gabriel Garcia Marques.) Despite this affinity for other subjects, Colgan still knew as much about literature when he graduated high school as I did when I finished my master's.

Before I met my husband Timothy, I never thought I'd end up in a place like Kellyville. Charlottesville, Virginia was the most rural place I'd ever lived before he brought me down here. If you've ever been to Charlottesville, you know it's not exactly country living, despite the idyllic setting. When we met, Tim was a medical student at Vandy. He had just taken a three-year "vacation" from his studies in the beautiful Pacific Islands, serving as a marine medic on Saipan and Iwo Jima. The man cut an amazingly dashing figure in his uniform, and I was instantly smitten. I never regretted it, though I wondered sometimes if he did.

I met Timothy two days after he returned to Nashville to complete a two-year residency. I was just starting a masters' program of the same length. We set our wedding date for a month after graduation about three weeks into the first year. Even before Timothy started his residency, he knew that he wanted to serve poor rural communities where medicine was failing the people. He warned me that this would never make us rich and that we'd never live in glamorous locations.

What's funny is that Tim was born and raised in northern Wisconsin. His original idea of underserved communities was informed by childhood experiences of geographical remoteness, often worsened by winter weather, and the neglect of Native American communities and reservations. The South presented a range of problems alien to his experience, but his passion to help those who needed it the most never wavered.

The first place we went after graduation was Meridian, Mississippi. Timothy was hired as a general practitioner working for an old man with very old-fashioned ideas, about both medicine and life. The office he worked in was a "whites-only" practice. Tim hadn't thought much about it before we moved to Mississippi, but it quickly annoyed him. Still, good man though he was, my Tim wasn't much of an activist, and he worked for Dr. Wilcox for four years without making any waves. I worked as a substitute teacher in Meridian for the first year, but then I had a very difficult pregnancy with our daughter and stayed home until we moved to Kellyville.

In the spring of 1951, Timothy got a call from a doctor in Kellyville whose partner was retiring. I think Tim was ready enough to get away from old Dr. Wilcox that he didn't give it much thought, even though I was quite skeptical of moving to an even smaller town. Unlike the practice in Meridian, the one Tim joined in Kellyville treated both black and white patients. There were separate waiting rooms and bathrooms, though. True to his enlightened but quiet ways, when Tim became a full partner in 1958, he convinced Dr. Anderson to take down the signs designating which race belonged in which room, but, honestly, it didn't make much difference in anyone's self-selection of where to sit.

My first year teaching in Kellyville started the same fall we moved to town. At first, I taught eighth and then ninth grade English. When Ms. Quentin retired, I took over tenth and twelfth. Not everyone took English their senior year, so one teacher had to do that class and another one.

I would not have been surprised if I had spent my entire career in Kellyville and never known a student like Colgan. Because twelfth grade English was optional, I got to teach almost all the smartest kids to pass through our school system in a fairly intimate classroom setting. When I say there was never another student like Colgan, I don't mean to imply that there weren't some great kids at KHS before and after him. Even at the same time as Colgan—P.J. Campbell was one of the five best students I ever had, and it's even possible I would remember him as being the most extraordinary if Colgan hadn't been there. That, however, would have been the type of phenomenon I described above. If Colgan hadn't been there, P.J. would only have been the big fish in a small pond—that guy on your softball team that you think could have made the majors.

I first met Colgan about a month into his ninth grade year. I had seen him before – he was hard to miss since he was already taller than most of the seniors and he had a bright shock of red hair. But at that time, he hadn't fully grown into his body yet. Yes, even the great athlete was a bit clumsy when he began his time at Kellyville High. One particular morning after first period, I was standing in the hallway greeting students and I saw the tall red-headed freshman coming my way. He was holding a book up and reading as he walked down the hall. I couldn't tell what the book was from where I was standing.

I glanced away to say good morning to one of my students, and when I looked back, Colgan had tripped over something and was falling face first onto the floor. He took three other kids down with him. I rushed over there and got everybody up and had to take him and one other kid to the nurse for minor first aid.

As we were walking up to the nurse's office, I said, "Young man, I admire your dedication to reading, but perhaps it should not be done whilst attempting to navigate the hallways."

"Yes ma'am," he said sheepishly, but with a bit of amusement in his voice.

"What were you reading so intently that you could not watch where you were going?"

"Frank Herbert's *Dune*, ma'am."

This response did not immediately engender my admiration, as I have never been a fan of science fiction. Colgan did eventually get me to read it, and I must admit that, though I find the subject matter trying, it is a very well-written novel.

"Ahh, so a fan of science fiction, are we."

"Yes ma'am, but I'll read anything I can get my hands on."

I said something about it being a good idea to do so while seated and thought the conversation was over. However, while the nurse was applying first aid to the other student, Colgan looked at me and said, "You're the senior English teacher, right? What are *you* reading?"

I was astonished, not by any sense of impertinence, but by the sudden realization that no student had ever asked me that before. I felt a little ashamed that my current reading wasn't something more interesting, but I told Colgan that my classes would be reading *Jane Eyre* next month, and that I was currently rereading it to prepare for teaching it. I mistakenly assumed, with some regret, that this mention of a novel generally considered dry and academic would shut down the conversation.

I was wrong. Colgan's eyes lit up and he asked me if I had read Jean Rhys's prequel to *Jane Eyre*, called *Wide Sargasso Sea*. I said that I had, but I kept to myself that I was floored that this fifteen-year-old boy in front of me had even heard of it. (Turns out he had skipped a grade in early elementary, so he was really only fourteen.) This was a post-colonial, feminist novel published less than ten years earlier. I would have been shocked if there were one hundred white men in Alabama who had read it. Before that morning, I would have been absolutely certain there were no high school students in Alabama who had read it.

The nurse interrupted us fairly quickly, but I asked Colgan if he had time to come by my room during his lunch period, since my only period of study hall coincided with the ninth graders' lunch. He promised he would and I took the other young man to class while he got bandaged up.

I had been teaching Jane Eyre for about fifteen of the twenty years I had been at Kellyville. Even after my guidance, no student displayed as thorough an understanding of it as Colgan did during our conversation that day. It didn't even matter to me that he said he hated it (and claimed that Rhys did too, which I disagreed with.)

That conversation with a gangly fourteen-year-old kid really did change my life. I never taught the same book two years in a row the rest of my career. I did not abandon Jane Eyre (or any other book) because I agreed with Colgan that there was enough morally wrong in Bronte's treatment of women or mental illness to justify ignoring the book. Rather, this child reawakened the reason I loved literature in the first place.

That was what was special about Colgan. He wasn't just brilliant; he honestly loved to learn, and his attitude was infectious. He raised the level of every class he ever participated in, and he made every one of his teachers better at their job, too. I know he did for me. Colgan started coming to my classroom before school a couple of mornings a week to talk about books. He kept it up the entire time he was at Kellyville High. My daughter was away in college, and my husband had been taken by cancer five years earlier, so Colgan soon became my best friend. In many ways, he was the closest thing I had to a soulmate after Timothy. The relationship was so close that it was undoubtedly "inappropriate" from a purely professional standpoint, but it contained nothing of a remotely romantic or sexual nature.

When Colgan went to Texas, we wrote long letters to one another. In some ways, I probably guilt-tripped him into doing it by reading and suggesting multiple epistolary novels and repeatedly lamenting the death of letter-writing skills. You should note, dear reader, that such skills were fading quickly even before the advent of e-mail. The letters between Colgan and me were almost always about books, though occasionally he would write of details of life on campus—his classes, interesting people he met, an occasional aside about football.

I still have Colgan's letters, hundreds of handwritten pages of them, in a box I keep in the pie chest (I never had much use for china anyway). I wish I had copied the ones I sent him; I'd love to be able to leave money and instructions for the whole correspondence to be published on my death.

The last letter I received from Colgan was sent from San Rafel Blanco, Guatemala. It was postmarked nine days before we learned that Colgan had been kidnapped, and it arrived two weeks before the funeral. I scoured the letter for any sign that my young friend anticipated or feared his own demise. In truth, perhaps, I was looking for some indication that the reports could be wrong, that Colgan could still be alive. There were none. The letter was mostly about a Brazilian writer named Jorge Amado. Colgan had been introduced to him by his martial arts instructor in Austin. Amado's fame in the U.S., such as it was, rested on a book titled *Dona Flor and her Two Husbands*, but Colgan's favorite work was a modernist political novel from the forties called *Cacau*. It was apparently the story of workers on Brazilian cocoa plantations developing a class consciousness.

Amado, as I later learned, was a member of the Brazilian Communist Party who had spent several years in exile behind the iron curtain. I often wondered about the irony of Colgan being kidnapped and killed by communist rebels from El Salvador. I honestly don't know how Colgan felt about politics, beyond a vague sense of a hatred of war, and the idea that the way American politicians present the world to their citizens was far too simple. Other than that, there was nothing overtly political in anything he ever wrote me. Many of the letters of the last couple of years of his life focus on a love of Latin America's people and literature.

There were other football stars, before and after Colgan. Every year somebody was crowned the valedictorian as the best student. Coach Brooks, and the fact that Colgan was the only player of any sport who ever drew national recruiting attention while I was at Kellyville, tell me that Colgan the athlete was at least different in degree than every other player we ever had. My own experiences tell me Colgan the student was levels of magnitude different in degree than the other good students at KHS.

So, yes, I eulogized Colgan by focusing on his unique and very real achievements. I don't believe I was wrong to do so. Yet, after hearing P.J. speak, I realized that he was right too. Colgan was different in degree from the other students I've known, but he was also different in kind. I believe P.J.'s statement that he never saw Colgan be mean or cruel to another child. I also never saw that happen. In the end, that is both the highest praise that a teacher could offer and the truest measure of what made Colgan unique.

CHAPTER 8

THE OPPONENT

There was another "sport" in which Colgan Toomey was at least as dominant as he was in football. I know because I was pretty damn good at it too, and he kicked my ass every time we played. My name is Kim Collins, and I am a sociology professor at the University of Alabama. But back then I was Kimberly Leidecker, a chubby (ok probably more than chubby), freckle-faced nerd who, I can say with some confidence, remains the highest scoring quiz bowl player in the history of Murphy High School in Mobile, Alabama.

Honestly, I'd like to go by Leidecker again, but I've published things with my ex's last name and would rather not confuse my academic colleagues. For a bunch of people with PhD's, they're actually highly susceptible to that.

At the time I graduated from High School, I was the highest scoring female quiz bowl player in the history of the state of Alabama. In fact, as far as I know, up to that point I was the only girl anywhere in the state that had led a team in scoring.

For those of you who don't know, quiz bowl is sort of like Jeopardy with teams. It's based on "college bowl," which was still on TV when I was in high school. Basically, two teams of four nerds with little electrical buzzers in their hands try to answer questions. At the time, quiz bowl was the best outlet to be found for the competitive energies of a five-foot-two, 200 plus-pound tomboy. I was too short and too fat for basketball, and they wouldn't let me play football.

I joined the quiz bowl team in ninth grade and was the best player on the team by the next year. Two of the senior boys quit when Mrs. Furman named me captain. By my junior year, I was almost certainly among the best players in the state. Unfortunately, however, I was in the same region with Colgan Toomey and P.J. Campbell.

Murphy was one of the biggest schools in the state. A lot of people describe their high school as being a prison, but Murphy kids can say it honestly. Our school was literally a remodeled Spanish prison. I couldn't tell you how many kids were in my class, but I guarantee it was more than Kellyville had in their whole school system. At that time, however, the state did not divide schools by size for quiz bowl, instead just grouping them geographically by regions. The state was divided into just eight regions, and all of southwestern Alabama, from Gulf Shores up to about Demopolis, was in the same region. To go to the state tournament, you had to win your region. They only took eight teams for the whole state.

I realize it's a bit rich to hear the kid from the big school complaining about this set up. Most of the little schools never had a chance against the likes of Murphy and McGill-Toolen, the big Catholic school in Mobile. My junior and senior year, I would have bet a lot of money that the best three teams in the state were all in our region. We beat McGill in the Mobile County tournament both years and beat them at their invitational my junior year. They beat us at regionals my junior year. My senior year we lost to Jesuit from New Orleans in the finals of their invitational, but we won one in Montgomery that included most of the biggest schools in Alabama.

But neither us nor McGill ever came close to beating Kellyville. I don't think anyone really came that close, not in Alabama anyway. They didn't go to Jesuit's invitational – I bet Jesuit could have given them a run for their money. At McGill's invitational, they got a fairly close game from St. Anthony's, which was from somewhere in Mississippi. Kellyville beat them by about 100 points. They beat us by about 200 and everybody else by more than that. Choctaw County got beat like 740 to 10. One of the other small schools never even buzzed in against them. The only other tournaments Kellyville attended were the state ones. They probably didn't have the money to travel to other invitationals.

Colgan Toomey, of course, was Kellyville's best player. (He was apparently their best player in every sport they competed in, with the possible exception of girls' basketball.) He was ridiculously fast on the buzzer, especially on science and literature. I saw him answer a question on some obscure element, strontium maybe, on two words – the name of its discoverer who wasn't, at least to my knowledge, famous for anything else. He regularly got literature questions from the names of minor characters, or authors from obscure books no one had heard of. If you told me he was psychic and reading the moderator's mind, I absolutely would have believed you.

When a really small school does well in quiz bowl, it's almost always because they have one great player. The rest of the team usually just sits there and watches him (and at those little country schools, it always seems to be a him, though I'm sure there are exceptions). In most of these cases, the second-best player on the team wouldn't make the roster at a place like Murphy.

Kellyville was different. They certainly had a great player, but I honestly believe their second seat would have been almost as good if Colgan hadn't been beating him to the buzzer on most things. His name was P.J. Campbell, and, in addition to being a worthy competitor, he was my first crush.

There were three or four other girls on our team over the course of my high school career. Every one of them developed an obsession with Colgan Toomey. He was tall and muscular and handsome, and somehow managed to be exotic despite coming from a town of two thousand people in a swamp in southern Alabama. I understood why everybody liked him—maybe it was just the contrarian in me that led me to choose a different path.

In contrast to his friend, P.J. Campbell was short, not more than 5'7", slightly chubby, and walked with a permanent limp. He had a hell of a smile though, and his excitement for the game was so genuine. Colgan seemed so polished and political, like he was a professional charmer. P.J. was just more real. Part of it was the way he played, and the questions he got. When Colgan knew something, he knew it dead cold in like half a sentence. P.J. was a great guesser; there would be some sort of tricky question that you had to puzzle together, and he would always buzz right before the time ran out and shrug his shoulders and kind of turn his head sideways and ask in this questioning tone "Is that such-and-such?" He always seemed to think he was wrong, but he almost never was. It was so cute.

Colgan and P.J. made a great team because Colgan got all the academic stuff, and P.J. got all the pop culture and weird puzzle questions. To this day I've never seen anyone who knew movies and television like P.J. Campbell. It wasn't the skill set best suited for a great high school quiz bowl player, but it complemented Colgan's perfectly. I've seen P.J. play bar trivia a few times in Tuscaloosa the last few years, and he's better at that than he ever was at quiz bowl. He'd be great on a game show.

Every tournament that we attended with Kellyville, from my sophomore year on, I tried to corner P.J. and get him into a conversation. He was never rude or mean, but he always said he had to catch up with his team, or he had to talk to Colgan about something. For awhile, I almost bought into the other girls' theory that he and Colgan were gay, since Colgan didn't seem interested in them either.

Our invitational at Murphy took place near the beginning of December, the last tournament of the fall semester. Kellyville attended the tournament of course. Some of the little schools feed everyone lunchroom pizza when they host tournaments, but since there were half a dozen fast food restaurants within three or four blocks of our school, we just gave people an hour to get their own lunch.

Our game with Kellyville was the last one before lunch. I actually had a decent game and kept it close for awhile, but they pulled away in the second half. When I went to shake P.J.'s hand after the match, I asked him where they were going to lunch. "Uh, McDonalds, I think."

"Mind if I tag along?" I asked, giving him the best smile I could.

P.J. just stammered but he nodded yes, retreating to his team gathered in the corner of the room. I just stood there looking at them, awkwardly waiting for their huddle to break. Their coach said something about how well they were playing that morning and then finally said "Let's go to lunch."

I had hoped that P.J. would say something to the coach but he didn't, so I just walked up beside her in the hall and said "Y'all are going to McDonald's, right?" She said yes and that they would be delighted for me to join them. She'd probably heard me ask P.J. after the match.

At that lunch, everyone was probably awkward and shy compared to their normal selves, including me. But I remember it as a session of witty banter worthy of the Algonquin Round Table, with me serving as Dorothy Parker, of course. Mostly, we talked about movies. P.J. was certain that, while One Flew Over the Cuckoo's Nest was the superior film, Rocky was a shoe-in for the best picture Oscar. Colgan argued vociferously for either Cuckoo's Nest or Dog Day Afternoon, and apparently hated Rocky. At least that's the way I remembered the conversation, but years later, P.J. told me they must have been talking about something at least slightly different, because Cuckoo's Nest and Rocky actually both won best picture in different years.

Anyway, I liked Rocky fine, didn't tell them that I hadn't seen either of the other two movies just mentioned, and feared that they'd laugh at me when I told them my favorite movie of the year was Shampoo. One of the other kids on the team – I'm not sure I ever knew his name and I'm quite sure I never saw him buzz in – did actually laugh. To my surprise, however, P.J. defended the pick, saying it was a very well-done film and might win some acting awards. As it turned out, only Lee Grant got a nod for best supporting actress, but it got a couple of technical nominations.

P.J. also really recommended a movie called Barry Lyndon, saying it was "based on some book only Colgan ever read, but it's Kubrick, so it turned out to be really good." I told him I thought it was still playing at one of the theatres in town, so I would have to check it out. He said he was jealous since it hadn't even come to the little one-screen theater in Thomasville, and he'd had to go to Montgomery to see it. I told him if he'd come to Mobile the next time he wants to see something that's not playing back home, I would be happy to go with him.

Colgan chuckled, which I didn't particularly appreciate, but P.J. blushed, which I took as a good sign. I didn't know how to follow up though, so I just sat there smiling at him, hoping he would say that he would be coming down next week to watch something. He didn't though, and the conversation moved on. I figured out that hints, no matter how direct, were never going to work. I would have to work up the guts to ask him.

The regional tournament happens in the middle of the spring semester each year, with the state tournament happening a little bit before the end of school in mid-May. So the regionals happen a little bit before prom season starts. My senior year, Kellyville hosted the regional tournament. On the bus ride up there, I decided that I was gonna convince P.J. to go to prom with me, either at Murphy or Kellyville, I didn't care which.

As always happened at tournaments, everyone gathered in the school auditorium before the games started. We got there early enough that they hadn't started the meeting yet, so I marched right up to where Kellyville's team was sitting and asked P.J. whether he'd rather take me to prom here or at Murphy. He blushed again, but he didn't say anything. His coach was walking up to the microphone to start the tourney, and he recovered his composure and told me he'd let me know which after our game with them.

It was Colgan that convinced him to actually go to Kellyville's prom with me. They had apparently been planning for P.J. to dress up like a chauffeur and drive Colgan and his girlfriend around that night. Talk about the ultimate third wheel. None of them, including P.J., had apparently considered the idea that P.J. might have his own date. To Colgan's credit, he had immediately relieved P.J. of driving duty when this possibility manifested itself. After they beat us by about 250 and ended my chances of ever getting to go to state tournament, P.J. walked up and said, “I would love to take you to our prom if you can get up here. It’s on May 14th. The best place to meet is the Panther Drive-In.”

The actual prom date between me and P.J. ended up going about like you’d expect for the first date in the lives of a couple of awkward nerds. To be honest, I remember the details of all the work I did to get that prom date perfectly, but I hardly remember the actual night. It wasn’t bad, really, from what I recall, it was just awkward and formalistic, and I guess neither of us felt enough of a spark to justify driving the two hours for a second date.

CHAPTER 9

THE HIGH SCHOOL SWEETHEART

My name is Steffanny Snodgrass Miller. That's right 2F's, 2N's nobody ever gets that right, but hell, having a name that's impossible to spell is still better than being named Snodgrass. At least when I got married, I picked up a regular, boring name. That's about the only good thing about my ex-husband.

Anyhow, Colgan Toomey was the best damn lover of my life. My God he was fine. Tall and tan, rippling muscles in his arms and legs. Every girl in school wanted Colgan. He had hair that was red, but not carrot-top orange. You'd probably call his hair auburn on a woman. I swear he could make me cum just by flashing those sea green eyes. God, there were waves for days inside his eyes, I just kept falling every time until he caught me.

I loved the way he made me feel. There's never been anyone else like him. I shouldn't say that; I mean Tommy's been good to me, helped me try to get my shit back together. I mean this is only like the second time since we moved in together that I've tweaked out. Thinking about Colgan does that to me though; it makes me want to get so completely fucked up that it feels almost as good as him inside me. I guess I've basically been chasing that high ever since then. God, I know that's fucked up.

I remember our first time, I'm pretty sure it was the first time for both of us. When we met, both of us were 15; I was in ninth grade, but Colgan had skipped a grade so he was a sophomore. He was so smart and so good at explaining everything we did in school to me.

We had been on a few dates – which meant his dad took us to the Panther Drive-In and sat outside in his truck while we ate and maybe talked a little bit and then his dad took me home. But we kissed for a few minutes every day before school. It's almost silly now to think of us out behind the gym sucking on each other's tongues, but I still get a thrill just thinking about it.

But anyway, back to the first time. It was a Thursday afternoon right after school–I remember the date exactly, November 17, 1976. Colgan was a junior and I was a sophomore. Colgan walked me up onto the porch and we could see that the door was open. My dad was passed out drunk on the couch. He usually worked 6-3 at the paper mill and got home right after I did, but it turned out he had been laid off that day.

I saw dad lying there and I just immediately turned around and wrapped my arms around Colgan and kissed him for all I was worth. He was so surprised he almost slipped off the porch. Then I reached behind me and pushed the door the rest of the way open, practically dragging him inside. I saw him look toward my dad, so I whispered "I don't think he's waking up anytime soon." There was an empty bottle of Jose Cuervo on the table next to his hand.

We crept along behind the couch until we could turn up the stairs. Damn I'm getting wet just thinking about that afternoon. By the time we were upstairs I had made up my mind that this boy was gonna pop my cherry this afternoon whether he wanted to or not. I grabbed his arms with both hands and practically threw him on the bed when we got to my room.

Colgan seemed a bit bewildered at first, but he didn't exactly complain about the situation. Once I had him on the bed, I leaned over and kissed him passionately as I started unbuttoning his shirt. As soon as I got done with his shirt, I unbuttoned his pants, and I heard him gasp a little inside the noise of our kiss as I touched his already-hardening penis for the first time.

Everybody says the first time hurts for everyone and it's always awkward and all that. If that was true for me and Colgan, either the memories of all the other better times afterwards or all the drugs I've done since then have erased it. I remember sheer ecstasy from the moment he entered me, and from that moment I wanted to feel it over and over and over again.

Colgan was gentle but powerful, touching every part of my body and soul with those big hands and what came with them. That first time we dove right in, but he quickly learned a million ways to set my skin and soul on fire. After that first day, there wasn't a day for the next year and a half that he didn't make me orgasm some way or another. And there was hardly any place in town we hadn't done it. One time I even hid in the locker room and gave him a blow job when he told Coach Brooks he had to take a piss right before a ballgame. I wanted to hide in there til halftime too, but Colgan wouldn't let me.

Colgan was mostly a good kid, upstanding citizen, boy scout type, but I really think he liked me being a bad girl. He loved that I was a freak of course, but he also never minded me smoking (including marijuana occasionally, but he only got high with me a couple of times, said he didn't really like the way it made him feel). I remember the goody two-shoes cheerleaders in his class hated me so much, but I loved it. I'm sure Colgan wouldn't have approved of the shit I got into later, but maybe that never would have happened if he'd been around.

I'm not blaming Colgan though. I can't. I used to think it was all my own damned fault, sometimes I still do. But even if it wasn't all my fault, it sure as hell wasn't Colgan's. Even though I begged him to go somewhere closer than Texas. I begged him, but I told him it wouldn't matter. I told him I would be there for him no matter what and I would come to Austin the next year. Then everything went straight to hell within a couple months of Colgan's leaving.

I tried, I really did. I loved that man with everything I had. For the first month and a half, I wrote him letters every day. Pages and pages every day. But I was a stupid kid, and I liked to party. I was lonely and self-absorbed when Colgan wasn't around, and I self-medicated myself with weed and alcohol for my depression. I've basically been doing it ever since, the drugs just got stronger.

I can honestly say that I know that night itself wasn't my fault. I've seen too many other victims get wrongly blamed to give a free pass to the guy who raped me. But damn, it's taken a lot for me to even get to that point, and I still feel like I did everything else wrong, before and after that moment.

I never should have even been at that party. I should have been working my ass off to make sure I got into Texas so I could be with my man. But instead I was drunk and trying to find someone who had a joint at a bonfire in Thomasville after we had played them in football. It was one of the guys on their football team. I thought he was just paranoid about being seen with weed when I asked him about it and he started leading me into the woods behind the pasture where we had the bonfire going.

I have no idea how I found my way out of the woods after he was through with me. I remember walking around in a daze and eventually stumbling back into the party. I'm sure everyone just thought I was stoned off my ass, and I can't really blame them. It's not like I actually told anyone and they didn't believe me.

I think it was the next Monday when I found a program from the game in the floorboard of Rachel's truck. I looked the guy up by the number I remembered on his letter jacket, 91. His name was Donnie Thompson. Right now, as far as I know, he's still a deputy sheriff in Clarke County. Ten or twelve years after that night, he was one of the officers who busted me for cooking meth. I'm pretty sure most of the time I ended up catching was for spitting in his face when he was trying to cuff me.

After that night I felt like I couldn't face Colgan. I still don't really know why though. In a life full of stupid shit I've done, that might be the stupidest – not giving him a chance to make it at least a little bit better. I'm not saying he really could have fixed anything. I don't know if anyone could. But I still really don't know what made me, in the time of my greatest sadness, turn away from the one person who had always made me happy.

I guess it was partly shame, or maybe just a kind of knowledge. Maybe now that I knew the worst about guys in general, I couldn't accept the good things about Colgan. It might have been different if I hadn't gotten pregnant. But honestly, I'm not sure it would have mattered. Yeah, it meant that a bunch of other people knew that something had happened. But I would have known anyway. No matter what, I would have known.

I hid my pregnancy from my parents until almost Thanksgiving. My mom just figured it out one day. I have no idea how long she kept her knowledge to herself before she came to talk to me. We decided that I would drop out of school after the end of the semester and go stay with her sister in Montgomery, then I would give the baby up for adoption and maybe come back and finish my last semester next year. It didn't work out that way of course. I mean I went to Montgomery and I gave the baby up for adoption, but I never did go back to school.

The last month or so in Kellyville was a daze. I mostly stayed in my room, skipped school most of the time. Hell, I was dropping out anyway, so what was the point. A few discerning friends probably figured out what was going on, but no one ever tried to talk to me about it. Rachel and Julie were generally like "What's wrong" and "We're worried about you," but I just told them I wasn't getting letters from Colgan anymore and let them think that's why I was depressed.

The truth is, I still got letters from Colgan every other week or so. At first, I had written him every day, and his weekly letters back never seemed enough. For the first couple of weeks after I was raped, I tried to at least match his one letter a week, but my letters got farther and farther apart and by October I just gave up. His letters eventually went to every other week, but never farther apart than that. I later found out he called my mom multiple times, but she always just said I was out. If my parents had had any sense at all, they'd have pushed me toward that boy, not helped me fall away from him.

I wanted to write him one long letter to tell him what was going on, but I couldn't bring myself to do it. I finally decided I owed it to him to let him know somehow, though. I thought about writing to his dad, but I had no idea where he had gone in his quest to join the church. Their house had been empty since a few days after Colgan left for Texas. Eventually someone rented it, but I can't remember now if it was before or after Colgan came home over Christmas. I already knew that at Christmastime he was going to stay with P.J. and his mom.

I don't think P.J. ever liked me very much. Maybe he just knew I never had the kind of potential Colgan did. Later on, after it became more common, I thought for a little while that he was gay and had been in love with Colgan himself. But the truth is, he was probably just a regular kid who was a little miffed that his best friend suddenly started to spend part of his time hanging out with a girl instead of him. I didn't really have anything against P.J., but I knew he didn't like me.

So there was something masochistic in the decision I made to tell P.J. instead of Colgan. I knew I was probably walking into a minefield, since Colgan would have told him that I had stopped writing. Hell, he might have told P.J. that he didn't want to be with me anymore anyway and he was glad that I stopped. More than that, my pregnancy was already starting to show, and, more than anyone else probably, P.J. knew that Colgan hadn't been home, and I hadn't been out to Texas. But somehow, I convinced myself that I had to face P.J. and tell him everything.

I went over and sat on Colgan's back porch and cried on the day that P.J. came home from Tuscaloosa. I could see his front door from there, but I had no real clue when he would be coming back. I had tried to cut back on smoking after I found out I was pregnant, but the pile of butts at my feet got pretty big before I saw him come home about 4:30 that afternoon.

Part of me wanted to rush right over and spill my guts when he arrived, but I decided to wait until his mom went to bed. I knew she was usually up really early cooking breakfast at the café, so I figured I wouldn't have to wait too late for her to shut down for the evening. As soon as I saw the light go off in the living room, I decided to walk down to the back of the house and knock on P.J.'s window.

P.J. came out on the back porch. I could tell he was absolutely overwhelmed by the situation. He was the only one I ever told the whole story, at least for a long time. Tommy knows most of it, I think. I never told him the part about how great Colgan was, of course. But anyway, I knew I was putting P.J. in an impossible situation. I mean, what was he supposed to do, this wasn't exactly something he could decide for Colgan.

I don't know what I wanted from him. I think part of me wanted him to cuss me out and tell me to leave Colgan the fuck alone. He didn't do that of course. He told me I needed to talk to Colgan. He said he would be home the day after Christmas. "What if he doesn't want to see me?" I cried. P.J. said he had no idea what Colgan would say, but he knew for certain Colgan would want to know.

I didn't argue, but I wasn't sure I believed him. I couldn't believe Colgan would want anything to do with me. But I think I was even more afraid that he would forgive me. He didn't deserve that. I mean what was he going to do, marry me and take care of someone else's kid? Even if he was willing to do that, or even if I gave the kid up for adoption, I just couldn't put the responsibility for putting me back together again on him. I knew he didn't deserve that.

That's probably true that he didn't deserve to be stuck with me. But I do wish I had given him the chance to make that decision. Maybe if I could have given him a reason to come back to Alabama, he wouldn't have gone to South America and gotten himself killed.

CHAPTER 10

THE BEST FRIEND'S UNCLE

I don't know what my sister's boy P.J. has told you about me, but I'm really not a bad guy, and, save the first couple years after I moved back to Kellyville, I'm not a drunk either. I just have a little less need for human contact than I used to, and a little less than most people, I suppose. When the guy who claimed to be your best friend for 25 years steals your wife and together they screw you out of your business, it might affect your faith in the human race too.

But like I said, I'm really not a bad guy. By the time I moved to Kellyville, I certainly preferred sitting alone in my library and reading to pretty much any other activity. I wanted to do nice things when I could though. For example, I let the boy scouts camp on my land whenever they wanted as long as they stayed away from my house. I even kept my boat tied up in the slough at the back of my property and let the boys use it when they wanted. If you knew where you were going, it wasn't hard to get into the Tombigbee from there.

Colgan and P.J. were in the boy scouts as soon as they were old enough. Like every activity he participated in, Colgan soon became the rock star of the group. He earned every merit badge that it was possible to get as soon as he reached the requisite age. Eventually he would earn his Eagle Scout, the first boy in the history of the Kellyville troop to do so. The next year, he helped P.J. complete his as well.

The two of them were basically inseparable, and they spent most of their weekends in the woods. Unlike most of the kids in rural Alabama, Colgan never liked guns much. He did target shooting with the other scouts for his merit badges, but for hunting, which was undoubtedly the most common local pastime, he taught himself (and then P.J.) how to use a bow and arrow.

Predictably, the two of them each brought down their first deer the same weekend. I think they were in sixth or seventh grade. Michael Toomey found an old black man at the paper mill who was willing to teach them to clean and dress the animals. Michael wasn't opposed to hunting, but he was adamant that the meat be used. At 13, Colgan could not only fully dress and butcher the deer, he could cook eight or ten dishes with the meat. I wouldn't have been surprised to see him wearing a jacket made of deer hide.

What amazed me more than anything, though, was how such a big kid could move in what seemed to me like complete silence. P.J. used to tell stories about him sneaking up on turkeys and even rabbits. He caught a rabbit by hand one time. He and P.J. built a fire and roasted it on a stick. Later that day, they found a warren of three small rabbit kits in the roots of a hickory tree that had been half uprooted in a storm. It had somehow stayed alive but was leaning into a hillside. Colgan was sure that these babies were the offspring of the rabbit they had killed. He took them home and bottle fed them. Two of the three survived and were his pets all through high school.

There was a story that went around during Colgan and P.J.'s junior year that Colgan had killed a buck by jumping out of a tree, landing on its back, and slitting its throat. Colgan never confirmed it, and maybe it was a fabrication, but it seemed exactly the kind of thing Colgan would try. He was always looking for a bigger challenge. He had instinctively rejected guns as too easy. It did not surprise me that he would eventually reject arrows as well. If he thought he could do it with his bare hands, he would probably try.

I remember when I first heard that Colgan had been kidnapped. My sister started beating on my door about nine o'clock one night. It was the middle of summer, so I wasn't quite asleep yet (I tend to rise and fall with the sun in my old age.) I came downstairs as quickly as I could muster. Angie was still wearing her uniform from the diner. P.J. had apparently called her at work after receiving a call from Michael Toomey.

She was agitated enough that I couldn't figure out what she was saying at first, so I led her into the sitting room and poured her three fingers of scotch. After a pretty good gulp (I've seen Angie drink maybe three times in my life), she calmed down enough to tell me that some Salvadoran rebel group had kidnapped Colgan.

My first thought was that those commie bastards had no clue what they'd gotten themselves into. I figured this would end either with a bunch of dead guerrillas or something like O. Henry's famous story The Ransom of Red Chief, with the Salvadorans making a big donation to Doctors Without Borders to take Colgan back. I couldn't imagine those guys getting the drop on Colgan, much less keeping him long enough to collect the ransom.

I told Angie that Colgan was smart and resourceful and a survivor. I knew she loved that kid like he was her own. She and Michael and P.J. and Colgan were more of a family than most groups of four people where the adults were married and the kids were blood related. I never heard of any kind of physical relationship between her and Michael, but they clearly loved each other at some level, even if it was just platonic.

I know it had been hard on her when Michael went to join the monastery, especially when it came on the heels of both P.J. and Colgan going off to college. Everyone who was important in her life moved away within a few weeks. At least P.J. came home every once in a while. Colgan made it back to Kellyville maybe twice after he left for Austin. Michael, of course, never came back, except for Colgan's funeral. Angie just poured even more of her soul into that diner, but I knew she was torn up inside. Losing Colgan again seemed like too much for her.

To our knowledge, Colgan was in captivity for about a month. Angie went twice to Montgomery to lobby the Alabama legislature to convince the Reagan administration to accede to the guerrilla's demands and get Colgan back. It was a fool's errand. The country was never going to change its foreign policy to recover one kid from backwoods Alabama whose family had no money or political connections. Nonetheless, she was planning a trip to Washington to go straight to the feds when we found out Colgan had been killed.

This time, Michael showed up at my door too, and the three of us drank a bottle of scotch that night. Before he joined the monastery, Michael Toomey had been the coolest, most collected, most poised man I'd ever met. I don't think he'd ever raised his voice in anger, and he'd raised a pretty rambunctious teenager, or two, really. That night he blubbered like a baby, even before the scotch hit him.

Michael said it was all his fault, that Colgan was running away from him because he joined the Church. I tried to reason with him, ask him what exactly was his fault? That he had raised a son who wanted to go to Latin America and help the less fortunate? Or one who had the intellect and the grades to get into med school and use that as his method of helping them? I just couldn't understand the idea that either Colgan or Michael had done anything wrong.

Michael still seemed to believe that Colgan shouldn't have been there. I don't really understand why. Maybe it was that there was plenty that needed to be done to help people in this country, and maybe it was just the twisted logic of a man beset by grief. I can be rightly accused of wallowing in self-pity sometimes, but my self-pity was basically self-aware, and I knew that Michael had faced sadness and loss on a level that I would, thankfully, never comprehend. As I led him and Angie to separate guest bedrooms that evening, my final thought was that I hoped his God provided a solace that he, like me, seemed incapable of finding in other human beings.

P.J. showed up the next day. In contrast to Angie's wailing and Michael's self-loathing, P.J. existed in a state of disbelief. According to him, the news from El Salvador was wrong; Colgan had escaped and the people that had kidnapped him didn't want to admit it. Furthermore, the CIA (which had confirmed to Michael that it believed the claims of the rebel group) was biased because they had a stake in the game—they, and the rest of the U.S. government wanted to trot out the idea that the Salvadoran rebels had killed a couple of brilliant American med students so that Americans would overlook the atrocities of the regime our country was propping up. Then he started going into all the awful things the Salvadoran junta had done to its people.

His mother and Michael eventually sat him down and told him he had to calm down and accept the truth. Of course, nobody wanted to believe it, but Colgan was dead. I don't know if he was just working his way through the stages of grief or if Michael said something that finally made it sink in. By the mid-afternoon, he was despondent rather than defiant. The speech he wrote for the funeral was one of the most depressing things I've ever read. I'm kind of glad he went off script, though at first I was worried that he would revert to a political rant about how awful the Salvadoran regime was. Most Americans, especially in the South, didn't want to hear that on a good day, much less when they believed one of their own had been killed by the godless commie rebels opposing that regime.

CHAPTER 11

THE PRISON GUARD

I have seen many men come through the doors of Santa Maria Prison. Men who thought they were macho, big men, strong men. All of them wept in the arms of Santa Maria. All but one. One man, a gringo they say, though perhaps a demon from hell. Some, though, might call him an angel from heaven. His only name was El Colo Loco.

I had already been a guard at Santa Maria for many years before Saint Romero was killed and the world went crazy and everyone in El Salvador went to war with themselves. I just kept doing my job, not because I hated the rebels or loved the government, but because it was the only job I'd ever known.

I didn't hate the prisoners even when they were actual murderers and thieves and rapists, and I wasn't going to start hating them now that they were just people who didn't agree with D'Aubuisson and Duarte. I was lucky that I was already an old man. They didn't expect me to beat anyone up or rip out any fingernails. I just cleaned up after them.

I remember when they brought him in. It was toward the end of June in 1990. I remember because it happened right about the time that Costa Rica made their run to the World Cup quarterfinals. Everyone gathered around the old black and white TV in the guards' room; we even let some of the regular prisoners come, but not the rebels. That would never have been allowed. It was amazing to see a CentroAmericana team beat two European squads—one was Sweden I know; I am too old to remember the other. If Costa Rica could do it, maybe someday El Salvador would do well. Alas we are still waiting. El Salvador has never won a World Cup game; we haven't even qualified since before that day we were watching Costa Rica and dreaming.

But back to El Colo Loco. He came two or three days after the Ticos won their last group game. The soldiers who had taken over most of the prison jobs heard that an important rebel had been captured well before he showed up. The sick bastards started getting excited because they knew this would be somebody they could use all their tricks on. They took bets on how long he would take to break and who would be the one to make him beg for his mother.

Nobody ever won that bet. I didn't see El Colo the first day. Maybe not the second or third day either. I don't remember for sure. Their first torture session was nonstop; they worked in shifts, poking him with electric cattle prods, putting their cigarettes out on his skin, slicing his hands with hundreds of tiny cuts. He never gave in. I heard them say that even after they had to hold him to keep him upright, he spit on the Commandante when he walked into the cell. I never knew what it was they wanted to learn from that man, but I am certain that they never did.

When I finally saw him, El Colo Loco lay in a heap in the middle of his cell. I was told to make him get up onto the bed, so I could clean up the floor. One look told me he wasn't standing up on his own any time soon. I squatted beside him and gave him a close look. I couldn't tell exactly how tall he was, but even balled on the floor, I knew he was probably the tallest man I'd seen. We Salvadorans are a short people, stocky and dark like the low granite hills that make the backbone of our country. This guy was completely different. Orange-red hair and skin that, even with a good summer tan, was several shades lighter than mine. I remember wondering where the hell this guy was from – Spain? Argentina maybe?

As I was squatting there wondering, a scream from another cell woke him and he reached out and grabbed my forearm. His eyes opened, a surreal sea-foam green, somewhere between emerald and peridot. I said something to the effect of "we need to get you up on the bed."

He let go of my arm and said he could do it. He spoke perfect Spanish, but I couldn't place the accent. He looked at his hands and I knew he wouldn't be able to push himself up. He looked at me, and somehow, in spite of everything, he smiled.

"I was wrong," he said, "I cannot do it alone. Will you help me?"

Somehow, the way he said it, it made me feel honored to help him. Here was this guy, stuck in a prison, bleeding from most of the parts of his body, unable to get himself off the floor, yet still he had this presence, this insane ability to make someone else feel special and make them want to do his bidding. I honestly believe that if El Colo had ever asked me to help him escape or wanted me to do something for the rebels, I would have done it. He never tried. In fact, after I helped him onto the bed that day, he never asked me for anything.

But after that, every time I walked by his cell, he asked me if I wanted him to pray to St. Romero for me. The first time I said no, wondering if anyone else would hear about it, but he said that's okay, I'll just pray to the Virgin for you. He held up a rosary circle he had made of knotted toilet paper.

I thanked him for praying for me and thought that would be the end of it, but every time he saw me for the next few days, he asked me if he could pray to Saint Romero for me, and I finally relented. He held my hand through the bars and said a simple prayer just asking the Saint to watch over and protect me. Every time I saw him for the next three years, he said the same prayer.

Eventually I learned that El Colo was American. At first the soldiers didn't want anyone to know that. One of the main things the government always said was that there was no reason for people to support the rebels because the Americans were on Duarte's side, and they would always prop him up no matter what. Later though I heard rumors that the government was going to trade El Colo back to the Americans for money or tanks or fighter jets or something.

I also found out that El Colo had been a doctor or medic when he started with the rebels. Apparently, the great mercenary had never been a soldier before he came to El Salvador. Later, I met someone who said that El Colo saved his life. This man said El Colo never even fired a shot during all the years of the rebellion. The squads he commanded blew up army barracks, helicopters, and even a naval warship, but El Colo himself never carried anything more lethal than pain killers and surgical knives into battle.

Eventually I heard stories of El Colo saving the lives of both his rebel compatriots and seriously wounded government soldiers. But the most famous story, the one the guards and the other prisoners told me more times than I can count, was the story of Suchitoto. Suchitoto was a village in the northern part of Cuscatlan province, a little vacation town on Suchitlan Lake of the Rio Lempa. Right across the lake was the Chalatenango province, the rebel stronghold in the north.

El Colo's squadron got word that a major government or army official was staying at the fancy hotel on the lake in Suchitoto. The rebels had eyes and ears among the staff at the resort. El Colo devised a plan to row across the lake on a raft, late at night, grab the official, and get him back across the lake to Chalatenango before sunrise. The man turned out to be a general in the Salvadoran Air Force named Alvaro Martin.

The kidnapping almost went off without a hitch. They had General Martin bound and out of the hotel when a group of soldiers on patrol showed up and cut off their escape to the lake. No one knows whether the soldiers showed up at random or whether someone at the hotel switched sides and tipped them off. In any case, the soldiers showed up in a jeep and blocked the squad's path to the raft. They jumped out and leveled their machine guns at the rebels but El Colo stepped in front of his compatriots holding General Martin with his arm around his throat.

"Kill me if you must," he shouted in Spanish, "If you think you can hit me without killing your precious general. His name is Alvaro Martin; you may have heard of him. You start shooting and he dies. But you can have me and him both if you let my squad just go on down to the water and row back over to Chalatenango."

When the soldier in charge hesitated, El Colo's grip tightened on the General's neck. "Or I can just break this guy's neck. Yeah you'll shoot some of us afterward, and some of us will shoot some of you, but any of you who lives will be carrying the body of General Martin back to your supervisors." The soldiers relented quickly and yelled at the rest of the rebels to get back on the raft and be gone.

You may be thinking that this is the story of how El Colo got caught and came to the Santa Maria prison. You are wrong! El Colo did not get captured that night. No one knows for sure what happened after the soldiers watched the rest of the squad push off into Lake Suchitlan.

No one on the rebel side saw El Colo that night, and he never said a word about what happened. The squad went back across the lake and reported that El Colo had been captured. The rebel commander didn't seem to care a whole lot; he was more worried about losing all the medical supplies El Colo usually carried.

The next morning, one of the rebels on patrol by the lake came upon El Colo finishing stitching up a wound on General Martin's right calf. Not only had he gotten away from the squad of soldiers, he had taken General Martin with him, and somehow swam him across the lake while the general was bleeding from a stab wound. Either that or somehow he convinced the soldiers to drive him around the lake and drop him off, letting him keep the general. Neither one seems particularly probable, but one or the other must have happened. Even if he had help from some of the staff at the hotel, it was a pretty amazing story. The rebels began to believe that El Colo could work magic.

General Martin was kept as a hostage for over a year and then exchanged for a rebel prisoner. That one had been in Santa Maria for awhile. He was nothing like El Colo. He was an Italian Communist dandy named Giacomo Baggiani who claimed to be a philosopher and thought he was a hero because he had once snuck some of Antonio Gramsci's notebooks out of an Italian prison in his underwear. He said he came to El Salvador to "inspire the revolution." From what I could tell, he sure as hell didn't come to fight in it.

Anyway, even after he was released, General Martin would never tell anyone how El Colo had captured him. The one time he was asked about it, the general said "That man is a rebel and an enemy of the state, but he saved my life. I hope he is captured. I hope his cause his defeated. But I cannot hope for his death." That was not exactly the kind of propaganda the government wanted so there were never any more quotes from General Martin about his time in captivity. The whole story made El Colo one of the known leaders of the rebellion. A few months later, his squad sank a navy ship with explosives and his legend became known throughout El Salvador.

When El Colo finally did get caught, there was much less mystery to the story. His squad had raided a government outpost and thought they had killed everyone but one wounded soldier. The squad set about getting all the weapons and supplies they had come for while El Colo tended to two wounded men, one of his own, and the one government soldier. When the squad got everything together, they went to put it in the truck, while two men stayed with El Colo and put the wounded squad member on a field stretcher.

When his own man had been taken out to the truck, El Colo moved to the wounded soldier. While his squad members were outside, a group of regular army soldiers showed up and got into a firefight with the rebels. The rebels were hugely outnumbered and before El Colo had any idea what was going on, they had been overwhelmed and the soldiers were running into the room where he was tending to their colleague. There was no miraculous escape this time, and El Colo showed up at Santa Maria the next day.

This was, of course, according to prison guards who had talked to soldiers who said they were there when he was captured. One never really knows how much truth you get from these people. El Colo and I came to talk about many things, but mostly about God and Saint Romero. He never tried to tell me that the rebellion was right in all things, but he gently emphasized some of the awful crimes of the government, adding to what I saw with my own eyes.

We learned of the Chapultepec Agreement in a staff meeting early one morning. All of a sudden, the rebellion was over and everyone in El Salvador was supposed to be friends again. Some of the rebels were just let out of Santa Maria onto the streets. El Colo was different. I think the government was afraid to admit to the Americans that it had imprisoned and tortured an American citizen. So instead of releasing him, we held on to him even after the accords were signed. Then he was taken out in the middle of the night and dropped off on the other side of the Guatemalan border.

Over the years after the peace agreement there would be "truth commissions" and government reports and stories written from every conceivable angle, but the truth is not something you can know. Each person's truth must be believed. Each of those beliefs carry meaning. Reality isn't what stands up when the biases are taken out of the stories. It is made of the biases themselves. They are its building blocks.

My truth, my reality, is that no matter what bad things he may have done, El Colo was both a great man and a good man. He was the most fascinating man I ever met, and the only thing that I would change about my interactions with him, is that, if I had known he was leaving, I would have said goodbye to him.

CHAPTER 12

THE COLONEL

I worked for thirty years at that God-forsaken place. I honestly thought I was making a positive difference in the world. Part of me wants to ask forgiveness because I knew not what I did, but the truth is I don't deserve forgiveness. I had every tool I needed to figure out what was going on, but I was willfully blind to it. Even after I opened my eyes, I was willfully dumb.

We'll get back to the School of the Americas later. I think you'll understand things a little better if I tell you a bit about myself first. My name is Colonel Harlan Lawson. I was an enlisted Marine in World War II, was almost cut in half by a grenade at Tarawa, then patched up over the course of a little over a year at a hospital in Hawaii. Then I got out just in time to be wounded again at Iwo Jima. That one wasn't nearly as bad though, I was pretty much good in five months, and the war ended right after I had rejoined my unit, while we were preparing for the invasion of the Japanese home islands.

I had enlisted on my eighteenth birthday, which fell about halfway through my senior year in high school. The recruiting officer in Tahlequah, Oklahoma was a bitter fifty-year-old who had had both legs blown off at Belleau Wood during World War I. He probably knew that my dad didn't want me to sign up until I got through with high school, but he didn't give a damn. I may be ascribing too much to the personality of that asshole, though; I'm not sure any recruiting officer in November of 1942 would have cared what a kid's parents thought if he was eighteen and ready to go.

So anyway, off I went, before graduating high school, to Marine Corps basic training and my eventual station in the Pacific. Dad, as you might expect, was pissed at first, but quickly forgave me. He got elected to the Tribal Council of the Cherokees the same year I enlisted, and somehow he was able to convince the Corps to let him and mom hop a ride to Hawaii while I was in the hospital.

Despite the defiant shenanigans of skipping out on the second half of my senior year, Dad told me he was really proud of me, and all he asked was that I get my diploma when I got home. I promised I would, so when the war ended, I went to this special program at Northeast Oklahoma Junior College where you could finish high school in one semester and start college the next. I completed the year there, but I was already applying to other colleges before I finished the high school portion.

That's when Dad and one of my old commanding officers showed up to meet me coming out of school one day. They had decided that I was academy material and I was going to seek an appointment whether I wanted to or not. Now, I've taken a lot of flak in the years since from some of my old Marine buddies for ending up at West Point, even been called (in jest I presume) a traitor to the Corps for going Army. I assure you that, at the time, I wanted to go to OU to try to play football, but if I had been given the chance to choose a service academy, it would have been Annapolis.

In the years following the war, there was some uncertainty about the whole appointment system, and sometimes officers were just grabbing men out of the field that they thought were academy-worthy. I don't know if my old commander just didn't have that kind of pull, or if he and Dad made the decision that I was going to go the old school route of seeking an appointment through a member of Congress. In any case, it was Dad who really had the inside track to get me into an Academy.

Like a lot of mixed Native Americans, I hadn't put a whole lot of interest into tribal politics. I thought of the Tribal Council as sort of an honorary thing and not that big a deal. But it was a big deal to our part-Cherokee Congressman, a guy named William G. Stigler, who was the reason I ended up at West Point. He had served in France during World War I before getting elected to Congress. His service, of course, had been in the Army, and he wasn't about to give a kid in his district an appointment to anywhere but West Point.

So, after I finished my one year at Northeast, I boarded a train with one trunk containing everything I owned, about to be a 22-year-old plebe and wondering if I had made the worst mistake of my life. I had no idea whether my experience in combat would translate into any affinity whatsoever for the simulated pageantry of the academy. I also had grave doubts about the preparation I got from the public schools of Tahlequah, Oklahoma.

The academics were tough, I will grant you that. But I don't think they were any tougher for me than they were for most of the others, even if they were from New York or Boston or Chicago. There were a few brilliant ones of course, who didn't have to try in any class and took grades for granted that I had to bust my ass for. But I did bust my ass, and nobody finished that far ahead of me.

I suppose the social aspects would have been even rougher than the classes if I had been the only one that wasn't a gunner straight out of high school. In the late forties though, at least a third of every class was guys who had been in during the war. Most of them were Army though, and they had fought in Europe. Three guys that lived in my hallway were with McAuliffe when they fought out of encirclement at the Battle of the Bulge. I think I heard the whole "Nuts" story three hundred times my first year.

I wasn't the only marine though. There were even a couple of guys that had been at Tarawa, nobody from my unit though. The Academy bunked me with a Navy fella originally from Maine. Joshua Claybrook was his name, and he could sail anything that floats. He wouldn't say why he ended up at West Point, but it was clear that his heart was in Annapolis. It was just like the Army to send a promising young officer like him to a place as far as you could get from the sea. In his case, it was Fort Riley, Kansas. Joshua served his one required tour there and scurried home to Maine. He runs a charter boat service for tourists to Mount Desert Isle now. I wish I had had the good sense to go home after my initial commitment was done.

Instead, I stayed in until they wouldn't let me do it anymore. I even got a special extension to stay in at fifty-five, but mandatory retirement caught up with me at sixty-two, forty damn years after I showed up at West Point. Most of it spent, I am ashamed to admit, doing the devil's work at that god-forsaken school.

Before that though, like most of the people in my class, I fought in Korea. I got my Captain's bars at a place called Chongchon River right after my birthday in 1950. I never thought I'd miss the fucking jungle of the Pacific islands until I spent a winter in Korea. Even West Point was tropical compared to that frozen hellhole. We also got our ever-loving asses kicked by the Chinese in that battle, but our brigade was the one that prevented the Eighth Army from being completely encircled and covered the retreat. So, the two guys above me and I all got promotions out of the deal.

By the end of the war, I had been bumped up again to major, and someone decided that it was a good idea to put me in charge of training new recruits. Actually, though, I wasn't in charge of shit when I first got to Fort Gordon, Georgia. My job was to procure boots for the newbies. Everybody I know that worked with new recruits hated it. There was a reason our jobs sucked – they wanted us to be complete assholes to the newbies. They were also in the process of making us more sadistic, because one of my responsibilities after I'd been there for awhile was to design the "course of study" for new recruits. Basically, I got to help pick out what they had to do.

But anyway, like I said, it sucked, so as soon as I got a chance I signed up to go to Ranger school at Fort Benning, which was still in Georgia, but on the other side of the state. Ranger school is six weeks of absolute hell. I guarantee you when I got done with it, I never wanted to see Fort Benning again. I sure as heck never thought I'd be one of the birds running the place.

It was a long time before I actually came back. I was in the special forces now, and my unit was doing a bunch of bullshit that I'm technically not allowed to tell you about. We were in Vietnam before anyone had heard of the damn place, and by the time the grunts got over there, we had moved on. South America, the Middle East, even a couple forays into Eastern Europe.

But it seemed like most of our time was spent in Central America. I went into Nicaragua so many god-damned times I speak Spanish with a Nicoya accent. Eventually I got promoted out of my damn squad and sent to a place called the School of the Americas, which at the time was located at Fort Gulick in the Panama Canal Zone.

Panama would eventually kick us out, and we went back to Fort Benning of all places, but not before I helped train the most sadistic bastard I've ever met in my life. His name was Roberto d'Aubuisson, but he earned the nickname Blowtorch Bob, from an "improvement" he made on the techniques of torturous interrogation he learned from us.

Like I said, this guy was a pretty sick bastard. There were later stories from El Salvador that he would toss babies into the air and whip out his machine gun to see if he could shoot them before they fell. I don't doubt it for a second. He was the one that ordered the hit on Archbishop Romero, and he led the death squad that murdered the entire village of El Mozote.

The real problem was that everyone who knew this guy knew he was off his rocker. He once said that the Salvadoran government needed to kill at least half a million peasants to restore order, and it really didn't matter which ones. Yeah, we knew he was a bastard, but he was our bastard, and at the time, that was the only thing that mattered in the foreign policy of the United States. If you were against the communists, you were with us, no matter what you wanted to do (or actually did) to your own people.

The things we condoned through the School of the Americas and the people we unleashed on Nicaragua, Guatemala, El Salvador and numerous other Latin American countries were fundamentally unconscionable. It took me far too long to come to this realization. I should have resigned my commission when we left the Canal Zone at the latest.

But I didn't. I didn't have the guts. I went back to Fort Benning and I became the administrator of the whole damn thing. I guess I somehow made myself feel better because I didn't deal with the damn torturing bastards directly, but instead lobbied the bastards in the Pentagon and Congress for more funding to "train" them. Then I went out and hired some of the best young officers we had to do the dirty work I was glad I wasn't doing anymore.

I firmly believe our country should apologize to the people of the countries that we destabilized, that we unleashed terrible dictators and murderers upon, and to those, in America and abroad, that we taught that this was perfectly okay in the name of fighting communism. I am personally complicit in all of those things, and I am finally willing to admit it.

CHAPTER 13

THE RECRUITER, AGAIN

I set aside my misgivings about his willingness to focus on football in the euphoria of Colgan Toomey choosing Texas. I mean, hell, somehow, I, Dixie Dawkins, had landed quite possibly the best recruit in the country that year. I actually doubt he would have been ranked at the top if the recruiting services that do rankings had existed then, but he probably would still have been a 5-star.

But when Toomey and his dad arrived on move-in day in August, my fears were rekindled. They had road-tripped in a rented van from Alabama to Austin, a last chance for father-son bonding before Dad went off to become a different kind of Father. It had not gone well, apparently, and the two weren't speaking to each other when they arrived. I had no idea how many miles had passed in silence between them.

By the time I saw Toomey that morning, he had apparently grabbed what he considered his most valuable possessions – a gym bag hung from his left hand and he had a guitar case on his back. I also noticed he hadn't cut his hair since his visit in March. He did greet me exuberantly when he came into the football dorm where I was checking in the players, but he apparently expected his dad to bring in the rest of his stuff. I had to tell him he better get his ass out there and help him. He didn't argue or anything, just nodded kind of sullenly. I still wasn't ready to tell the other coaches of my doubts about him.

And throughout fall camp, he didn't give me any reason to. Physically, the kid was everything we expected him to be, and some things we didn't even expect. He was the fastest freshman on the team at a dead sprint, and only a couple of the upperclassmen, one of whom finished second in the

100-yard dash at the NCAA finals the year before, could beat him. One day in a scrimmage, Colgan threw an interception on a tipped ball. Before I knew what was happening he had hurdled a wide receiver that got blocked and then laid out the 250-pound linebacker who intercepted it. That linebacker went on to be all-Southwest Conference that season. He said the hit from Colgan was the hardest one he took all year.

Coach Akers told me the decision to redshirt Toomey was one of the toughest he made that year. To be honest, it probably shouldn't have been the toughest. We had a pretty good battle going on for the starter at quarterback. There were two seniors who had each started most of a season for us, both of them becoming starters due to injury halfway through the year. The one that everyone thought would start for us was Mark McBath, last year's starter until he got hurt against Oklahoma in the Red River Shootout.

That Oklahoma game was a hell of a story. I was still at Penn State but I remember watching it on TV because we had a bye week. OU was number 1 in the country, and Texas was ranked 5th. Earl Campbell had about ten touchdowns the first three weeks. Nobody had given a second thought to Texas's quarterback – heck, all he had to do was turn around and hand it to Campbell. Then McBath got hurt seven plays in, broke his ankle. Then the second stringer comes in and he lasts a quarter before he tears up his knee.

So off the bench trots Randy McEachern. Turns out he had never worked with the first team offense before that day. I think Randy threw about seven passes that day and completed less than half of them. But he didn't screw anything up, and the Longhorn defense was stout. Campbell got the only touchdown of the game, on a drive that I think included all of McEachern's completions, and Texas pulled the upset 13-6.

Randy McEachern continued his serviceable play the rest of the year. One game, against Arkansas, he even led a fourth quarter drive that relied mostly on passing, and he got named player of the game. He never had a lot of yards, but he usually didn't have to, since last year's team had Earl Campbell. In the Cotton Bowl at the end of the season, it became pretty clear that it would be tough to win just relying on him – Notre Dame's defense was good enough to at least slow Campbell down, and Randy threw three interceptions.

We didn't have the luxury of a superstar tailback anymore though, and it was a pretty tough decision between McEachern's steady mediocrity and McBath's slightly better running and passing skills. One of our biggest problems that season was that we never really made the decision. Both of them were great kids, both fifth-year seniors who had given their heart and soul, not to mention their bodies, to Longhorn football for about a quarter of the time they had been alive.

That was part of the problem in choosing between them, but the bigger problem was that Coach Akers (who had been an offensive coordinator before he took a head coaching job and still considered that his area of expertise) and Coach Manley, the current offensive coordinator, never could seem to get on the same page.

Anyhow, none of this really matters since y'all want to hear about Colgan and he was redshirting the whole time we couldn't choose between Mark and Randy. Nobody cares that we had a mediocre season with Colgan on the bench. By the middle of it, everyone was looking forward to next year's quarterback, but there were still huge doubts as to who that would be. Colgan was in competition with a kid named Donnie Little. Little only got in a couple of mop-up snaps behind Mark and Randy, but in so doing, he became the first African-American to play quarterback at UT. Donnie hadn't done anything truly spectacular, but he was clearly a talented kid, and he had some Texas high school records, so a lot of people were really excited to see what he would be able to do.

There was also, unfortunately, a contingent of people who were extremely opposed to starting Donnie at quarterback. Some of them even looked at Colgan as a sort of "great white hope" that would prevent the abomination of a black kid leading the offense at UT. I have often wondered whether this played a role in Colgan's decision not to return to the team after his injury. I know that it bothered him to be the hero of what he saw as a bunch of racist rednecks. But before he got hurt, I'm a hundred percent sure that he wanted to beat out Donnie fair and square and be the starting quarterback. He just never wanted it handed to him because of the color of his skin.

After the injury, I'm not sure he wanted it at all. And maybe part of that was just discovering other things in life. I heard he got a hot exotic girlfriend, for example. But I think part of it stemmed from the things he heard after he was hurt – he may have heard them before, but he was focused on getting the starting job and didn't pay them any attention. He was on crutches the rest of the season, but he did a lot of helping out with the trainers, just taping people up and stuff on the sidelines. He told me that at the Baylor game that year, a fan yelled at him "Hey Toomey, why'd you have to go and get yourself hurt and let that damn nigger be quarterback."

I'm pretty sure the coward wouldn't have said it if Colgan had been able to walk at the time, and I'm even more sure Colgan would have been in the stands in a heartbeat if he had been able to. Colgan's official reason for giving up football was that he wasn't sure he'd ever be able to come back and be any good, and he didn't feel comfortable taking up a scholarship if he wasn't going to be the player he thought he should be. I just had a feeling that maybe he was sticking it to that asshole fan by stepping aside and ensuring Donnie Little would be the starting QB. Or maybe he was just tired of putting in so much effort to please a bunch of racist assholes. I can't blame him for feeling that way, but I wish I could have convinced him to keep playing for his teammates and himself and not to worry about the minority of fans who were losers.

It probably didn't help that Colgan knew to a certainty that his father would never be there to watch him play a down of college football. I don't blame the guy for answering when he felt like God was calling him, but there's no question in my mind that Colgan felt abandoned, even though he would never talk about it.

If I remember correctly, Colgan took seven game snaps as the quarterback of the Texas Longhorns. They all came in the first game of the 1979 season, a non-conference tilt against Iowa State. Colgan had been doing pretty well in practice, but so had Donnie. I'm ashamed to say I think Coach Akers started the white kid just to avoid trouble. But we planned from the beginning to play both of them.

So Iowa State got the ball first and got a first down or two but then we stopped them. Colgan's first snap, he turned out the wrong way coming out from under center and couldn't hand off. He actually should have lost about four yards, but he juked the hell out of a defensive end and spun off another guy before diving forward for one of the more exciting one-yard quarterback runs you'd ever see. The next play we called an option; the end closed on Colgan, so he had to pitch it. I think the running back, probably A.J. Jones, got three or four yards. On third and five, the tight end dropped a pass Colgan put right on the money.

The next time we got the ball, we put Donnie Little in at quarterback. He didn't do anything spectacular, but Jones had a couple good runs and we got about 30 yards and kicked a field goal. Colgan got the next series, but it was only one play. Our defense had intercepted ISU and returned it to the four yard line. Colgan turned around and handed it to AJ and he went off tackle left for the touchdown. We were up ten zip, but Colgan really hadn't gotten to do anything.

ISU then mounted a long drive that ate up the rest of the second quarter and scored a touchdown. They missed the extra point, though, so we went into halftime up 10-6. We knew we'd have to open up the offense a bit in the second half if we wanted to pull away, and we decided to start the half with Colgan under center again.

As it turned out we got the briefest of glimpses of Colgan's brilliance before it was taken away (forever, as it turned out.) On the first play of the second half, Coach called a play-action pass. Colgan faked the hand off, drifted right, and laid a perfect ball over the wide receiver's outside shoulder. The whole sideline went nuts and we were sure we had a touchdown, but ISU's safety caught McKenzie around the five yard line.

The next play, we ran AJ up the middle for next to nothing. Then Coach Manley got a little more creative. We called a naked bootleg, with the tight end running a drag route back to the left while everything else but he and Colgan went right. Most of the ISU defense was fooled, but one safety sniffed it out and sprinted for the QB. The tight end was alone in the end zone, but I guess Colgan didn't think he could get the ball over the guy running at him. So he pump fakes and spins back toward the middle of the field, several yards behind the line of scrimmage now and reversing back to the side where everyone was.

My head was probably in my hands at this point, but I've watched the film so many times that I can't remember what I was doing during the actual play. Anyway, Colgan spins again away from a defensive lineman and starts running toward the other sideline pointing at a wide receiver. He pump fakes another guy and then AJ puts a linebacker flat on his back and Colgan hurdles him. At this point he's back to the line of scrimmage, which was probably about the four. He stiff arms a dude onto the sideline and is now tiptoeing trying to stay in bounds. Somehow, Colgan regains his footing and pirouettes almost to the goal line. Two guys are waiting for him. At this point, the average football player dives low and hopes the ref rules him across the line in the pile. Colgan decided to try to leap both guys.

Somehow, Colgan got high enough that he took a direct hit on each side of his knee from both players' helmets. He then flipped over into the endzone and landed on his back. Even though he had scored, there was no cheering on the sideline. It was clear he was hurt, but at first I thought it was at least possible that he just had the wind knocked out of him when he landed on his back.

I actually think that happened too, but he caught his breath about the same time the trainers got to him, and at that point, he grabbed his knee and started rolling back and forth. He was all the way on the other side of the field, by the ISU sideline. Two of his teammates and the main trainer lifted him up and started to carry him back to our side. He kept putting his good foot down and trying to get them to let him try to walk. Finally, they propped him up and he tried to take a step. Well, he did take the first step, hopping quickly on his good foot. But then he tried to put his other foot down and collapsed in a heap. I think the whole stadium heard him scream.

CHAPTER 14

THE BEST FRIEND, AGAIN

The day Brother Michael told me he was dying would have been Colgan's 35th birthday. I still had never missed my semi-annual trip to the monastery, though for two years I had to fly from L.A. to Nashville and rent a car to get there. Now I was back in Tuscaloosa, patching together my collage of a dream deferred, with Mama living in an assisted living facility next door to my apartment complex.

Michael and I had long since stopped exchanging letters between our visits. Maybe we just got lazy; if that's the reason, I'm sure it was one hundred percent my fault. But I think there was more to it. The core of our relationship was our faithfulness to these visits. Me doing everything I possibly could to get to this blessed little corner of Tennessee twice a year and him standing outside waiting for me, ready to hear what was really my lapsed Protestant version of a confession. We knew that we would go over everything that happened every six months. There simply was no need for communication between these sessions.

When Michael told me he had been diagnosed with pancreatic cancer, though, I told him there were some things worth picking up the damn phone for. He just shook his head and said he only found out a couple of weeks ago, and he knew I would be here soon, so there was no reason to alarm me.

I told Michael everything you're probably not supposed to say to a person who has received a terminal diagnosis—that he was healthy and young (only 56!) and that if anyone could beat this he could. I even asked him if there were some rule at the monastery that said he couldn't get treatment and told him I would help pay for it if he needed. He just shook his head and told me he was ready to see Sarah Anne and Colgan.

I had been struck, over the past few years, by how much closer in age Michael and I seemed as I got older. In some ways it only makes sense; by the time I had a sense of age at 5 or 6, he was about five times older than me, but by the time I graduated college he wasn't even twice as old. Now fifty-six just really didn't feel that far from thirty-six, and his impending death scared me for reasons beyond the loss of our ritual.

I also marveled at the fact that, just as the age difference between Michael and I seemed to shrink, the eight years between he and my mother seemed to widen exponentially. She was the one who had all the health problems; now, somehow, she was going to outlive Michael. I didn't want either of them to die, of course, but that just didn't make any sense.

He had told me as we took our customary walk around the monastery grounds. I asked him if he minded if we went back to the chapel so I could light another candle, this one for him. He said he would never discourage a man from prayer or try to deny him access to God, but there needn't be any candles lit for Michael Toomey.

Still, he gently led me back to the chapel, knowing I was probably in some kind of shock. When we came through the door, I didn't want to do what he had just said he didn't want, so I asked him to pray aloud for me. I will remember his simple prayer until the day I die.

"Father, watch over my friend Peter. Let him find the ability to speak to you as he has spoken to me, for I know that you will be a far, far better counselor to him than I ever could have been."

I don't know if I have ever really been able to talk to anyone, much less the divine, the way I could talk to Michael. But Colgan's listening ability had been close, and as we stepped back out into the bright winter air, it was my talks with his son that were on his mind.

"Peter," he said, stopping suddenly, "do you remember what you told me at Colgan's funeral about your conversations with him during your first couple of college years?"

"Sure. I don't think I'd have stuck it out in Tuscaloosa without those talks."

"Did you know that, at the same time, Colgan was not speaking to me at all?"

"I thought you weren't allowed to talk to anyone while you were trying to get into the monastery. That's what Colgan told me."

The big man slowly shook his head. "That was never the case." The words came languid and sad as Michael began walking again. "Though I was restricted from having visitors during my novice period, I wrote Colgan many letters and tried to speak to him on the phone. He had completed two years at Texas before he chose to respond to me."

I honestly had not known that the rift between the two of them had been so deep. "Wow" was all I could think of to say. I found it hard to believe that Colgan could have been so angry at Michael and never told me. At the same time, I knew beyond a shadow of a doubt that Michael was telling the truth. So, while Colgan was keeping me sane during my first two years at Bama, he wouldn't even talk to his dad? That still didn't make any sense. I thought they had patched things up by the time our senior year ended.

I looked up at Michael. "I honestly never knew. I was always amazed that Colgan was a thousand miles from home and dealing with a career-ending knee injury, and he was the rock that kept me going. I can't believe he was shutting you out at the same time."

Michael nodded slowly. "If you don't mind me asking, what did you two talk about during those years?"

The question was so open-ended I had no idea what to say. "Well, I mean at first we just mostly talked about football, maybe a little bit about school," I laughed.

Michael just nodded, clearly expecting me to continue. "For a long time our freshman year, we thought Alabama and Texas might play for the national championship. Turns out I don't think that was possible because of the bowl tie-ins even if we both did go undefeated. But they lost to Arkansas toward the end of the year anyway."

"I remember giving Colgan crap about Bama going undefeated. He would say, 'wait 'til I get on the field next year; we'll win a national championship for sure. Then he blew out his knee and never really got a chance to play.

"I found out quickly in college how much better my life was in high school because of Colgan. When you are a kid who is perceived as being different from everyone else, having the stud athlete and coolest kid in school as your best friend makes a big difference. Colgan insulated me from the ridicule I would have received.

"At the college level, it wasn't so much ridicule as just indifference. For the most part, people didn't go out of their way to be mean like high school kids might, but nobody saw much point in becoming friends with me."

I looked up at Michael. I don't think I had ever really talked to him about my "disability" before. Even though he was someone I could talk to about anything, it was something I never had to talk about with him. I was so lucky that the people I was close to growing up just never made a big deal of it, so I never really had to think about it. But when I left Kellyville, I went from being universally known as either "Colgan's best friend" or "the diner lady's kid" to being "that creepy crippled kid with the camera."

Even now, though, there just wasn't any point in delving into all that with Michael, so I moved on. "I really wasn't ready for the work level in college either. It wasn't that the classwork was particularly hard, there was just so damn much of it. And on top of it, I was not only at every practice the players were, I spent hours every week editing the film of those practices. By the middle of the season I was even doing the first pass on the game films after the other student film guy quit. But despite all the work, I always made time for a couple of hours on Sunday afternoon to talk to Colgan. It was my only real break of the week, and it really did keep me sane."

Again, Michael just kind of sat there nodding. I knew he was listening, but I felt like there was something particular he wanted to hear about. I guess he was thinking about what he would talk about with Colgan when he got to heaven—I knew neither of them ever had any doubts about that, and, even in my doubting state, I knew that if heaven existed it had a place for these two—and I was a window into the one part of his son's life that he hadn't really been a part of.

After we had walked in silence awhile, Michael, following his innate sense of monastic time, turned us back toward the main hall so that we would get there by lunchtime. After we turned, he put his hand on my shoulder to steady himself for a moment, and I caught a glimpse of fear, which was something I had never seen in that face.

His breath caught for a second and he exhaled slowly and rather loudly. "The one thing that Colgan would not speak to me about after we reconciled was his decision to leave the football team and focus on his studies. Perhaps he thought I was criticizing him, but I fear that the decision still pained him, and he just didn't want to talk about it, even with me."

"It really was a tough decision for him. The rehab guy, who became Colgan's martial arts teacher, said that he could probably play again but he would miss a whole season. At first, Colgan told me he would come back better than ever, still joshing that he would destroy Alabama a bowl game. But as the rehab wore on, he told me that he wasn't sure he could ever go out on the field knowing he wasn't at his best, and he wasn't sure he'd ever be at his best again."

"Then when it came time to decide whether to accept his scholarship for the third year, he said he couldn't do it; he'd be taking it away from someone who deserved it more. He said he had come to the decision that the team would be better without him."

Michael nodded. "That sounds exactly like what Colgan would say. I fear that he never played football for the fun of it. He played to be the best, and to help his teammates win. It's not that there's anything wrong with that, I guess, but sometimes I feel like I gave Colgan way too much of a sense of duty and not nearly enough of joy."

I thought for a moment. Sure, Colgan did have a bigger sense of duty than most kids of my generation (the 'me generation' as it came to be called), but it's not like he didn't know how to have fun. And football was definitely part of that, at least at first. "I don't know, Michael. I think in high school he certainly had fun playing football, although that may have been diminished a bit by the focus that was put on where he would play next. A lot of big recruits feel that I think – they don't get to enjoy what they're doing in high school because they, and everyone around them, are always thinking about the next level."

"And a lot of them, like Colgan I think, when they get to the next level, the pressure goes up tremendously. Maybe they've always felt a responsibility to their teammates, but now suddenly, they aren't really volunteers anymore. They've got an organization that's given them something of great value, a scholarship to, in Colgan's case, a pretty prestigious university. He felt like he owed them something after that, and maybe that did make football less fun for him."

"But more than that I just think that, compared to most star football players, Colgan was interested in, and good at, a lot of different things. The time you have to put in to play football at a major college level really does take away from the overall college experience – hell, the time you have to put in to be the film guy for a major college football team takes away from the experience. But most football players are just there to play football, so it doesn't really matter to them. Colgan was always more well-rounded than that."

It was the kind of answer a parent would want to hear, but I knew I couldn't leave it at that. I couldn't just give Michael an answer about how awesome Colgan was, just like I couldn't stand up and basically read Colgan's resume at his funeral.

"I also think that the injury really scared him. He faced the real possibility of not only never playing sports again, but being unable to walk normally for the rest of his life if he hurt that knee again. I'd like to think that growing up with me would have helped him deal with that if it actually happened, but it probably also made him realize how difficult it could actually be to be handicapped.

"Plus when he made the decision to quit football, that was about the time he met Patrycia."

Michael perked up at the mention of her name. "That was the girl from El Salvador, right?"

"Yeah. I'm not saying she made him quit football or anything like that, but I guess he just realized he wanted more time for other things."

"I knew of Patrycia's existence before the breakup, but he didn't tell me much about her until after his opinions had become colored by what happened in San Salvador."

I nodded. I had met Patrycia Saldana once, when I took a bus out to Austin the summer between my sophomore and junior years. It was easy to see why Colgan was taken with her. She was exotic and tan, with black hair well past the middle of her back and legs that went for miles, as much taller than me as Colgan was taller than her. She was elegant and, well, for lack of a better word, I'll call her "fancy," like what women in Kellyville said about people on TV.

Her family was one of the most prominent in El Salvador. They had presumably sent her to the University of Texas to capture the heir to some oil baronetcy and would not be happy when she returned with an Irish kid from Alabama who would inherit literally nothing. (Michael had given the land and two houses that were all they'd ever owned to my mother when he joined the Church.) Well, they would be unhappy, except that the kid would be Colgan, so I assumed he would be able to charm their socks off.

That apparently didn't happen. Colgan told me he was going to propose to Patrycia when I left Austin that summer. By the middle of the fall semester, they were engaged. Over Christmas she went home and told her parents all about him, and they made plans for him to come to San Salvador for Spring Break in 1980. I'm hardly an expert in Salvadoran history, but some serious stuff was going on at that time, and somehow it caused a major dispute that ended the relationship between Colgan and Patrycia. He never really said much about it.

Michael seemed to be a little more knowledgeable about it than I. He ran his hand through his hair and said thoughtfully, "It is a very difficult thing to feel that you have to make a moral judgment against someone you love, to feel that you cannot remain true to yourself and accept something about the other person. I know that it was not easy for Colgan to walk away from that girl. I believe he still thought about her the rest of his life."

"I think so too" was the most that I could add to this insight.

I looked up and thought that Michael's illness, which didn't seem to have affected him much physically to that point, must have messed up his super monk time sense because we were about to pass the raised walkway into the cafeteria and the bells hadn't gone off yet. The ringing, of course, began as soon as this thought crossed my mind.

As we ate a meal of fish and steamed vegetables in silence, I thought about what Michael had said about Patrycia, and how hard it must have been for Colgan to leave her over some aspect of the political situation in El Salvador or her reaction to it. It made me wonder if Michael even knew about what had happened to Colgan's high school girlfriend Steffanny. I meant it when I told her that Colgan needed to hear about her rape and pregnancy from her, but I eventually broke down and told him, of course. He was angry and upset, not at Steffany, but at the fact that he hadn't been able to protect her.

And he was angry because he felt powerless to protect her going forward. By the time he knew about the whole situation, she had been shuffled off to Montgomery. She hadn't told me the details of what was going to happen with the baby, and I think Colgan felt like he would just be an outsider messing up their family decision. As far as I know he never talked to her again, but I think what happened to her stayed with him.

The other thing I remember is how it was the first time I'd ever heard him say anything violent. He clenched his fists until his arms were shaking and said that if he ever found out who did this, he would tear them to bits with his bare hands. It was pretty scary actually.

I looked over at Michael and wondered again if Colgan had talked to him about it. It never really came up again between Colgan and I, but I think it really did affect him. I can't imagine what he would have told his dad about it, or what Michael would have said.

After lunch, my conversation with Michael returned to the usual fare of our visits. I told him about returning to what was essentially my first job, as a media specialist for the University of Alabama's athletic department, only now I was getting paid and the kids I was supervising were using cameras I would have had no clue how to operate in 1979. I had accepted that I wasn't ever going to be a hot shot Hollywood director, and working inside the athletic department beat the heck out of producing the sports segment for the local news. It paid a lot better too.

When we were leaving, I gave Michael a big hug and told him I'd see him in July. I think he probably knew that was unlikely. His farewell to me that day turned out to be his final words to me, and they showed me that perhaps his greatest sadness, in this man that I admired so much in large part because of how he had kept his faith and kindness and humanity in the face of so much grief, was one that he had never spoken of to me. One that, despite everything that had happened to him, centered on something that didn't happen.

"Peter," he said, "tell your mother I love her very much and I hope she can forgive me."

CHAPTER 15

THE ARCHBISHOP

"When I give food to the poor, they call me a saint. When I ask why the poor have no food, they call me a communist."
– Dom. Helder Camara, Archbishop of Olinda y Recife, Brazil.

I have seen this quote attributed to me, but I did not say it. It was an archbishop from Brazil. A good man, I met him once, Archbishop Camara. It was in Rome, I think; we were young then, priests going for their doctorate. I doubt many would have believed we both would become archbishops. Perhaps a part of me wishes I had been more like him, wishes that I had said it. In truth, I am neither a saint nor a communist, though I have been called both.

The people who call me a saint are deluded by their need for some sign of divine endorsement of their cause. That is not to say that God does not endorse both the freedom of the masses and some level of alleviation of their earthly suffering. He abhors violence, but the people must be able to defend themselves. I do not need to be a saint for all of this to be true.

The people who call me a communist are intentionally deluding others. They use the label like it somehow justifies the brutalization and murder of all who supported me or claimed my name after my death. (And plenty of people who never had anything to do with me at all, for that matter). Maybe for some in the international community it did justify it. The Salvadoran government and military certainly had plenty of powerful friends throughout the Civil War, and those powerful friends gave them plenty of powerful weapons.

The truth is, I tried not to be a political person. I tried to simply serve my God and His people. It was not possible in a place like El Salvador. The prophet Micah said that what the Lord requires of us is to do justice, to love mercy, and to walk humbly with Him. But in El Salvador, the doing of justice required fighting those who intended and performed injustice. The loving of mercy meant opposition to the policies of oppression and destruction. And walking humbly was a constant struggle when the masses yearned for and thronged and virtually worshipped anyone who gave their needs a second thought

Colgan Toomey was one of the people who thought I was a saint. I never met him, but apparently my death affected him in a strong way. He began praying to me just days after my death, and he continues to do so, though with somewhat less frequency, to this day.

There are those who are still trying to make me a Saint. Pope Francis has declared me a martyr, a name I can accept, for I do know that I was murdered for my role in the Church and my attempts to be its faithful servant. I would rather, if they were going to shoot me, that they had come to my home at the archdiocese, or grabbed me in the street, or done it anywhere but in the pretty little chapel in the Hospital of Divine Providence. I forgave them immediately for defiling my body. It is not my place to forgive them for defiling that sacred space, and I fear that I could not do it if I were asked to. Yet I know that One far greater than me does forgive them.

I knew as soon as I saw the flash of light from the gun that I was dead, and I knew why. The day before, in my homily, I had reminded members of the Salvadoran military of their duties as Christians not to engage in the oppression and torture that the government heaped upon its enemies. I knew the government would not take this well. I even thought they might have me killed. I did not imagine it would be so soon or that it would be during mass.

I know no better than anyone else exactly what happened at my funeral. Existing in the eternal does not give a soul the omniscience of God. Whether the government provoked the mourners simply because they were there to mourn me, or whether some already-existing violent revolutionary faction saw an opportunity to provoke the government into murdering mourners, I cannot say. I know that I learned that it is possible to feel sadness even as my soul worked its way to eternal peace with the Lord.

Much of what has happened since then has brought me sadness as well. It was certainly never my intention to lead or inspire a violent revolution in

El Salvador. I will readily admit, however, that the government needed to change the way it treated the people. I was one of the few people who was not afraid to speak that truth to those in power, and they killed me for it. I could have easily predicted the consequences of that action, even if those consequences saddened me.

Even before my body was laid to rest, Colgan Toomey prayed to me for intercession with the Lord. He was far from the only one doing so, despite the fact that, I must reiterate, I am not a saint. But it is not for me to determine the rightness or wrongness of any person's prayer, and, just as I did while I was alive, my only goal as a spirit has been to try to bring those who seek my counsel closer to God.

I think Colgan wanted me to appear to him in a dream and tell him exactly what he needed to do to fix El Salvador. Aside from the fact that it doesn't really work that way, the obvious flaw in the scheme is that I had no master plan to deal with all the injustices in my country. I believed when I lived that God did have a plan, and I know it even more strongly after death. But, as I said, the ascension of my soul to heaven did not automatically give me all the knowledge of God, nor did it make His ways any less mysterious to me. Just like when I was alive, my ability to communicate His plan to anyone comes only from the way He chooses to use me.

In those fateful days following my death, I tried to send to Colgan, and anyone else who sent their prayers through me, a feeling of peace. But I do not doubt that they sensed from me also a righteous anger at the way the Salvadoran government treated the people. Perhaps they even felt my bitterness at being murdered in the chapel. As I have said many times now, I am not a saint, and my thoughts are not always pure or free from anger and selfishness.

I do not honestly know whether the rebellion in my country caused anything other than suffering and death. I do think that El Salvador now, though it still has many problems, is not the place it was before the war. The government, though it still struggles with many forms of corruption, no longer tortures and kills people at a whim. Many of the poor remain in a desperate struggle for survival, but their leaders are simply ineffectual at helping them, not actively and intentionally making that struggle more difficult.

The prayers I most remember from Colgan Toomey are those that he prayed with other people when he was in Santa Maria prison. I don't know why he always asked me to be the one to watch over them, to help them find a feeling of peace. But I will always remember the way he lifted up the names of people who were literally torturing him. He didn't ask that they receive some kind of epiphany so they would stop hurting him. Instead his prayer would go something like this (it probably sounds better in the original Spanish):

"Most blessed and holy St. Romero," he would begin. I already told you he had deluded himself into thinking I was a saint. "Watch over Senor Morales [though he would use a first name if he knew it] and bring him the peace of our Father. Bring him all the possible blessings that can be bestowed upon humanity by our Lord Jesus Christ in this life and the next."

He always added in a prayer for peace in El Salvador, but it never had anything to do with which side would win. Sometimes he would even throw in a specific prayer for job success. Keep in mind that the job of the person he was praying for was usually to beat up Colgan and the other prisoners. Sometimes I wondered if he was just a masochist. But by the end of his time there, I was convinced that Colgan was really trying to hold love in his heart for the people who were torturing him. He didn't always succeed; no one could have. But he tried, and that's a lot more than most people would have been able to do.

CHAPTER 16

THE JILTED FIANCÉE

For a long time, even after he abandoned me, I firmly believed that Colgan Toomey was the love of my life, my soul mate, the heart of my heart, whatever other cheesy expressions you want to throw in there. I followed him around campus in Austin like a wounded puppy dog, and the fact that he tolerated my presence and found it hard to be unkind to me just made it so much worse. I cried for days when my father made me come home, because even though Colgan said he no longer loved me, I believed utterly in the idea that given enough time and enough of my wondrous presence, he would change his mind. Telling me to let go of that as the animating purpose of my life was like telling a shipwreck survivor to let go of his life raft.

I've figured out, of course, that I was incredibly naïve. The idea that someone I met at nineteen, while away at University in another country, would be the person I was meant to spend my life with is ridiculous on its face. Oh, I know that there are couples out there that marry that young and spend the rest of their lives together, outwardly happy. I think most of them happen in rural communities where divorce is so frowned upon that the parties never even consider it.

But if Colgan and I had married, I can't even tell you what country we would have lived in. My father would probably never have allowed the marriage anyway after Colgan disrespected him in his own house. You see, Colgan was at least as naïve as I was, just in different ways. He refused to try to understand the complexities of a place like El Salvador. The poor were suffering, just like they always had, and a priest got killed, and in his mind that was enough to justify throwing the whole country down the drain.

In America, when the poor get angry, they vote for Democrats and try to pass civil rights laws. They maybe raise your taxes a little bit, and give your money to programs to feed people. In El Salvador, no one even advocated for that. It's an all or nothing kind of place – a zero sum game as the mathematicians call it. The Salvadoran poor didn't want fairer laws and more food stamps; they wanted to kill everyone who owned anything and completely destroy everything that my family and the other families like us had worked so hard to build.

And the Church, what can I say about the Church in El Salvador? The Church claims to be concerned with the eternal and the spiritual, not the political. It should be a sustaining force, a protector of life and provider of order. In El Salvador it is none of these. Instead the Church is jealous and greedy, seeking to take power from the legitimate government by rousing the rabble with their ridiculous thoughts of liberation theology.

The idea that God would support a violent revolution that destroyed everything that centuries of good Christians had given their lives to build felt so absurd to me that I never understood why anyone believed it. I'm still not sure anyone did, but it was a useful excuse, something the communists could use to get their foot in the door with the few honest peasants they did run into.

I'm not saying El Salvador would have been perfect if the poor people and the Church had just shut up and let the government do their job. It would have been better, but of course not perfect. No country is perfect. The Salvadoran government made mistakes like the governments of every other country in the world.

El Salvador has always been a poor country; it has never been easy to keep the economy going and keep the country afloat. Look, I'm not stupid, and I'm not heartless. I do realize that some people suffer a lot more than others, and there might even be a better way out there, a system that both takes care of the people that have a hard time taking care of themselves and rewards hard work. But like I said, nobody in El Salvador is advocating such a system. The country has always faced a question of choosing order and stability, or violence and chaos.

My family simply chose order. Not only inside our country, but internationally as well. We, as individuals and as a country, have always been loyal friends of the United States, never giving any quarter to the Cubans or the Russians. It is the Americans who, in the end, demand that we maintain order, but at least the U.S. government sees the necessity of helping us have the tools to do it. To too many individual Americans, though, we become a pawn in your domestic politics. Every action of our military, taken often at the behest of your pentagon, gets scrutinized and criticized. The atrocities of the rebels, at least as bad, never get mentioned, because they didn't get their guns from you.

I never thought I would go to America and fall in love with a man who turned out to be a communist. I mean I knew Colgan was different from your average American cowboy jock. Most of the guys I met at Texas were rich, arrogant hicks whose worldviews were about as wide as their ridiculous hats. Colgan wanted to see outside of the small-town world that he was born into, and he was smart enough to do it. He was always interested in my life, the world I came from. I have often wondered how I did such a terrible job of explaining El Salvador to him and preparing him for what he would see there. Yeah, he was naïve, but isn't that my fault? I could have saved us both a lot of pain if I had been able to make him see what it was really like. But I never admitted of the possibility that our love wouldn't be stronger than the monsters ripping apart my country.

I remember the visit before the one where the world ended. Colgan didn't come, but I showed my parents the ring he had bought me. It wasn't a million-dollar diamond or anything, but it was reasonably impressive, and much more so to me, because, unlike my parents, I knew the person who bought it didn't come from a rich family. I let them believe he was the typical oil baron's or cattle rancher's kid that girls from El Salvador are sent to the United States to land. I did tell them he was fluent in Spanish though. I wish now he hadn't been. He might not have understood everything my father said or been able to tell him what he thought.

But that first trip, when it was just me and the ring, everyone was so excited. I showed them the pictures that Colgan and I had made at Sears. I even convinced him to cut his hair for them. Everyone was amazed that I had actually found someone considerably taller than me. I was the tallest kid in my class at school, even taller than my father. At 5'11 he was tall for a Salvadoran, and he had done the opposite of what he sent me to do and married a cattle rancher's daughter that he met at UT, though his find had been raised in Mexico. She was only an inch or two shorter than him, and I ended up being about 6'1. At the time I was so happy that I had been able to go to America for school, because all the guys in my country were so short!

I just knew that they would be even more impressed when they met Colgan. And they were, at first. We got to San Salvador on Saturday evening, and father's driver Martinez picked us up at the airport. I could tell Colgan was a little nervous. I remember he tried to start a conversation with the driver. Maybe I should have picked up a political connotation there; maybe Colgan was just being his friendly self.

When we got to the villa where I grew up, Colgan seemed genuinely in awe, but maybe he was shocked and disgusted by our supposed opulence in comparison to the rest of the country. Our villa was in a neighborhood called Santa Elena de la Montana. From the airport, which was more than an hour's drive southwest of the city, you had to drive through San Salvador proper and then climb into the mountains. It feels like you are getting out into the countryside, but then you come around a curve and see that our neighborhood overlooks the whole city. The American embassy stands at the entrance to our neighborhood, and the whole place is set off on a mountain top behind a thick wall of sunbaked pinkish bricks.

While we were driving through the city, Colgan asked a million questions that I tried to answer as best I could. Everything from what the current population was, to questions about the city's founders. I keep wondering if I could have figured out how Colgan really felt about the people running El Salvador, about me and my family.

But in the end, I just can't think he was lying to me. I think his feelings for me were as honest as his revulsion after the archbishop was murdered. Of course, I'm not saying that it was a good idea to murder Romero or that being upset about someone being killed is a bad thing. I just wish I could have made him understand that this wasn't a reason to throw the baby out with the bathwater, to give up on me and our whole country because the government did something stupid.

From Saturday afternoon when we arrived, until Tuesday morning when we learned of Archbishop Romero's death, the world was perfect. Saturday was a cool spring evening; our back porch faced west, overlooking the whole city. Some days you can almost see the sea. In my memory, I just assume that Saturday was one of those days. I remember holding hands with Colgan, the two of us sitting between my parents, watching the sun set on the other side of San Salvador.

Papa wanted to talk about the natural beauty of El Salvador, the birds in the forests and the mountains. Papa was a big bird watcher. His favorite was a medium-sized bird of prey called a caracara. They usually had two-tone bodies, brown or black on the bottom with a white chest and head and a black crest on top. They always had a splash of color right behind the bill on their cheeks. The cheek color was usually orange or yellow, but sometimes a bright purple, especially on young birds. The caracara, like many falcons, has adapted to live in urban areas, and, if you knew what to look for, could often be found inside San Salvador.

Colgan seemed genuinely interested as Papa told him about other birds that aren't found much in the United States, from the chubby little chachalacas with their constant cooing chatter to the large green parrot with a yellow stripe down the back of its neck that we called an Amazona. I remember we all laughed when Colgan, in turn, tried to tell him about the songbirds of southern Alabama's pine woods, but his Spanish, so good up until that point, failed him in the names of our feathered friends.

On Sunday, we went to the early morning mass at Santa Elena, the small but beautiful church in our neighborhood. You see, we were good Catholics too, even if we didn't always agree with the political stance of the Church in our country. Our little local priest wasn't much of an agitator though. Padre Tomas was a comical caricature of a priest, a Friar Tuck type, wide as he was tall and prone to dipping into the communion wine.

After mass, Colgan and I went for a walk around the neighborhood. I pointed out the homes of my childhood friends and boarding school mates. It was a fancy and beautiful neighborhood, and that March the first flowers were blooming on the squat little izote trees that lined the streets. We walked past sprawling Mexican-style haciendas with pink sandstone sides and brightly-tiled roofs, tall-columned French colonials, and one massive (and massively out-of-place) four-story Victorian with an octagonal tower and captain's walk. Colgan walked beside me, holding my hand, occasionally stroking my hair, and never saying a word against such opulence in a poor country.

We finally reached the American embassy at the front of the neighborhood. I have reconstructed this walk so many times in my head. It is only here that Colgan finally, maybe, gave me a clue that he thought there was something wrong with the way my country was run, or with my family's lifestyle. We had stopped by the outer wall where the stairs led down to the embassy building. You could see not only the whole grounds, but past the embassy and down into San Salvador.

Colgan had his arm around my waist. All he said was, "I wonder why it's not down in the city."

"Because all of the important people in the country live in this neighborhood, my dear."

Colgan looked perplexed for a second, looking around the neighborhood. Then he turned to face me and gave me a big kiss. In the end,

I honestly wonder if the plight of El Salvador's poor ever even crossed his mind until he heard of Oscar Romero's death. I am certain that their plight was never more important than his feelings for me until after Romero's death.

The next day, we slept late, and Papa had already gone to work. We were eating breakfast out on the porch when we were interrupted by my tia Blanca, who had lived with us since her husband, a colonel in El Salvador's air force, had died in the war with Honduras in 1969. Tia frantically called us into the house, screaming something about riots in the city. I think she thought we were going to be hit by a stray bullet or something if we stayed outside.

Papa had apparently called home to tell her to make sure we didn't come into San Salvador that day, because there were protestors and police on the street in front of his office. He was still on the phone, which Blanca, in her excited state, had left dangling from the wall. When I picked it up to put it back on the ringer, I heard him cough and realized he was still there. He didn't actually seem all that concerned about the protests.

"Your tia, bless her soul, believes that every conflict leads to war, and every war will lead to the death of those she loves. I can't blame her for feeling that way, but I'm sure this is just some minor, random disturbance, like a farmer's strike or something."

"You don't know why they protest, Papa?"

"They are always protesting something, Paty. But I heard it had something to do with a priest or bishop or something."

I promised not to go into the city that day and we said our goodbyes. It turned out Papa wasn't able to come home for two days.

As we watched the news coverage of the protests, I could tell that Colgan was getting a little upset. I know that it was shallow and naïve of me to assume that he was worried about our trip being ruined. But at that time, this trip was the most important thing, I thought, that had happened in either of our lives. Before the trip, he honestly believed, or at least made me believe, that he was going to El Salvador to win over the family of the woman he was going to spend his life with, and to plan his wedding to her.

We didn't talk much about the wedding, since it was soon overshadowed by other events, but we were actually supposed to have visited the cathedral in San Salvador that day. I never considered that I would get married anywhere else, of course. My parents were married in the cathedral; my father's uncle was the President of El Salvador at the time, and there were probably two thousand people there. I hadn't told Colgan yet that the same would probably be true of our wedding.

I had, however, showed him pictures of the cathedral. He loved the art and architecture of it, and he said he couldn't wait to see it for himself. Lord help me, I really thought he was upset that he wouldn't get to see the cathedral that day. I think I even said something about this blowing over in a couple of days and us getting to see that cathedral then. I wonder though, whether the connection to that building, where Archbishop Romero so often presided, was part of what triggered Colgan's strong feelings for him.

Romero wasn't killed in the cathedral. But he was saying mass when he was shot. He was in the chapel at the Hospital of Divine Providence. I know that this is one of the things that bothered Colgan the most. He just assumed that I would be horrified. And at some level I was. Like I said, I'm not a monster. I don't get pleasure from the government killing priests in the middle of mass. I also didn't think it was a good idea from a practical perspective.

At first when Colgan commented about how sad it was, I just agreed. He seemed a little sullen, but not really up in arms against the government. At first the protests were peaceful too, even though they shut down most of the center city and made it impossible for the people that worked there to leave.

I could tell Colgan was beginning to get angry, but I guess I was still being shallow and naïve and thought he was upset that we weren't getting to see the city. We were cooped up in the house and constantly hovered over by Tia Blanca and my mother, who decided, after 24 straight hours of protest coverage on all the network TV stations, to turn off all the televisions in the house and make us listen to old records of cumbia dance music, followed eventually by Papa's classical records, mostly Bach and Schubert.

It wasn't the fault of the music, but by the end of the day on Tuesday, we were going stir crazy. After helping Tia Blanca clean up after dinner, I found Colgan on the patio looking out over the city, large swaths of which were completely dark because the government had turned off the power.

"I don't know if this is going to blow over like your dad thinks, baby."

I wanted to ask him what in the world he knew about it, but I just said, "There are always going to be people mad at the government and protesting. I don't see why this will end up any different."

"They killed a priest at mass... in a country that's like 95% percent Catholic. And I don't think the government is willing to do anything to apologize for it. You know, willing to compromise and be more responsive to the poor people."

"The poor people here are communists, darling. It's not like America."

"They're still people."

I couldn't argue with that, so I tried to snuggle up beside him.

He walked toward the edge of the patio and started ranting. "I'm serious baby. I honestly think there are going to have to be major changes in this country. I know your family is invested in the government and I'm not trying to say you're bad people or anything like that." I braced myself for whatever the hell he was about to say that he had to preface with the idea that the family that he had been ingratiating himself into for the last few days "weren't bad people."

But the revelation was slow in coming. "I don't know Paty, exactly what the answer is. Hell, beyond a government that appears to condone murder, I'm not completely sure what the problem is. But it's not just that the poor people protest all the time. They've probably got a damn good reason."

"Someone in the government did something stupid. That happens in every country. It doesn't make everyone that supports the government guilty of murder."

"Maybe it doesn't, but maybe it does make them responsible for change."

"You don't understand El Salvador. 'Change' here would mean violent communist revolution."

"Why does it have to mean that?"

"It just does. That's what those people in the street want."

"They probably just want justice for Romero. Maybe a little more bread."

"That's not how it works here. Can we please talk about something else?"

He just nodded, but he clearly couldn't come up with anything else to talk about. He just stood there, silent, looking out over the half-darkened city, until I finally told him I was cold. Reluctantly, he turned away from whatever was gripping him about the scene below, and took my hand as we went back in the house. He still didn't say anything though, just kissed me on the forehead and headed to the guest room where he was staying.

I have to admit that, once again, I was really quite shallow in my reaction to all this. In addition to thinking he was frustrated that the trip wasn't going perfectly, I figured some of his sullenness came from the fact that we weren't able to have sex at my parents' house. But I knew there'd be hell to pay if mother or Tia Blanca caught us. I figured I'd just have to make it up to him when we got back to Texas. That pleasant thought took my mind off the situation at hand and I fell asleep content.

The next day there was a lull in the protests and Papa was able to come home. He hadn't slept much in the last two days though, and he was in a rather foul mood. He ranted about the protesters and the communists and the Church until my mother finally convinced him to go to bed. I was very happy that Colgan appeared to have the good sense to keep his mouth shut when Papa was going on about something.

That evening we had a nice meal and some music and everyone seemed to forget about the protests. We still didn't turn on the television, though. If we had, we would have known that Romero's funeral was scheduled for the next day.

We probably wouldn't have guessed though, that all the protests up to that point were a mere prelude, and that all hell wouldn't break loose until the next afternoon. Father stayed home from the city, thank God, and I remember him getting a call a little after noon telling him to turn on the news. When he did, I knew almost immediately that what started as a protest would soon turn into a war. Maybe that didn't happen every time like Tia Blanca thought, but it was going to happen this time.

I don't think we'll ever know who provoked who or what started the events that turned Oscar Romero's funeral into a pitched battle. Apparently, there were 250,000 people there from all over the world. Obviously, the government wasn't ready to handle the event. At some point, someone set off some smoke bombs near the cathedral. Most of the people that died were stampeded by other mourners, but a few were shot by soldiers or police. And a couple of the police were killed by protesters.

Even after the protests turned violent, still Colgan didn't seem to come unhinged. He still just acted sullen and sad, but all of us felt that way. I think we knew even more than Colgan did just how serious this had become and that there was a pretty good chance of our country coming apart. We even knew that the government hadn't done a particularly good job of handling the funeral and that, even if the protestors had set off the smoke bombs, the troops had to have better discipline than they showed. There were hundreds of foreign dignitaries in town, for God's sake.

I was cleaning the kitchen with Tia Blanca when the dispute between Colgan and my father started. I still don't know exactly what was said. Colgan later told me he merely suggested that some reform was necessary in the country, trying to feel out the opportunity for compromise and see whether I was right that there wasn't any way to change El Salvador gradually. It was either law and order or communism and chaos.

Papa, on the other hand, said that Colgan suggested that the ruling class had better start giving all their possessions to the poor if they didn't want to see their heads on a pike. All I know is that whatever was said started a screaming match and by the time I ran into the room from the kitchen, Colgan was stomping off to get his stuff.

I followed him to the room and asked him what the hell he was thinking talking to my father that way. He just looked at me and shook his head. "I never should have thought I could get along with rich people."

I just stood there staring at him. Finally, he looked up and said, "No, that's not quite it. It's not the fact that y'all are rich, it's that you apparently don't think poor people are actually people. Well I'm one of them, Paty, I'm a dirty fucking peasant, and I don't think I should stay here anymore. I'll talk to you when you get back to Austin."

I'm sure my mouth was wide open in a caricature of shock, but I don't think I moved at all as he stuffed a couple changes of clothes in his school backpack and brushed past me on his way out into the night. I walked down the stairs after him like a zombie. My father saw that he was leaving and got up and opened the door for him, sticking out his arm to block me from following. I didn't even say anything. I just turned around and went to my room.

I doubt it would have changed anything even if I had had some clue about what to say to either of them. The break in Colgan's personality was clean and total. He never treated me particularly unkindly after that night. We even cried to each other when we were back in Austin. But he said he couldn't be with me, and there was a flatness and a finality to it that opened up a gaping chasm between us. My life, my family, my country – they all fell into that same chasm.

CHAPTER 17

THE MARTIAL ARTS MASTER

My name is Kuniko Kurabashi, but here in Austin, folks call me Kenny (or coach K – I was the original Coach K, long before that Polish fellow at Duke). Darrell Royal used to say that I was his secret weapon and joke that I was the reason he won at least two of his three national championships. Well actually, he called me his secret ninja, but I was always a little annoyed by that. Even the white folks in Austin didn't question Coach Royal, though, so I sure as hell wasn't going to.

I did like the idea of being a secret weapon of sorts. There wasn't a whole lot of knowledge about kinesiology and physical therapy back then, and, even now, there are very few people out there who both understand those sciences and know how to integrate eastern healing practices and martial arts into the process.

Anyway, I was never officially on the coaching staff at UT. Instead, I worked by the player. Officially, I ran a dojo, next to my sister's restaurant, the Casa Japonesa – I'll get into our screwed-up family history in a minute. When a kid got hurt, or every once in awhile just when a promising recruit didn't live up to expectations, Coach Royal would give me a call and pay me double my usual rate to give the kid martial arts lessons. The physical therapy was worked in as we went. I'm sure there was some kind of NCAA rule against it, but learning the NCAA rules was never part of my job.

Austin has a reputation for being proudly "weird." I hope that my family contributes to that in an appreciable way. We came to Austin in 1938, when I was 2, from Brazil. I'm guessing you were going along fine, but that last word totally threw you off. You're like, "Wait, what? Brazil?" Yep. My sister and I were both born in Brazil, and my parents had come there from Japan as teenagers. There were actually quite a few Japanese immigrants to Brazil in the early 20th century. My father's family was one of the very first in 1907, and my mom's came in 1912.

My parents were pretty lucky among the Japanese Brazilians, since they had moved beyond working on the coffee plantations and owned a small farm. But by the mid-30's, the Brazilian fascists under Getulio Vargas had taken over, and were making life unpleasant for people they perceived as foreigners. My parents decided it was time to pack up and leave, just as their parents had decided about Japan. They sold the farm and never looked back. I honestly have no idea how they got into the United States. I've done some research and their immigration should have been illegal and impossible. Apparently, someone in Austin pulled some strings.

My father could have been a world-class chef if he had been born into the money necessary to get him there. He loved grand experiments in the kitchen, mixing foods from different cuisines and cultures. He had wanted to open a restaurant from the time we got to the United States, but his plans got a little derailed a couple years into the journey.

Despite not having been subjects of the Empire of Japan for more than thirty years, my parents, along with their children, none of whom had been born in Japan and the youngest of whom, my little brother, had been born in Texas, were rounded up in November of 1942 and sent to an internment camp. I guess whatever strings had been pulled to let us into the country snapped back and hit us in the face.

My earliest school memories were in this camp. It was in a place called Rohwer, Arkansas, which, to this day, has the most humidity of any place I've ever been. In the two and a half years we were there, I was an outcast among outcasts. For the most part, the problem wasn't that my parents weren't from Japan, it was that they weren't from California. Most of the other kids knew each other at least a little bit. Or at least they had common reference points they could talk about. I knew nothing about their world. I learned to fight early, and I got pretty damn good at it.

Most of my learning consisted of watching the older kids and imitating them. As I got older though, I became obsessed with Kung Fu movies.

Everyone always assumes that a Japanese guy who teaches martial arts learned them at a young age, presumably from his father. My father was an amazing man in many ways, but he couldn't tell Jiu-jitsu from Tae Kwon Do.

On top of that, he was essentially a pacifist. After we got back to Austin he enrolled me in martial arts classes not so that I would learn how to fight, but in the hopes that I would learn to control my anger and avoid fights. He took me to a place matter-of-factly called the Texas Academy of Martial Arts, where I studied Karate under a man named Henry Bernstein. I was a senior in high school before I faced another Asian in an official martial arts competition, and his family was from Thailand.

I learned Karate, and later Judo and a little bit of Kendo, from Mr. Bernstein as a child and teenager. It wasn't until well into my adulthood that I connected with the other birthright of my heritage, or at least birthplace. While I was in grad school for kinesiology, my sister, who had absorbed a bit more Brazilian culture than I, married a guy named Santos Oliveira, who was a little into Brazilian jiu-jitsu, and a whole lot into Samba and Bossa Nova music.

As I began to listen to the sensual rhythms of South American beaches, the concept of a dance-based martial art intrigued me. Although I would argue that I was never a true master of the art, Brazilian Jiu-Jitsu became the most popular discipline I taught, especially among the football players referred to me by Coach Royal. I think they just liked seeing a dorky, old (in their mind) Japanese guy dancing around to weird music.

My dad did eventually get to open that restaurant. He died a couple of years before I met Colgan, but he was able to pass it on to my sister, whose kids still run it today. I've even heard people use it as an example of how crazy Austin really is – where else would you find a place called Casa Japonesa. The chicken wasabi tacos are world famous, but the wagyu teppanyaki enchiladas with mango salsa are even better.

But anyway, I'm supposed to be telling you about Colgan Toomey, right? But what is there to say about him? My interaction with Colgan was just like virtually everyone else's. He blew me away. He was easily the most natural martial arts student I ever coached. I once saw him fight to a draw with a guy named David Watanabe, who would have won the 1980 Olympic gold medal in Judo if Team USA had gone to Moscow. David was better than Colgan in technique (one of the few that ever was), but Colgan's height and long arms gave him an advantage that could be easily overcome when he didn't know what he was doing, but was virtually impossible to defeat after he learned even the most basic technical theory. He learned a lot more than that, and he learned it in multiple disciplines.

I remember when Coach Akers, who had replaced Coach Royal a year or two earlier, first introduced me to Colgan, I was skeptical. And, in the end I had good reason to be. Colgan became a pretty damn good martial artist, but he never panned out as the football star he was supposed to be. Most of the players I worked with were obsessed with the question of when they would get back on the field. Colgan took his referral to me as an opportunity to dive headlong into the world of martial arts. After a year, he was asking me about Chinese styles I'd hardly heard of, that he found in books in the UT library. After three, he had virtually mastered all of them, at least from what I could tell from the books.

Of course, he wasn't even supposed to be in my dojo for a year much less three. Well, maybe a year would have been about right; it was a pretty nasty knee injury. Coach Akers said he took a direct helmet to both sides of his knee from below when he tried to hurdle two six-foot tall linebackers. I remember wondering how the hell he got his knee that high off the ground in the first place. I didn't realize at the time that my new charge was 6'6", but it's still darned impressive.

When Colgan first came to me, he was still on crutches. We spent weeks doing nothing but stretches and talking about how the body works. He had already decided he wanted to go to med school, so we talked about all kinds of kinesiology stuff that I had learned. It took four or five months before Colgan was able to do any contact sparring, and by that time he was already questioning whether he wanted to play football again. He said that he wasn't sure his heart was in it, and if it wasn't, he shouldn't be taking away some other kid's scholarship. At first, I told him what I thought Coach Akers would want me to tell him, that he was an amazing talent and he could be a real star, lead the team to great things.

Colgan seemed genuinely torn. He didn't want to let the team down, but football had never been the be-all end-all of his life, and that level of commitment was essentially a requirement at the major college level. When I saw how much he was struggling, I had to tell him it was okay if he didn't want to play football anymore. I'm sure this was probably a breach of contract or something, since I was technically getting paid by the UT athletic department to get him back on the field. I still think it was the right thing to do. I have no idea how much my comments influenced his decision; he was certainly smart enough to know he didn't need my permission, but he seemed to crave it.

Once Colgan decided to leave the team, he had to figure out how to stay in school without a scholarship. At first, he thought he might be able to make enough money playing music at night to finance his education. Who knows, he was pretty good, he might have been able to, but given what had happened with football, I told him that if he could find another way, he should, because it would be best if he could keep playing music because he loved it and not because he had to if he wanted to stay in school.

Colgan didn't tell me about his dad joining the Church until after he went to the financial aid office. I run a business for young people in a college town; I've seen a lot of students come and go. Colgan was probably the only one who could ever truthfully report his parents' income as $0. Needless to say, the financial aid office worked out a way for him to stay in school. I think part of it was merit-based academic scholarships, but he got a heck of a grant too.

I don't know how much the UT football team and community missed because Colgan left the team. He might have turned out to be a star, and he might have blown out his knee again and had trouble walking for the rest of his life. But I do know how much I gained. Colgan's affinity for martial arts went well beyond his athletic ability to physically do it. He embraced mental discipline and body control, and became my teacher as much as he was my student. He was also my confidant and pretty darn close to being my best friend, despite the years and cultural gaps between us.

I remember when Colgan introduced me to his girlfriend. In some ways the attraction was obvious; Patrycia was beautiful, tall, and athletic, as well as being intelligent and interesting and able to introduce Colgan to an exotic new culture. It was not surprising that Colgan would pick someone from whom he could truly learn. She was far from shallow, but I knew from the beginning that she just didn't have the depth of soul that Colgan had.

I kept my mouth shut, of course. You can't tell a 20-year-old in love that the object of his affection is just a rich kid on holiday, and not someone he could have a true and deep relationship with. I guess part of me wasn't fully confident of my own observations either; I didn't spend a whole lot of time around Patrycia, and Colgan didn't tell me everything. Still, I had a bad feeling about that relationship from the beginning.

That feeling never made any sense as they seemed to fall deeper and deeper in love, got engaged, and planned trips to meet her family. But after they went to El Salvador over Spring Break in 1980, everything changed. Colgan came to the dojo the next week and went straight past me as I was leading a class. He opened the door to my office and sat down in one of the chairs facing my desk. Out of the corner of my eye, I could see him leaned over with his head in his hands. I hurried through the rest of the lesson I was teaching.

I had heard something about the protests going on in El Salvador, sparked by the murder of a bishop or archbishop or something. To be honest, the only reason I had thought about it at all was to absentmindedly wonder whether it would delay Colgan and Patrycia's flight home. I knew next to nothing about El Salvador.

Colgan, though, was absolutely distraught. Patrycia's family was apparently very important in El Salvador, part of a small cadre of ruling families that ran the country. It made sense, given the fact that they had the money to send their daughter to college in the United States.

There were literally tears in Colgan's eyes when he said, "They think it's not only perfectly okay for 90% of the population to be starving, but that it's also okay to murder anyone who stands up for those starving people. It's complete bullshit, the fourteen families run everything based on privileges that go all the way back to Spanish colonial times. They control the military, and they use it to keep everybody else in poverty."

I started to say something, trying to commiserate with him, but he let out a small sob and said, "You know what the worst part is? Paty completely agrees with her parents. She says I don't understand her country. The 'good families' have to do what they do to prevent communism. Well if communism is bad, it can't be worse than what's happening in El Salvador now."

I told him that he should try to talk to her and understand her point of view, even if just to educate himself. He said that's what he'd been trying to do for a week. Any expression of sympathy for the working classes sent her into a diatribe about how hard her family and the other leaders of the country had worked to keep order, and how that damn priest was trying to wreck it. She certainly didn't sound like she wanted to see anything from his point of view. But, he said, she didn't want to break up either. She told him she would worry about her country and they could stay here.

"I just don't think I can be with a person that thinks that way."

That was the last thing Colgan ever said to me about Patrycia. But we talked about El Salvador many times, and about how money and power corrupt people, and about how America seemed willing to support anyone who claimed to be on our side against the Russians, no matter how dictatorial and oppressive the regime. I honestly am not a scholar of history or international relations or anything else really, but I had spent enough time disciplining my mind to know the value of seeing things from multiple sides, and to see the folly of seeing the world in black and white. I encouraged Colgan to learn about everything that mattered to him, to read about it from as many perspectives as possible, and to keep an open mind.

As Colgan got busy with his first year of medical school, his visits to the dojo were less frequent, but he still stopped by occasionally. He seemed much more focused on his studies that year, but what he had seen in El Salvador in 1980 was always a touchstone for him. His medical studies were still very generalized of course, since it was his first year, but he wanted to be an epidemiologist in the third world, an American version of Albert Schweitzer, whose writings he had studied extensively.

The Doctors Without Borders trip to Guatemala seemed like the perfect opportunity for him, a chance to develop his medical skills while helping people in a part of the world he really cared about, and where he spoke the language and could actually get to know the people he was helping. I cried when I saw his death reported on the news, but then they said it was guerrillas from El Salvador that killed him. I wondered if there was some sort of cosmic irony at play, or if maybe there was something more to the story.

CHAPTER 18

THE BROKEN CHILD

In my hour of greatest need, the Lord sent me an avenging angel. The angel tried his best to save my soul, but only my body survived. He must have been sent mostly to punish the men who hurt me. Foul, evil men who took advantage of a vulnerable child.

I was but a lamb, ready for the slaughter. I was a lost child of an absent father and a dead mother. I was a stranger of the Lord's tribe, wandering in the desert of the gentiles. The desert that would never end for me, where I would be sacrificed and left bleeding upon the sand.

I would like to speak only of my angel, the only godly man who walked into my life. The man who followed an appearance of the Virgin into the desert to try to come to the rescue of a fourteen-year old girl. The man who carried her upon his back through miles of parched and barren canyon land, so that the doctors might have a chance to save her. The man who avenged her with the sword.

But first I must tell you of that little girl, and of the awful demons sent by Satan himself to destroy her.

I was given the name Alicia Gonzales, and I was born in the Year of our Lord 1978 in San Salvador, El Salvador. It was a place of emptiness and despair, though it might be seen as an oasis of peace in comparison to the desert of death. My parents left El Salvador during the worst of the fighting, when I was only 6, and took me to live with relatives in Quetzaltenango, Guatemala.

But then my father escaped Guatemala too and went to a place called Texas. When I was a child the name of this place rang out like the angels were calling God's people to the promised land. I lived to see Texas myself, and I know now that it is no more a land of milk and honey than is El Salvador or Guatemala.

My father would send us enough money to keep my mother and I alive, but he could never come visit us. He said that if he came home, they would not let him back in to the land of Texas. Over and over again he said he would send for us when he had the money. Always, it came back to money.

After my mother died, my father finally said it was time for me to come to Texas. He even told me I would have a new mother there. He supposedly sent money to my uncle, who came to pick me up in Quetzaltenango and dropped me off with the demons in Guatemala City. Little did I know that I myself was the payment for smuggling my uncle's sons to Texas. I don't know if my father never actually sent any money or if my uncle just kept it in his pocket.

I do not have to tell you what happens when a couple of criminals are given total ownership of a 14-year-old girl. It doesn't even matter that I wasn't particularly pretty. What I will say is that they were smart enough to wait until we got over the Mexican border and were hiding in the jungle, so that I couldn't possibly go to the authorities.

I do not know how long we were traveling through Mexico. There were places we walked and places we rode in the back of a canvas-covered truck. It was always hot, and after the first few days, dry and dusty. The land stopped being green and was covered with a sickly yellow. There were twelve migrants that went with us, along with the two criminals.

One night when we were camped in a low ravine, I heard the two demons worrying that a man was following us. One feared that he had been following us all the way from Guatemala, hiding in the shadows, basically getting a free trip. The other said that wasn't possible they would have seen anyone following behind them so far. I prayed that the man following us would kill the demons.

It was two nights later when I discovered that I was with child. I tried to tell myself that I was a little bit like the Blessed Virgin, because I had gotten pregnant without ever willingly lying with a man. But even in my tormented teenage state I knew I was nothing like her.

I knew I had to hide the baby from the demons. They would kill my child and probably me too if they knew. By the time I realized the baby was there, I was already getting sick every morning. I prayed that the demons would not see, or that they would not know what it meant.

Whenever they wanted me, the demons took me off into the desert, but only a short distance from camp, usually where one could stand and see what was going on in the camp while the other had his way with me. But I remember on that night they just kept pulling me further and further away, out into the desert, even over a ridge where I knew there was no way the camp was visible from where we were.

The demons had always been violent men, oppressors who made sure that I knew who was boss. But generally, if I kept my mouth shut and did what they made me do, there was only the occasional slap or shake. But on this day, they seemed more intent on beating me than on their typical perverted pleasures. Somehow, I knew that they had learned about my baby. I prayed and prayed for God to take me but keep my baby safe. I was a stupid child, of course, since I was not more than a few weeks pregnant and my baby could not possibly have lived outside of me.

But, in a way, God answered my prayers. I did not see the man who rescued me until after he had killed both of the demons. He came like a ghost, right as the last light from the vanished sun disappeared in the west. One moment, the demon was standing over me, punching me in the stomach, and the next, his throat was being slit by a silent avenger. Both of them were dead before they ever knew what the Lord had sent as their punishment.

The angel, who was tall and thin with long red hair pulled back in a ponytail, said nothing at all about the dead demons as he scooped me up effortlessly and began carrying me in the direction away from the campsite. He stopped only once, to make me drink some water, as he carried me for what felt like miles. When I tried to speak to him, he just told me to be still and conserve my energy.

I don't know how long he carried me, but I was completely unconscious before we reached the little hospital in San Patricio. While I was sleeping the Virgin appeared to me and told me to name my baby Maribel. For a long time I thought this vision was a cruel trick. Our Lady must have known that my baby would not survive. She was probably already dead by the time I had the vision.

But perhaps she knew that I would need a name, something I could call out when I mourned the little girl who never was. A symbol of everything that was pure and good, when everything around me was evil, and even when I did evil things.

Maybe the name also carried this focus, this symbolism, for my angel. He too had done evil things, he said, but it did not stop him from doing something good for me. I saw him only rarely after that, and not in many years now, but I knew that he prayed for me, and I hope that he prays for me still.

CHAPTER 19

THE MEDIC

My name is Antonio Rutledge. Colgan Toomey helped me fake my own death, then saved my life twice, then got me killed. Okay, so the last one really wasn't his fault, but I thought it sounded better that way.

When I met Colgan, I was 21 years old and about to start medical school at the University of Texas, having graduated valedictorian of my class at Prairie View A&M, a historically black college between Houston and College Station. PV later became famous for having the longest losing streak in the history of college football – we lost 80 straight games, didn't win one from 1989 until 1998.

We weren't much better than that when I was "on the Hill" as the school's campus is known. I was on the team my first two years, though I never saw the field. Colgan and I later bonded over the injuries that prevented our glorious careers as college football stars from materializing. Mine was a shoulder that kept separating, sometimes just from throwing the ball hard. Anyhow, we won six games total my first two years and then went 0 and 11 my junior year, after I had left the team. I like to think I was contributing something without even knowing it.

I don't think, at the time, that I realized how big an achievement it was to get into Texas's medical school. School had always come easily for me, and, growing up on a relatively remote air force base near Mission, Texas, I was pretty insulated from the discrimination that had kept people like me out of schools like Texas well into my lifetime.

Since Prairie View was an HBCU, I think most of my classmates were thinking about all this at the forefront of their decision to choose a school. It honestly never crossed my mind. I came to PV because they gave me a football scholarship, and it was a pretty good academic school too. I didn't learn much about civil rights until I was in college there. Colgan and I used to laugh about the fact that the white kid from Alabama had more connection to the Civil Rights movement than I did.

My racial identity has always been a little fluid. I'm dark enough to pass for black, especially anywhere where there aren't a lot of Spanish-speaking folks, and my dad is African-American. My mom, though is half-Spanish – like actual Spanish, her father's from Spain and her mother was from Equatorial Guinea, a Spanish colony in Africa. I wish I had gotten to know my Grandmother, but she died when I was a few months old. Even if I was a little darker than some of them, I grew up just another Hispanic kid from the Valley. (In Texas, that's the Rio Grande Valley). It was just luck that my Spanish first name, which came directly from my grandfather Antonio Quevedo, was one that black folks from other parts of the country had started adopting by the time I went to college.

The story of my parents didn't have quite the drama that Colgan's did—no waking up in the hospital with an angel hovering over you—but it did parallel it in some ways. My father, James Rutledge, was from Cleveland (Ohio, not Texas), and he wanted to fly from the time he was five years old. The air corps was still part of the Army back then, and he signed up on his 18th birthday in June 1945. The war ended a week after he finished basic training.

Dad always joked that he would never have been able to fly anyway; he couldn't see well enough. Besides, pilots had to have a higher level of education than just high school and the month of electrician classes he took to fill the time between graduation and his birthday. Though he never talked about it, I think his race would have presented an obstacle as well. The Tuskegee Airmen were amazing, and deservedly famous, but I'd be willing to bet a good chunk of change that they were a small percentage of the black men who wanted to become pilots during the war. Most of the others never got the chance.

Dad did manage to get himself assigned to the air corps though, and stayed in when it became the Air Force, spending over 30 years in total as an airplane mechanic and radar tech. Like Colgan's Dad, he went down South on a temporary mission, though his came from Uncle Sam, and he never made it back to Yankee land. I'm sure when he reached this remote outpost in the borderlands, he didn't expect to be there for the rest of his days. In fact, he was about to be transferred to California when he met my mom. It wasn't exactly hard to get someone to switch assignments with him, when he decided he wanted to stay. Since most people wanted to get out of our dusty, remote base as soon as possible, he was running the maintenance department within a couple of years.

When they met, Mom was teaching biology at the high school halfway between the base and the town of Mission. She was also moonlighting at the base, teaching Spanish to the airmen. Dad was fond of saying that half the class tried to ask her out, but he was the second one that she accepted. The first was a pilot who died after his plane experienced a mysterious mechanical failure. He always told that last part with a devious twinkle in his eye, but I have to assume he was joking.

Colgan and I met at an admitted students' day at UT med school in the spring of 1983. He was in his first year, but he also went to undergrad there, so he knew his way around Austin and was given the task of showing us the town.

We went to a restaurant and three bars that night and at least one person at every one of them knew Colgan. I'm sure part of the reason was that he was just physically hard to forget, a slender but muscular six-foot-six with a red braid that went halfway down his back. He looked a little like a young Willie Nelson had been blown up to a larger picture.

After dinner at a Mexican place on Guadelupe, complete with a couple of margaritas, we headed down Sixth Street to find some live music. Eventually we ended up at this honky-tonk type joint with a giant rotating boot on top. Most of the others took a sideways glance at me, and one girl stopped dead in her tracks and turned to look at me. I wanted to look at this white chick and say "you're from Connecticut; I think they'll like me better than you."

I think Colgan saw me roll my eyes at her. He said, "You folks that aren't from Texas might not understand this place, but I promise they won't hurt you, right Tony?" Despite her feigned concern, I'm pretty sure Miss Yale didn't have a clue what my name was because she leaned over and said, "I can't believe he's bringing you here." I put on my best Texas accent for the response: "it's ok sweetheart, this ain't my first rodeo." I don't think she said another word to me the rest of the night.

In contrast, Colgan and I became fast friends, starting, I suppose, with the fact that I let him call me Tony without correcting him. As I got to know him, this didn't surprise me at all. Colgan just had this way of putting everyone at ease. That comment from the Yalie (I don't even remember her name) might have been the most negative thing I ever heard anyone say about him.

After about three songs, the band in the honky-tonk took a break. The guitarist made a beeline for the long standup table at stage left that the out-of-place wannabe med students had occupied. He still had his guitar slung over his shoulder when he got there.

"Big C!" he joyfully called to our guide. "Haven't seen you in forever, man!"

"Well, you know, learning to save the world takes up a lot of my time, brother. How you been? Y'all sound good."

"Man, most of the time we sound like a second-rate house band at a lousy kicker joint in Amarillo. I'm just glad somebody decided to put one of those in Austin. I can't handle the weather up in the panhandle."

I looked around and noticed that most of our group had drifted to the bar or the bathroom. Aside from Colgan, all that remained was myself and a Chinese guy from California who had gone to either Stanford or Berkeley.

"You better watch out, Danny, I think Steve here's from the panhandle." Colgan indicated our bay area companion, who started to protest, and then began laughing hysterically.

Danny, as the guitarist was apparently called, stuck out his hand and said, "No offense, pardner." This set off an even greater fit of laughter in the Stanford kid, who I'm pretty sure was not actually named Steve. He did manage to shake the fella's hand though.

Colgan next looked at me – "And this is Tony, he's from Prairie View."

"Antonio Rutledge," I said, sticking out my hand. "Nice to meet ya."

Danny shook my hand and said, "You may have gone to school in Prairie View, but I'll guarantee you're from the Valley. I grew up in Brownsville."

"Mission," I confirmed.

"I knew it! Anyhow, Big C, you need to get up there and play with us.

"Man, it's been forever. Ain't no way I could keep up with y'all."

"Bullshit, man, if you're out of practice it might mean we can keep up with you."

Colgan laughed and said, "yeah right," but I could tell that he agreed with the basic truth in Danny's statement. Apparently, our guide was a musician of some renown in a place where live music was the heart and soul of the city.

When the band took the stage again, someone had produced an extra guitar (a nice Fender, so I doubt it was just lying around behind the bar) and Colgan joined them on stage. It's possible he set all this up to impress the new students, but it's equally possible someone just loaned him a guitar, because he was really, really good.

The first song they did, a version of "I Fought the Law and the Law Won" closer to Bobby Fuller's than Hank Jr.'s, sounded pretty much like they had sounded all night. But then they all huddled up and apparently decided to let Colgan show off some, letting loose with a version of Free Bird that brought down the house. I found myself wondering why this kid was bothering to go to med school. Surely being a rock star would be more fun.

Maybe he wasn't really as good as I thought. It's not like I heard him jamming with Stevie Ray Vaughan or someone. (Hmm, that makes me wonder if they might not have run across each other there in Austin.) Anyway, at the time, when Stevie Ray had just made Austin's scene the hottest thing on the planet and Sixth Street was crawling with big time agents, I feel like he could have gotten a band together and finagled himself a record deal.

But for all the musician's bravado and willingness to party he showed, Colgan was, by all accounts, a serious med student as well. His first semester grades had been in the top ten percent of the class. I later learned he really was fascinated by the concept of medicine; the ability to understand the mysteries of life and to help improve the lives of individual people. His vision of medicine always had a social component too. If he had stuck with it, I think he would have worked for a charity in some third world country somewhere.

But I guess it's time to get to the blood and guts of the story, the salacious part where two wholesome, red-blooded American honor students become crazy commie revolutionaries. I don't know how much Colgan planned what he did, but for me, it really did start out as a chance to go on a mission trip and do some good in the world.

One of the professors had told me about the Doctors Without Borders trip during the admitted students' day. He said a couple of the students would be going to Guatemala with the aid group to basically be gophers and watch what the doctors did. I told him that if there was a spot for prospective students to let me know.

But when such a spot came open, it was Colgan who called me in my dorm room right before school ended. "Tony, my man," he asked when I answered the phone, "are you up for a tropical vacation?"

It took me a minute to place the voice, much less figure out what he was talking about. "Sure, why not," I said hesitantly.

The mission really was a great opportunity to see real doctors at work and help some folks out in the process. We would basically just be orderlies and janitors and such, but we were allowed to watch whatever procedures were going on, and the MSF folks (Doctors Without Borders is originally a French organization, so they use this acronym for "Medecins Sans Frontieres") were willing to do post-op recaps with us like a teaching hospital in the field.

I have to give Colgan the benefit of the doubt that if he had known he would be trying to recruit me into the FMLN (the Salvadoran rebel group we later joined), he would have told me. The Doctors Without Borders mission was supposed to last six weeks, and we were down there for a month sharing a tent and getting to know each other before he decided to bring me in on the plan. Hell, I don't even know if he had made the plan before that week.

The area of Guatemala we were in was just a couple miles from the Salvadoran border. We snuck to the border to meet the guerrillas one night about midnight. We met with them like three or four times before they and we were both comfortable with each other. I'm not necessarily saying I did the right thing, but man, there was some bullshit going on down in El Salvador. The people running that country really were evil, and the United States' decision to support them was a mistake. The FMLN (I honestly don't remember what that even stands for) guys that we met were good people who had been pushed over the edge and felt like they had to fight for their very existence and that of their nation, which had become a brutal dictatorship.

When young people do something that seems stupid in hindsight, everyone always wants to know why. But why is never the question that the kids are asking on the front end, or at least it wasn't for us. We saw injustices, Colgan more of them firsthand, because he had been in El Salvador before with his ex, and the question we asked was "what" – what can we do about this?

Most civil wars in the second half of the twentieth century are about ideology – right vs. left, communist, capitalist, etc. El Salvador's had that aspect, and I won't say that Colgan and I weren't moved by the plight of the poor and willing to accept that, at least in El Salvador, capitalism had completely failed to the extent that it seemed like Communism couldn't possibly be worse. But to a couple of idealistic Catholic kids, it also felt like a religious war. The unrest that led to the civil war started with the brazen murder of an archbishop while he was saying mass, for God's sake (or more accurately against His sake, I suppose). Later the same year, three Maryknoll nuns and an American laywoman were raped and murdered by members of the Salvadoran military. The same military the U.S. government was propping up and giving weapons to.

I won't say that I understood Liberation Theology very well, but it was enough for me that there seemed to be people that could rationalize Marxist philosophy within the Church. None of the Salvadorans I met seemed to believe in the "Godless Communism" that I had been warned about growing up. Their beliefs were based instead on Jesus's focus on the "least among us" and his unswerving commitment to taking care of the poor. I have to admit though, I later met some Cuban mercenaries (and a crazy Italian who thought he was a philosopher) that put much more stock in Marx's dictum that religion is the opiate of the people. But mostly I met a bunch of desperate men (and a few women) who just wanted to create a country where they could live in peace and have enough to eat.

On the night we actually left, they had originally just asked us to steal some of the medical supplies and come join them. Colgan, however, convinced them to cross the border and kidnap us, and that way they could have all the medical supplies they wanted, rather than just what we could carry. He made it clear that we weren't going to join them if they hurt anyone in the MSF camp though.

The plan went off without a hitch. The guerrillas came about two in the morning and got everyone out into the cleared circle at the middle of camp. When they told us to gather up the medical supplies for them, Colgan and I started protesting. The leader slapped him with the butt end of a rifle, and he went down in a heap. I jumped like I was going to help him and started arguing with the leader in Spanish. Somebody grabbed Colgan and stood him up, and two men tied our wrists and led us off while the rest of them ransacked the camp.

The next day, Colgan wrote up a press release saying that we were in the hands of the National Liberation Front of El Salvador or whatever it was FMLN stood for, and we would only be released if the United States renounced its support of the Salvadoran regime within 30 days. When the deadline came and went, he wrote another one saying we had been killed. I don't think anyone back home ever doubted it for a second.

There was almost no one in the insurgency in our part of the country who was trained in any kind of medical field, so Colgan and I quickly became two of the most valuable people around. The weird thing was that Colgan, who had the idea to join the darn rebels in the first place, refused to train with or carry a gun. Nonetheless, I started noticing even the squad leaders coming to him for advice. Apparently, he had a natural knack for military strategy, just like most everything else he ever tried.

But me, I was just a medic. I won't say I didn't participate in fighting, I absolutely did, but that was only when things broke down and we were all just trying to save ourselves. About the second mission we went on was the first time I saw a man die. He was shot through the throat by about six machine gun bullets. The fighting had moved on a bit, so I dragged his body where we might be able to find it later for his family. Then I prayed for him and took his AK-47. Colgan was either a hell of a lot braver or at least a little bit crazier than me. I never once saw him carry a weapon, even when we knew we were going into pitched battle.

This crazy bravado became central to his legend among the rebels. Soon everyone knew about El Colo Loco, the giant red-headed gringo who would take on the entire Salvadoran army with his bare hands and live to tell about it. The way they worshipped him was pretty hilarious if you knew the guy behind the Legend of Colgan Toomey. I always wondered if they would make him president of El Salvador or something if we won. Maybe I could be the foreign minister.

CHAPTER 20

THE ARCHBISHOP, AGAIN

I, Oscar Romero, served as a Catholic priest all of my adult life. As I told you before, I eventually became the Archbishop of San Salvador. I heard confession from thousands of penitent sinners and thousands more who were just going through the motions. I heard people confess to murder, rape, and countless unspeakable things. On multiple occasions, I went to the authorities when I knew that the person speaking to me would continue to hurt innocents. We're not supposed to do that; you probably know that. I never ratted on someone after the fact. But if I thought an innocent person was still being harmed or was about to be harmed, my conscience would not allow me to keep that confidential.

I never thought I would continue to hear confession after my death. But almost immediately, mixed in with the prayers for intercession, there were confessions. I have said before that those who believe I am a saint are deluding themselves to give divine provenance to their cause. Their prayers for intercession with God would probably be more effectively addressed to a far more worthy soul. However, I have come to believe, probably against sound doctrine, that, when a living priest is unavailable, confessing to a dead one has some value.

Colgan Toomey was certainly not the only person who sent daily confessions winging their way to me in the afterlife, but he was perhaps the most faithful in doing so. Many of the penitents who sought my spirit's counsel were engaged in the violent struggle of the Salvadoran Civil War. While most of them fought for the rebels, there were even some government soldiers who sought forgiveness for fighting against their countrymen, and for participating in atrocities they knew were wrong. I could not absolve them from the pangs of their own consciences simply because they were "just following orders." But where they did feel remorse, I tried to send them both peace and the courage to stand up to their superiors when they were asked to do something that was obviously morally wrong.

I'm not sure the soldiers I heard from could have made much of a difference. I doubt the ones who were shooting civilians, kidnapping and raping the wives and daughters of rebel soldiers, and generally terrorizing the Salvadoran people were confessing their sins to anyone. Maybe some of them were; maybe they coopted a few collaborationist priests that just absolved them of anything as long as it was done in the name of order and anti-communism. But I certainly wasn't hearing from them.

Colgan Toomey, however, began saying confession to me even before he returned to Texas in the days following my death. One of the things he confessed to was that he did not want to go to the fat little government priest in the fancy neighborhood where he was visiting his girlfriend's family. He told me that he knew he shouldn't talk about a consecrated servant of the church that way, and he probably wasn't supposed to be trying to confess to a dead man, and he was really confused by everything that had happened. Even if I had been alive and standing before him, I could not have definitively answered his questions about which side God would (and the Church should) be on in the war in El Salvador. All I know is that God abhors both violence and the conditions that El Salvador's working people suffered that led to it.

If I could have sat down with Colgan and tried to help him understand, I would probably have told him to go back to his country and work on both making sure that similar things didn't happen to the working classes of the United States and trying to get his country to stop funding and arming dictatorships all over the world. I don't know if he could have made a difference by doing that. It is possible that he really did make a difference in El Salvador by the help he gave to the rebels. There was a good chance, early on, that the government would crush the FMLN and implement even harsher control over the country. Colgan joined the rebellion at a crucial time; his actions helped it survive and eventually fight the government to a draw.

It is hard to overestimate how extraordinary that statement really is. To think that Colgan's contribution could have affected the course of the war seems ludicrous. He was a foreign kid with no military or strategic experience who never picked up a firearm. He fought with strategy, planning, and healing, and it is a testament to his intelligence, his perseverance, and his courage to acknowledge that his actions really did affect the fate of the nation he adopted.

When he first returned to Texas after my murder, Colgan's prayers were the confused and tortured rants of a broken-hearted nineteen-year-old. Nothing else could have been expected. He cared for Patrycia, and he had no desire to be unkind to her, but before he visited El Salvador he had looked upon her as virtually perfect. He worshipped her and thought she could do no wrong. What happened in San Salvador burst that bubble irrevocably. Whatever his feelings for her, it was impossible for Colgan to imagine a life with someone who could condone the actions of the Salvadoran government.

In Austin, Colgan's parish priest was a studious, jocund fellow name David Harrison. Father Harrison was a good man who spent his life helping college kids cope with being away from home and making sure they understood God and their parents would forgive them the occasional night of drinking or missed class. He told Colgan exactly what you would expect a college priest to—his advice was that there were plenty of other fish in the sea and that Colgan should focus on his studies.

That was fine advice as far as it went. Priests, of course, are notoriously bad at giving love advice. We have no idea how relationships work, and sometimes I think we just assume that if any two people do what they are supposed to do otherwise and treat each other nicely and with respect, they can make a marriage work. Simple observation of the world ought to tell us this is not true. But because most of us have no idea what else is required to create romantic love, we stick with essentially just telling people to be kind to one another, or trying to scare them into following the commandments, depending on what kind of priest we are trying to be. This is also what keeps us believing that there are plenty of other potential mates out there, no matter how strong your feelings for the one you just lost. In our mind, all you have to do is find someone who is a decent human being, who is a good Catholic, and who'll be nice to you. I've known too many good Catholic kids who settled for just another good person because they assumed if they were good, God would provide whatever else was needed to make a good marriage. In some cases, I think He did just that, but in others, the couple was just never meant to be together.

Anyway, this is a problem that priests aren't equipped to fix. Colgan's discussions with Father Harrison just made him frustrated and despondent. He adopted a fatalistic attitude, assuming that he had been given one chance to choose between individual romantic love and doing what was right in loving his fellow man. Somehow, these two forms of love became opposites in his mind, and he believed that everyone had to choose one or the other. Having chosen humanity over Patrycia, he saw no reason why he should be given the opportunity to choose again, and he certainly saw no point in pursuing it. This, honestly, is something priests ought to understand a little better, since we renounce romantic love to pursue our calling to serve God. Colgan never shared all these feelings with Father Harrison, so I cannot say how the Father would have counseled him. If a young man in El Salvador had come to me saying these things, I would have steered him to the priesthood himself. I don't know if that would have been the right choice for Colgan, but I doubt it.

Colgan would be even quicker than I am to deny that he is any sort of hero or saint. And to tell you the truth he would probably be even more right about the latter. Most of his actions in the war were essentially motivated by anger. He believed that his anger was righteous, and, at some level, he was probably correct. But the Church still teaches that wrath is a deadly sin, and that acting purely out of anger can never be the right answer. Colgan recognized this, and he often asked me to help God bring him peace and remove his wrath. I tried to do so, and I feel like it helped him be calm and cool in the heat of battle. But his motivation remained anger – anger at the Salvadoran government for the way it treated the people, anger at the military atrocities it perpetrated, anger at those who ran his own country and propped up oppressive governments around the world with money and weapons…

Anger at those who killed me. This is the anger I felt like I should have been able to take away, and I would have if I could. I continued to learn and grow as a soul after my death, and I learned relatively quickly to forgive all those who had wronged me and to release that anger. Yet it was a constant source of torment that I seemingly could not help others to do the same. I tried my best to send feelings of peace and forgiveness to everyone who sought my intercession or counsel, but I could still feel the rage and hatred in so many hearts, and the fact that these feelings were connected to my life and death slowed my progress as I worked toward eternal salvation.

Even though Colgan was immensely capable of clearing his mind and acting without any rashness in difficult situations, his motivation remained anger. He was angry at his girlfriend Patrycia and her father when he first prayed to me. Even as he showed utter calm and patience to his tormentors in Santa Maria prison, he remained angry, not at his own treatment, but that he could not be outside the prison helping the rebels.

Colgan also believed in the path of vengeance. He firmly believed that the government of El Salvador deserved every effort he could make to bring it down. This did not mean that he allowed the ends to justify unspeakable means. He would never have condoned the massacre of civilians in government-favoring areas, or the torture of prisoners of war. The rebels in general did a lot less of that than the government forces, but no one could seriously believe that there weren't war crimes on both sides. I feel that Colgan would never have participated in these actions; he would never have told other rebels that it was ok; but at the same time, he believed that the people who suffered from them deserved what they got because they supported the government. That is not a belief I would share.

Yet for all his anger and vengeance, which absolutely were traits I would try to counsel out of him if I could, Colgan did not translate that into cruelty or gratuitous violence. As his primary role in his rebel unit expanded from medic to strategist, he tried his best to kill only when necessary. It was, unfortunately, common in my country's civil war for both sides to kill prisoners, shoot civilians, destroy property for no reason, and torture people for information. Colgan never did any of those things.

He also confessed to every life he ever took, at least to me in private prayer. I don't know that the confession of such a sin matters all that much. It takes an awful lot to absolve someone of killing another human being. I know God is capable of forgiving it though, so I must learn to be as well.

When Colgan arrived at the Santa Maria prison, he prayed to me virtually constantly. There were times when he seemed to realize that the anger and vengeance that had driven him outside those walls would not serve him well in prison. I tried my best to pass on the peace I knew that the Father was sending him, but I take no credit for his reception of it. It astonished me how well he was able to accept that grace and peace from God. His soul probably craved it after staying angry for so long.

What remained special about Colgan in prison, was what had been special about him from the beginning. It was his ability to think about others, no matter what was happening to him. He reached out to the guard, Señor Amaya, with an understanding and generosity of spirit that honestly surprised me. I knew that Colgan was capable of dealing with an awful lot of physical pain, but to be able to translate that not into anger but to compassion for the old man and a sense of shared experience was truly beautiful.

I fervently believe that God was the source of Colgan's peace and his compassion. However, I do also acknowledge that the techniques of concentration and centering that he learned in his martial arts training were helpful. God teaches people in all sorts of different ways, and not all of them are through priests. That can be a hard lesson for the clergy to learn. There may be other religions that use a particular technique, but that does not mean that it should be off-limits to Christians, or to Catholics specifically.

Colgan's experience at Santa Maria prison was something that no human being should have to endure. But it also allowed him the time to pause and find at least a little bit of peace within himself. If, somehow, he could have reintegrated into normal society after that, I think he could have done amazing things with his talents. The Devil, however, was not through with Colgan Toomey, and he had many more ordeals to pass through.

CHAPTER 21

THE MEDIC, AGAIN

In my last chapter, I started out by saying that Colgan Toomey helped me fake my own death, saved my life a couple of times, and then got me killed. Like I said then, the last part wasn't really his fault, but it's a nice symmetry. I realize now though, that I only talked about the first of those three things in that chapter.

Before I was killed, I don't think Colgan or I ever regretted joining the Salvadoran rebels. I mean we probably should have regretted it I guess. We may have been rash, but we weren't stupid. We understood the danger of just choosing to be in a war zone, much less becoming medics in a rebel army. We both thought there was a really good chance that we'd never survive the war. I don't remember ever discussing what we thought would happen if we did survive it.

As far as I know, everyone back home thought we were dead. When Colgan wrote the original ransom note, we knew, of course, that the United States would not pull the rug out from under the Salvadoran Government. We were already planning to write the second note that said the rebels had been forced to kill us because their demands were not met. We had discussed whether this might bring down the wrath of the U.S. government on the rebels, but we decided that there was no appetite among the American people for active intervention in El Salvador. Reagan would keep funding the government and giving them military supplies, but there was no way he was going to put American troops on the ground. We were basically right about that.

We never discussed the legal ramifications of being dead. We both knew our family and friends would believe that we had been killed, and, of course, I was sad about what they would go through. Colgan never really talked about it though. We never thought about the fact that the U.S. government would issue death certificates, or whether we would be allowed back into our home country after the war was over. We never thought about the war being over, I guess. Day-to-day survival required our utmost attention the vast majority of the time, but even our longer-term thoughts focused on the war itself and what our strategy might be for improving the rebels' position.

It always irked me a little bit that Colgan's Spanish was better than mine. I mean I'd learned both Spanish and English as a baby, and I'd spoken both languages all my life. But I had to admit that I hadn't used it much between the time I arrived at Prairie View and going to Guatemala. So Colgan's really was a little better than mine, though it was possible that Colgan just communicated a little better with the Salvadorans because he had more experience with their dialect.

Beyond the linguistic facility, though, it was Colgan's overwhelming personality that had him sitting in on planning sessions with the local commander within a month or two of joining the rebels. At first, when we were always at the same campsite, he insisted on bringing me along. Colgan had a magnetism that attracted the rebel leaders, and they were grateful for the medical supplies we had provided. But what overcame their reluctance to let this foreigner be part of their closest councils was his unmistakable personal courage.

A little over a month after we joined the rebel camp, right after we sent out the letter that said they had killed us, Colgan and about five others got separated from the main group of about 20 (which included me) after we had raided a small-town police station for weapons. On our way back to the camp, a group of national police—these guys were often even more vicious than the regular army—had created a roadblock between the town and the rebel-held area.

The guy in charge of the raiding party selected some guys to go around the roadblock and tell the main rebel group about it so they could attack it from behind. Colgan piped up and asked to go with them. He had apparently been talking a lot with one of the guys who got chosen, who spoke up for him and convinced the commander to let him go.

So Colgan and the rest of this group cut away from the road planning to sneak through some fields and then into the woods to get around the road block and let the main rebel camp know what was going on. They made it about to the tree line when someone spotlighted them. We watched as they sprinted into the woods while a group of national police broke off from the road block and gave chase. We had no idea what happened next, as we retreated back down the road and found a place to hide while we could figure out our own path around the road block. We were still close enough that if the main rebel force attacked the barricade, we would hear it.

One of the men in Colgan's group got killed that night, and three others were temporarily captured. One eventually made it through the woods to the rebel camp. And then there was Colgan. Apparently after the police began chasing them, he went up the nearest tree. I have no idea what he was planning to do; maybe he thought he could swing back to camp like Tarzan.

As the three captured soldiers told it, they were being force-marched back to the road block by four policemen when one of their captors suddenly collapsed with a surgical knife in the back of his neck. Despite being handcuffed to one another, they took this as a cue to try to fight back. In the ensuing melee, the other three policemen were killed. None of the captives knew that the "loco gringo" had thrown the knife and then jumped out of the tree to attack the policemen until he pulled his knife out of the guy's neck and popped their handcuffs with it.

The four of them had no idea whether either of the other two members of their team had reached the rebel camp, so they headed off in that direction. They soon found the body of the man who had been shot. Colgan pronounced him dead and put his body over his shoulder so that he could have a good Christian burial. I would soon learn that the rebels typically did not have the luxury of recovering their fallen, so they seemed especially grateful to Colgan for carrying the man out of the woods.

By the time they got the body back to camp, the main rebel force was leaving to attack the road block. Colgan immediately volunteered to go with them. The national police roadblock folded quickly when they saw a group several times their size approaching from behind, but the rebels did take a couple of prisoners. Colgan's only contribution to that attack was to treat one of the prisoners, but his earlier heroics had begun to cement him in rebel lore.

Two days later the Commandante invited Colgan to a meeting planning an attack at a place called Citala. It was a border crossing between El Salvador and Honduras and taking it would allow the rebels both easier access to supplies and the chance to get some cash by collecting taxes on the cross-border traffic. The rebels were always conscious that they were trying to set up an alternative government, not just defeat the regime militarily. The Commandante said he wanted to make sure the border traffic wasn't disrupted too bad and wanted to lower the customs tax by ten percent.

We knew that the border post itself would be guarded by Salvadoran Army regulars. It was a pretty isolated spot, though, and we didn't think the garrison would have more than a handful of soldiers. The rebels' main activity prior to this attack had been further north and west, along the border with Guatemala. The area was extremely rugged, mountainous and rural, and the poor, largely indigenous population of the state of Chalatenango, along with the far northern part of Santa Ana state, were hotbeds of rebel sympathy.

Colgan raised the idea that maybe starting some kind of commotion on the Honduran side would be a good way to distract the Salvadoran Army posted at the border station. At first, the Commandante seemed extremely skeptical of this plan. There were elements of the Honduran government that were sympathetic to the rebels and he didn't want to upset them.

But the area around Citala wasn't held by the rebels yet. It was just kind of empty country. So Colgan came up with a way to start minor trouble in Honduras and blame it on the government. We had a few old uniforms from the Chalatenango State Police. One of the squadron leaders had brought them with him when he defected to the rebel side. Colgan kicked up this plan where he would sneak into Honduras alone on foot a couple of miles north of the Citala border station. We would need a spotter with binoculars in a tree near the border line to watch what happened to him. Colgan said if he got caught, to just break off the plan, and he'd find a way to get back to us later. (I'm not sure anyone believed that last part.)

Assuming Colgan made it into Honduras without incident, there would be four guys in state police uniforms waiting to "chase" him at a point closer to the border station. We later scouted this out and found a perfect place where a small creek crossed the border just over the hill from the customs house. At this point, the Hondurans were supposed to see what was going on, so Colgan was just going to come running out of the woods and across the creek, and when the others saw him, they would give chase into Honduras. He would run over the hill and onto the road that went through the border station.

At this point it was assumed the Hondurans would get pissed that four Salvadoran state policemen were playing Keystone Kops on their side of the border. They would probably complain to whatever garrison was on the

Salvadoran side, thus distracting them from the attack of the main rebel force on the customs building. It was hoped that Colgan and the other four would then just be able to run back across the border.

The whole plan was insane. So, of course, it worked like a charm. Not only were the Salvadoran soldiers "distracted" by the incident, they got in a huge argument with the Hondurans about whether their state police had a right to come over the border chasing an "escaped prisoner." By the time the main rebel group came within sight of the border station, both the Hondurans and the Salvadorans were in the middle of the road yelling at each other.

When he saw this, the Commandante took off on a dead sprint for the customs house and we followed. The soldiers in the road were stunned, and at least half of them were unarmed. They surrendered without firing a shot. The only casualty that day was that one of the guys dressed as a state policeman was wounded by a Honduran soldier after we took the station and as the "distraction" group was crashing through the woods to our south trying to get back over the border. It was just a minor wound on his leg though.

The Citala operation was a huge success. Much of the surrounding countryside in Chalatenango state soon became rebel held territory, and even the mayor of one of the nearby towns, La Palma, switched sides. The rebels had enjoyed similar success south of us along the Honduran border, in the province of Cabanas, which had seen some of the worst activity of government death squads. Within months, we had combined with two other groups and were moving to take the state capital, the city of Chalatenango. Colgan had become the trusted confidant of our Commandante, and even the soldiers who were at first suspicious of his unwillingness to carry a rifle trusted him completely now. By the time we had taken Chalatenango, the national leaders of the rebellion knew who he was.

So I've told you about how Colgan got in good with the rebel leadership, but I still haven't told you about the times he saved my life. The first one was about six months after we took the border station at Citala. We had moved further south and were fighting in the Morazan department. It was slow going, basically house to house fighting in a medium sized city called Ciudad Barrios. We never knew whether a particular house contained rebel sympathizers, government soldiers who had taken it from the locals, or just scared people who had no idea which side to be on.

The Salvadoran Civil War was brutal and nasty on all sides, even if I didn't always see that. There were a lot of civilian casualties, and they were often intentional. On the government side, this was done with a purpose and plan of intimidating the local population. I firmly believe that on the rebel side it was almost always the result of an untrained army being presented with situations where they couldn't tell who the enemy was. That doesn't mean the rebels didn't intentionally shoot people when they had no idea whether the person was armed or whether they belonged to the enemy, and that was wrong.

Anyway, Colgan and I were with a group of guys sweeping a neighborhood that had supposedly already been won in Ciudad Barrios. We quickly found out it wasn't anywhere near secure when we got ambushed from what looked like a car repair shop. One of our guys was killed and another wounded. Colgan carried the wounded man to safety after we had disposed of the two ambushers. I pulled the dead man out of the street and flagged the location where we would find his body and then ran to catch up with the squad, which had turned a corner in front of me.

The remaining members of our party were understandably jumpy after the ambush, and they made a mistake that still haunts me even after my death. I want to believe that it is at least possible that a government soldier set up the situation. Someone kicked a soccer ball out of a cross street and it bounced off a building and rolled toward us. Two of the members of the squad ran forward to that cross street and, looking in the direction from which the ball had come, saw someone leap out of the street and hide behind a wooden flower stand.

Unfortunately, the flower stand provided virtually no protection from AK-47 rounds. By the time I got to the corner yelling "hold your fire" in Spanish, whoever had been behind it was almost certainly dead and buried in a pile of splintered wood. The squad ran forward to secure the next cross street, while I went to see who was left in the rubble. It turned out to be a boy of about seven, wearing a Dallas Cowboys jersey. His face still haunts me, and the connection to Texas, the home I'd probably never see again, made it that much more difficult.

At the time I imagined a little kid whose dad had gone to Texas for work or something and who grew up on stories of the mighty Cowboys, his dad bringing back a precious souvenir to remember him by while he was working so far away. That narrative is possible, but it's more likely that he got a Cowboys jersey because the team donated old merchandise to organizations that passed out food and clothing in Central America. Which of these is true doesn't really matter at all, because I still see that kid, his chest covered by half of a single blue star and everything below his rib cage just basically gone.

I never forgot that image, but I had very little time to think about it right then. If the government soldier who had set up a position on the roof two blocks further down had been a real sniper, it would have been the last thing I ever saw. Luckily, he missed the first shot and I had the opportunity to at least give him a moving target. Apparently, the guy had some kind of order to shoot the Americans, or perhaps the medics, because he probably had a clearer shot at two of our soldiers closer to him, but he fired several shots at me and then started shooting at Colgan as he came running back around the corner. I don't remember where he had gone, probably helping wounded or something.

To this day I'm not sure how Colgan got onto the roof with the "sniper." One minute he was running down the alley being shot at and the next he had somehow climbed up behind the man who had been shooting at us. The last shot that the soldier got off ricocheted off a building and hit me in the thigh. Colgan snapped the guy's neck with one of his jujitsu moves and then literally took a running leap off the building to come and stop my bleeding.

The bullet, which had been slowed by its carom off a building, had merely grazed the fleshy part of my thigh. There was a lot of blood though, or at least it looked that way to the person whose blood it was! Having never been shot before, I was freaking out, assuming I was dying. Colgan quickly laid me back, determined no bullet needed to be taken out of the wound, and put on pressure and a bandage to stop the bleeding. It probably wasn't his medical care that saved my life – I don't think the wound was that bad. But if Colgan hadn't taken him out, the guy on the roof would have been taking pot shots at a sitting target as I freaked out about my leg.

The second time Colgan saved my life had nothing to do with Salvadoran soldiers. I had gotten a cut on my leg marching somewhere at night, and it became infected, probably with staph. We had a lot of first-aid type supplies, but almost nothing in the way of antibiotics. Colgan convinced the Commandante to raid a hospital because we were running low on supplies.

In that hospital, Colgan found some antibiotic cream. He cut my leg open where it was infected and packed the wound with the cream. It hurt like hell and I basically couldn't walk for three days. At first, I was pissed at Colgan for doing it, but it almost certainly saved my life, or at least my leg.

Like I said before, my eventual death wasn't actually Colgan's fault. We weren't even in the same unit anymore. He had gone with a group of he most experienced rebel soldiers—some of our original unit, a few lefectors from the Salvadoran army, and about a dozen Cuban "advisors"—o the coastal department of Sonsonate, home of the country's largest naval ase. There wasn't a whole lot of military value in taking out a navy ship – t's not like the Cuban navy was gonna bring in a bunch of soldiers if we ould just disable their opposition on the sea – but it would look amazing, plift the morale of the rebels, and demoralize the government soldiers.

I heard about Colgan's triumph in blowing up a cruiser the day before was killed. By this time, the guerilla war in Chalatenango state had pretty nuch ended, and there were pitched battle lines, especially along the border vith San Salvador state, where the rebel-held areas came within 20 miles or o of the capital.

Because of that, there's not a lot of individualized story to tell about ny death. We were in an entrenched position and the Salvadoran Army lecided to attack. It was a bit of a surprise and everyone just jumped into he nearest firing position. Three of us were in a nest shooting away at the ncoming soldiers when we got hit with a mortar. All three were killed, but he rebels ended up holding the position.

CHAPTER 22

THE NURSE

The man told me his name was Colo. I don't know if he was American or Guatemalan or Salvadoran. He could have been from South America or Europe for all I know, which is that he didn't have Mexican papers and he spoke perfect Spanish.

The night he brought that girl into the emergency room is still burned into my memory. She couldn't have been more than about fifteen, and she might have been a couple years younger than that. She had been beaten within an inch of her life. When she came in, she was passing in and out of consciousness and her blood pressure was about 75 over 40. We were sure she would die of internal bleeding.

My first thought was that our little hospital in San Patricio was not equipped to deal with this. We basically had a big round emergency room with six cots and then two operating rooms and an x-ray room. Down the hall from that was a small kitchen and six overnight rooms. We didn't have any kind of imaging system that would tell us where the internal bleeding was on this poor girl.

I'm not sure we had ever dealt with this kind of trauma before. Over the course of a normal month, we set a couple broken bones, gave some antibiotic shots for various infections, sent people home because they had the flu, and maybe, once every few months had a serious life-threatening condition like a stroke or heart attack. Car wrecks weren't even common in our area, because so few of the people had cars.

At the time the girl showed up, two of the back rooms were in use. One held an old man who was dying of being old, but had the money to do so slowly and comfortably in the hospital instead of painfully at home. The other temporarily housed a doctor whose wife had kicked him out.

The girl's breathing was ragged and irregular and her oxygen levels were all over the map. She needed a tube. There was no way to know she was pregnant by looking at her. But while we were about to insert her tube she sat up and screamed "save my baby" in Spanish. I took her hand and told her we would, but I knew it was a lie.

I am almost certain that the baby was dead before she arrived at the hospital. At the time I was certain the girl would be dead soon thereafter. I'm still not sure to this day how she survived. Maybe it really was a miracle like she said. She kept ranting that the Lord had sent an angel to save her. We just thought she had seen some vision while we had her knocked out with morphine. Or maybe some of us thought we were the angels who had saved her life.

By the time I figured out she meant the big red-headed guy, she'd been in the hospital about a month. For almost three weeks she was on the ventilator and was rarely even conscious. It took me about a week after that of her ranting about "her angel" every time I was in her room to figure out she was looking for a specific person. After that, it didn't take long to remember the guy who had brought her in.

The problem was that he'd been gone for weeks by the time I realized she wanted him. For the first three days after they arrived he slept in the lobby. Every couple of hours he would ask about her, but there was never any change. What's weird is that we tried to get her information from him, and he had no clue. He didn't even know her name or how old she was, but he had apparently carried her for miles across the desert from where she was attacked. Then, despite having no apparent connection to her, he camped out for days in the lobby.

Eventually we realized that he hadn't eaten anything since he'd been there. A couple of the nurses brought him food from the kitchen on their lunch hour. I took him to an empty room to let him take a shower. He was kind of cute once he got cleaned up! When I got off that evening, I spent an hour talking to him and rebraiding his insane amount of luxurious red hair.

On the third day, two federales (cops from the Mexican national police force) showed up to talk to him. At the time we didn't know that he had killed the two men who were attacking the pregnant girl. (She hadn't woken up yet, and he hadn't told us anything.)

Colo was sleeping when the cops came in. He clearly didn't want to talk to them. But when they asked, he was oozing politeness and said they needed to hear his story and that he would have come to them, but he wanted to make sure the girl was okay. The cops started out nice and sweet just asking him who he was and what he was doing there. He gave the name Oscar Romero and said he lived in San Salvador. There was a town called San Salvador south of us in Hidalgo state. I think the cops assumed that's what he meant.

All of us that worked in the hospital were a bit smitten by this red-headed stranger, so the girls at the front desk strained to listen to him talk to the cops that day. They heard a hell of a story. He said he had been camping out in the desert south of here and noticed a group of people who seemed to be human smugglers. As he tracked them, he heard screams from a young girl and was moved to try to help her. For two days and nights he stayed behind them.

On the third evening, he saw the two men take the young girl away from the rest of the group and over a rise dotted with low sage bushes. He crept up behind a boulder and saw that the men were beating the young girl. Here, the stranger gave no details but said only that he got the girl away from the men and brought her to the hospital.

The federales did not ask what happened to the two men. They had probably found the bodies before they interrogated him. Eventually they asked the stranger when he would be going back to Hidalgo. He said only that he would leave when he knew the girl was well again. The cops finally began to lose patience. They asked him what kind of job he had that would allow him to leave home for so long. Looking at his clothes, he clearly was not a wealthy man.

Colo replied that he was a poor farmer and his brother and son would take care of the farm while he was gone. The cops asked for their names. The girls couldn't remember what he said but the cops knew he was lying. That's when they demanded his ID or papers. They made him stand up and searched him. He had no wallet, no money, no identifying documents of any kind.

That's when one of the cops finally figured out that San Salvador probably didn't mean the little town in Hidalgo. They told him he didn't look Salvadoran and asked him where he was from. He told them he was from everywhere there were victims of oppression who would come together to fight that oppression.

The federales, though not particularly bright, did show a higher amount of restraint than a lot of Mexican cops. They just told him if he couldn't produce his ID papers, they would have to arrest him. He calmly stuck out his wrists to be handcuffed. As they marched him out of the door, he told Carlita at the front desk that he would be back to check on the girl. The cops just laughed at him.

Twenty or thirty miles north of us, about halfway to the border, there was a federal prison where they kept border crossers who were caught on our side of the Rio Grande. The Mexicans went home after a couple of days (and were usually back in the U.S. within a week), but the Guatemalans, Salvadorans, and Hondurans were held at the prison until their country decided there were enough worth trading something of value for and then sent home.

I had decided that Colo was probably American, and I figured Americans who illegally came into Mexico probably ended up in the same place as Mexicans trying to get into the U.S. Actually, I had never heard of any Americans trying to illegally get into Mexico. And why did he tell the federales he was from San Salvador? The cops were right though, he certainly didn't look Salvadoran. None of this really made any sense, but one thing I was pretty sure of was that we would never see this mysterious stranger again.

I was wrong about that. Almost two months after the cops led Colo away, we were trying to determine what to do with the girl. Like him, she had no papers or identifying documents whatsoever. She also didn't have any money and had run up one of the biggest hospital bills I'd ever seen. I'm surprised the hospital administrator didn't call the cops on her and have her thrown in jail too.

The girl said her name was Alicia Gonzales and she had been born in El Salvador but lived in Guatemala before trying to make it to Texas to find her father. She was a weird girl, always talking about the wonderful land of Texas and the way "her angel" had saved her from the "evil demons." Like I said, it was several days before I figured out that her angel meant the big redhead who had slept in the lobby the first week she was here. I can't say that I had forgotten about him though. I still think about him sometimes…

Anyway, we had no idea what we were going to do with the girl. She couldn't stay there forever. We couldn't just let her walk out into the desert. We couldn't call up her father in another country and have him come get her. (Especially since he was probably in that other country illegally and wouldn't be able to cross the border.) Besides, the only information she had from her father was that he lived in San Antonio. The thugs that he had hired to take her across the border were supposed to bring her to him. The only option seemed to be to turn her over to authorities, but everyone was reluctant to do that.

Even though she was more than a bit odd, Alicia was a sweet girl, and no woman should ever have to go through what she went through. She was obviously horribly raped and beaten, but she never said anything about that. She never said a word about her own pain. It was always that God sent an angel to save her and her baby, Maribel. I wanted to cry when I heard that she named the baby. She said the Virgin Mary appeared to her in a vision while she was being carried to the hospital and told her the name. I couldn't believe the Holy Mother would be so cruel as to intentionally make her think the baby could live. But maybe the name served some other purpose.

Then, out of nowhere, Colo showed up again. We didn't even hear about his escape from the prison until the next day. This shouldn't necessarily have solved our problem—there was no good reason to release the girl to this drifter who didn't even know her name. But Ms. Gonzales insisted that she be allowed to go with him, and he promised to take her to her father. Everyone knew the hospital would never see a dime of what she owed, so we just let her go. I don't know what happened to her afterwards, but something makes me believe that Colo did the best he could to take care of her.

CHAPTER 23

THE MUSICIAN

Yeah, I remember Colgan Toomey. Dude owes me like 50 bucks 'cause I got his guitar out of a pawn shop in Corpus Christi or Galveston or someplace. Dude was a hell of a guitar player, but he was a strange cat, man. He would slip into these weird daydreams or trances and if you tried to talk to him he would respond with long strings of Spanish. I mean I'm from Texas, I've picked up enough words here and there to have a basic conversation, but sometimes he would go ninety miles a minute in a dialect that wasn't your basic Tejano. He was usually talking about someone or some place called Santa Maria.

Colgan was obsessed with finding a guy named Tomas Gonzalez. Half the time it seemed like he wanted to track him down and kill him, but the rest of the time it seemed like he was trying to return his daughter to him. This Gonzalez character had apparently come to the US from El Salvador but left his daughter in Guatemala--I know that doesn't make a lot of sense, but I'm a bit fuzzy on the details.

Anyway, something happened to the poor kid, Colgan would never say what. She nearly died, but she pulled through and made it to the United States. But apparently once she got here, she couldn't find her Dad. I have no idea where she met Colgan, but apparently he was helping her try to find Pops.

I also have no idea how a fifteen-year old kid in a foreign country by herself even survives. I mean did she go to school? How had she not been picked up and deported? Nobody had ever mentioned her Mom, but I had the feeling they wouldn't be trying so hard to find the father if she was around. All Colgan would ever say was that she lived in Laredo.

Everybody knows about Austin, but Texas in general has the best live music in the world. I feel like it's the only place where you can still make a halfway decent living playing local venues. Half the small towns here have dance halls with house bands made up of full-time musicians. You don't see that in most parts of the country.

So, it wasn't inherently odd to see a thirty-something fella still trying to make a life out of playing guitar in honky-tonks. But usually when you saw somebody doing that, at least the other musicians in the area knew who he was. With Colgan, there were only a few old-timers down in the Valley that said he used to play in Austin. Apparently, when he was in college, he was in a band called Big C and the B-Minuses. Despite the awful name, they were supposedly pretty damn good. Rumor had it that Colgan even played with Stevie Ray once or twice.

But, the story goes, Colgan gave up the band and music generally to go to med school. I've heard more than a couple people say it was a damn shame too, because Colgan had a gift. I think that's crazy; this business don't come easy for anyone. Well maybe if you're Brad Pitt gorgeous and related to a superstar. For the rest of us, we do this because we have to. Either the music inside will drive us mad if we don't, or we just don't have any other options for making a living.

So, if Colgan had a chance to go to med school, I sure as hell can't blame him for it. I just wonder what the hell happened. Did he do something awful and lose his medical license? Just get burned out with the long hours and watching people die? Did people sue him out of the business? Maybe he flunked out of med school and never practiced medicine at all. But if that were true, why didn't he immediately come back to music?

Colgan eventually admitted to me that he was the same guy that used to pick up in Austin when he was in college. But he never would talk about what happened between then and when he showed up on the scene again down in the Valley. Part of me says he's just a crazy Mick who always has to have a cause, always gets obsessed with something and pursues it to the exclusion of everything else. That's exactly what he did with this Gonzales character.

We ended up playing together in the backup band for a cat named David Roy Harris. He wasn't exactly a superstar, but he'd been on Austin City Limits a few times and had made more than one real honest-to-God studio album. I think I even heard him on the radio once, just the last few seconds of a song, so I couldn't be quite sure. He kept saying he was going to go back in studio with the band he had now, but it never happened. Our music was pure Texas, but it didn't really fit any other genre. Some songs sounded like Bob Wills or George Strait, and some sounded like Buddy Holly and a few were more like ZZ Top or Stevie Ray Vaughan. We would travel a kind of loop from Houston to Austin to San Antonio, then down to Laredo and over to the coast. Sometimes we played the biggest, best-known joints in H-town and San Antonio, and sometimes we played in dirt-floor saloons in towns without stoplights. Once we played in an actual barn in Beeville.

So anyway, everywhere we played, Colgan would ask the bartender about Tomas Gonzalez. I remember one time this fella in Seguin goes "Yeah, I know Tommy, he's right over there" and pointed at a rather large fellow in a biker jacket. Now Colgan was tall, and claimed to know all kinds of martial arts, but this guy was at least his height and twice his weight. I thought I was about to be witnessing a disaster.

But Colgan was all charm, so he didn't need the ninja stuff. "Good evening, Mr. Gonzalez," he began. "I don't know if you're the fella I am looking for, but if you'll let me buy you a round, I'd like to ask you a couple questions.

The big man just kinda grunted like he didn't really give a shit who paid for his beer as long as they kept 'em coming.

"What ya drinkin, amigo?" Colgan continued. Gonzalez just turned his bottle of Lone Star around for Colgan to see.

"A Lone Star for myself and my friend here," Colgan called out.

I didn't hear the whole conversation between them because Colgan leaned forward and talked lower – obviously a man's relationship with his daughter is a private matter. I think Colgan went back and forth believing that the girl's father intentionally abandoned her and believing he just didn't know where she was. But he was smart enough not to accuse this big-ass biker of abandoning his kid, and he was probably smart enough not to mention that the guy he was looking for came here illegally.

In any case, Colgan satisfied himself that this wasn't the guy he was looking for. I heard the big biker fellow tell him that if he saw this other Tomas Gonzalez he'd let him know about where his daughter was. I thought to myself that he honestly had a better chance of finding the guy than Colgan did.

Right before he left the band, Colgan got another lead in a little place called Pearsall, down in Frio County, south of San Antonio. Now Pearsall probably had about five thousand people in it, but in the music world, it was famous because George Strait grew up there. The place where we had our gig was the first venue King George had ever played.

Anyway, we were talking to the owner and some of the staff before the show and, of course, Colgan asks about Tomas Gonzalez. The bartender nods and says, "Yeah, there's a bunch of them Gonzalezes that live out on highway 140 toward a place called Frio Town. They're a bad bunch from what little I know of 'em, always causing trouble. If I'm remembering right, there's a couple of 'em called Tommy. You should talk to Jack when he gets here, he lives out that way."

Jack was the bouncer, and it turned out he'd had more than one run-in with one particular Tommy Gonzalez of Frio Town. He was more than happy to tell Colgan how to find him, even said he'd give him a ride up there the next morning. Now, one thing you gotta understand about musicians, including David Roy's band, was that we stay up late and don't wake up too early in the morning. It was usually midnight or one when we finished playing, sometimes later, and we'd hang out and drink, maybe smoke a little weed, and try to catch a groupie until the place shut down, usually around three or four. Then we'd stagger back to the hotel (usually one or two of us had already headed that way with a girl) and make plans to meet in the lobby at noon, plans which we were often as much as an hour late for.

Colgan wasn't particularly opposed to this debauchery, though I never saw him ingest anything stronger than beer. He snuck off with his fair share of ladies, too, more than his fair share if I'm honest about it. Hell, he probably got more action than David Roy himself. But man, when that boy was on a mission, he was all about it. Since he thought he had a good lead on this Gonzalez fella, he headed back to the hotel right after we quit playing. Said he was gonna be up at 8 to meet ol' Jack and ride out to Frio Town.

Whatever he found out there, it wasn't what he was looking for. I'm not sure what happened to Jack, but he probably just dropped Colgan off back at the bar. Anyhow, we were getting ready to roll about 1:30 and I'd already loaded Colgan's stuff in the van by the time he showed back up. I was like "man, we were starting to worry about ya pardner."

"Sorry," Colgan huffed. "It wasn't our guy."

A couple nights later we arrived in Laredo for a several-day run of shows at different places. We had the first night in town off, so several of us decided to go over the border to one of those wild Mexican night clubs and see the show. We invited Colgan, but he seemed to get real squeamish about crossing the border, said something about he wasn't sure either side would let him in. We had a pretty good laugh about that, since he was mostly a pretty straight-laced fella when it came to any kind of criminal activity. But something in his eyes when we laughed told me there was a real reason there, some kind of history with the border patrol or something.

I didn't think much more about it until Colgan abruptly quit the band two days later. There wasn't any kind of blow up or fight, we just finished the show one night and he said, "Well, that's the last one for me, boys."

We all kinda looked at each other and went, "what the hell?" Colgan had given absolutely no warning that he wanted to quit the band. I wanted to ask him if that meant he had found Tomas Gonzalez, but he just said that he had to go over to Los Artistas on the other side of the border and he probably wouldn't be able to come back for awhile.

That was the last I heard of Colgan Toomey. I don't know if he's still bangin' around over there in Mexico, or if he's dead or if he's gone off to Nashville and we're gonna see him on the hit parade next year. But I do know he still owes me that fifty bucks.

CHAPTER 24

THE BEST FRIEND, A THIRD TIME

Five months after the last time I spoke to Michael Toomey, we buried him in Kellyville next to his beloved Sarah Anne and the monument he had built for Colgan. Stubborn to the end, he never did contact me, he just assumed he would see me in July. He died on May 25th.

Angela Campbell, Michael's other beloved, if I dare call her that, was stoic and stone-faced at his funeral. But she cried all the way back to Tuscaloosa, and I believe that Michael's death was what started her descent into madness. I'm sure there's some sort of brain chemistry and genetic explanation for what Alzheimer's does and why, even if doctors don't really understand it yet, but for me, the best explanation was that my mom just couldn't make sense of a world that didn't have Michael Toomey in it.

I never found any evidence of contact between them in the long years after Michael left Kellyville. I don't know if they even spoke to one another after Michael joined the church. I don't know if they had some sort of secret relationship that he broke off, or if they never got around to starting one. I don't know if being together would have made them happy, but I know being apart brought them both a profound sadness, even as they maintained outwardly happy, productive lives, each dedicated to an institution, the

Panther Drive-In being as much a sacred place to her as the Monastery of St. Bernard was to him.

Neither Mom nor I has visited Kellyville in the years since Michael's funeral. She's basically on hospice now, with a nurse to take care of her 24-7. I doubt she'll see Kellyville again until she's laid to rest there. But I got a phone call yesterday that has me headed south on Highway 43 about as confused as Mom is most days.

The call came from Tanya Haynes, wife of Colgan's former backup and current head coach at Kellyville High, Matt Haynes. Matt was in the class behind me and Colgan, and Tanya was a class behind him, so I really didn't know her in high school. Matt was also a backup safety at UA while I was there, and he and Tanya were both education students. I spent a little time with the two of them during college, but I hadn't seen or spoken to either in years.

Tanya's phone call, at 9:00 p.m. on a Tuesday night in September of 2000, came completely out of the blue. I'm not even sure how she got my number. The subject proved even more surprising. Tanya told me she was sure she had seen Colgan at the cemetery in Kellyville.

"Wait, slow down Tanya. You know that's impossible. Colgan's dead."

"Six and a half feet tall with bright red hair ain't exactly common around here, P.J. If it wasn't Colgan, it was his spittin' image, by God."

"Tanya, it's been seventeen years. I believe you that you've seen someone that looked like him, but it can't be Colgan."

She told me she was absolutely certain it was him, so I asked her how. The answer set my spine to tingling.

"P.J., I saw him kneeling beside Michael Toomey's headstone." I don't know if Tanya heard the gasp of air I took in, but she continued. "My daughter and I were walking the dog along Pine Street, across from the cemetery. Suddenly the dog began pulling toward the street and barking, so I looked out into the graveyard. The man stood slowly and turned to us, then smiled and waved. I just stood there with my mouth open, while Julie waved back. Then Colgan took one more look at his parents' graves and began walking toward the woods at the back of the cemetery."

"Tanya, it wasn't..." I stopped myself. I didn't know what to think anymore. I stammered a thank you to Tanya for calling me and gave her my cell phone number. Then I put down the phone honestly wondering if it were somehow possible.

I had no idea what I would do when I got to Kellyville. Going to the Panther Drive In for lunch seemed like a reasonable choice though. But first something told me to drive through the neighborhood where Colgan and I grew up. I guess that something was just nostalgia, because I didn't find any evidence that Colgan had been there. Of course, I had no idea what kind of evidence I should be looking for. We had sold both houses after Michael died, since he left everything in his estate to my mom. They looked well-kept, ours probably better than it had been when I was a kid.

The sale of those houses not only paid for Mom's hospice care, they had allowed me to open a sports bar on Fifteenth Street in Tuscaloosa. At first, I wanted to call it Colgan Toomey's, but I decided that there might be a few people around who remembered Colgan turning down Alabama, so that might not fly too well in T-town. Instead, I just went with P.J.'s, even though I found it a rather boring name. I looked at the clock on my dashboard – P.J.'s might open a little late tonight. Thankfully it was just a random Tuesday night and not much was going on.

On the whole though, the bar business had been really good in the two years since we opened. It allowed me to be my own boss and even gave me a chance to do a little film work on the side. I didn't work directly for the University anymore, but I had built my own editing studio upstairs at P.J.'s. The only thing I really had to get done this week was a recruiting video for the business college.

As I drove past Colgan's old house, I thought about talking to the new owners, but what was I going to do, just walk up to the door and ask them if they had seen a tall, middle-aged red-headed fellow snooping around here? That would probably encourage them to shoot Colgan if they did see him.

I made a loop of the neighborhood and went back to the Panther. I was glad to see that the place had hardly changed since Mom left. It was still hard for me to be there knowing she'd never be able to see it again, at least not with any understanding of where she was. Everyone asked about her of course. I just told them she was holding up about as well as could be expected.

They also, of course, wanted to know why I was back in town. I decided against asking if anyone had seen anything weird at Michael Toomey's grave or heard rumors about Colgan being alive.

"Honestly just came by to see how the place was holding up… and take a trip down memory lane I suppose."

I figured if I was gonna eat at the Panther Drive-In, I had to throw my diet out the window, so I had a double cheeseburger with a side of red beans and rice. I had just finished and was contemplating which of my old friends might be able to give me a place to take a nap, when I got a text from Matt Haynes that snapped me wide awake.

"I think I know where Colgan is."

I sent him back a text that just said "Really? Where?" But he was teaching summer school and I had to wait fifteen agonizing minutes before he could respond.

The text was hurriedly written – "migrant camp… Mexicans, down off 12 toward grove hill."

What the heck? Why would Matt think Colgan was hanging out with a bunch of Mexican agricultural workers? But it wasn't any more absurd than any of the rest of this. Sure, Colgan wasn't supposed to be there, but he wasn't supposed to be anywhere. He died seventeen years ago. My head was spinning.

I thought, hell, I drove more than two hours from Tuscaloosa. Why wouldn't I drive ten more minutes to whatever I was going to find at this labor camp? Well one reason was that I didn't speak a word of Spanish. But when that popped into my head, I suddenly remembered that Colgan had been killed in Central America, where, duh P.J., they speak Spanish. I felt like I was turning into a real idiot hanging around with all the college kids in Tuscaloosa. Anyway, I knew I had to find this place and figure out some way to communicate with the people there.

Grove Hill was ten or twelve miles east of Kellyville, where 43 met 84. County Road 12 was the back way to get there, but I had no idea where this migrant worker encampment might be. I texted Matt saying I was going out there, but I didn't hear back from him. I'm guessing summer school class ended, and he was leading an off-season football workout.

The first time I thought I had found the place, I was driving along County Road 12 and saw five or six old trucks parked in the back of a field. I didn't see any signs of a shelter, but I figured maybe they struck their tents when they went to work every day. (I was completely naïve about how migrant agricultural labor works.) But when I got to the back of the field, I could see that there was a path leading down to Sutton's Creek, right above where it went into the Tombigbee. I could hear a couple folks talking down there (in English) and finally figured out these trucks just belonged to some guys that had gotten together to go fishing.

The place I was looking for, though, was only about a mile up the road. Turns out the migrant workers didn't live in tents at all. Several of the local farmers had pooled their resources and built a long bunkhouse with a low-slung metal roof and a kitchen and bathroom at one end. There weren't any old trucks sitting around either. The farm workers weren't going to drive here from Mexico, of course. Instead, it turned out there were two buses that took them back and forth to the place they worked. Neither of the buses was present when I arrived.

I pulled into the gravel lot next to the bunkhouse and looked around. This was a fairly sophisticated setup, not a bunch of hobos camping out and looking for work. Whoever hired these folks put some effort into providing for them. That meant that if they had hired Colgan, he was probably still here.

But none of this made any sense. If Colgan was still alive, he could have walked up to just about anybody in Kellyville and introduced himself. If they didn't recognize him, they would at least have heard his name. Maybe he just didn't have any money to get here, and he had to fall in with the farm workers for a ride. Hell, maybe it was the only way he could get back across the border, since the U.S. government presumed he was dead.

As I parked in the bunkhouse lot and got out of my car, I was preoccupied with the idea of how we would convince the government that Colgan was actually alive. I never thought about whether Colgan wanted them to know he was alive. I certainly didn't think about the fact that he might not want me or anyone else from his past life to know he was alive. In my mind, and in the mind of basically everyone in Kellyville but the youngest kids, Colgan Toomey was a town hero. We'd have thrown him a damn parade if we found out he was alive. Who wouldn't want that?

I opened the door to the bunkhouse and entered a rectangular room with about ten bunk beds arranged around the walls. The room next to it was identical, but as I entered it, I heard someone call out in Alabama-accented English "who dere?" The voice was vaguely familiar.

"I mean no harm ma'am. I'm looking for one of the workers."

My voice was evidently more recognizable to her. "By the Lord, is that P.J.? What chu doin' here, child?"

A white-haired African-American woman in her late 60's emerged from the kitchen with an apron on and dishwashing soap covering both arms up to the elbows. I recognized her as one of the ladies that had worked in the lunchroom at Kellyville High when I was there. I racked my brains for her name – Mrs. Baxter maybe? Yeah that was it, Ophelia Baxter.

"Mrs. Baxter, what a pleasant surprise!" The surprise in my voice was genuine.

"You can call me Miss O like you used to, child. You a Kellyville boy, so you're family. We don't need that formal talk. Besides, I ain't been a Baxter for a long time, no-how."

"It really is good to see you Miss O! How have you been doing?"

"Oh I get on okay, I guess. Same as I always have. This my 40th year at the High School an' they let me leave once lunch is over and come on out here to clean up. I'm proud of my years there you know. Every kid that ever come through Kellyville knows Miss O gonna make sure they got something good to eat."

"That's definitely something to be proud of, even if we didn't always appreciate you like we should."

She nodded and then took the conversation out of the realm of pleasantries. "I reckon you're here about Colgan." She sighed somewhat dramatically at the end of her sentence, so I figured whatever I was about to hear wouldn't be good.

"Well, I'll be honest Miss O, I don't know what to think right now, but someone said they thought he was here."

"Oh, he was here alright. Wouldn't listen to anything I told him that people would be glad he come back. Lord, he hardly let on he knew who I was."

"Tanya Haynes said she saw him at the cemetery at his parents' graves."

"I don't know what's wrong with that child, but that seems to be the only thing he came here for. To visit that cemetery."

"Isn't he working in the fields with the other migrants?" This seemed like a stupid question – why else would he have been here? But the whole situation was completely surreal.

Miss O shook her head. "I think he went out with them bout two days. They come here in groups. The folks out there now only got here Sunday. Colgan was with them when they arrived; I saw him that night. He pretended like he didn't know Miss O. But at breakfast the next morning I pulled him aside and gave him a good talking to. Then he went out to the fields. I imagine it must be hard for a man so tall to stoop over and pick beans and cotton."

She shook her head again, apparently engrossed in imagining Colgan's difficulties. I was about to ask her where Colgan was now, since he had been out in the fields with the workers just two days ago, but she took a sharp breath and went on.

"Tuesday evening when they got back, Colgan ate his supper but then he pulled me aside and said he was walking into town to visit his mama's grave. I didn't have the heart to tell him there would be two graves, but I guess he found out soon enough. Anyhow, turns out he took everything he had with him in that little backpack and ain't nobody seen him since."

I didn't correct her by saying Tanya and her daughter had seen him since then.

CHAPTER 25

THE STAR

My name's Cody Kelly. You may have heard of me. You might even like my music. Unfortunately, I'm a complete fraud. Like a Milli Vanilli level fraud. Although I promise I didn't lip sync, and I sure as hell couldn't dance like them. And they did win a Grammy, and I was only nominated for one -- but in my opinion I didn't earn the two Americana awards I won.

What's sad is that, before I met Colgan Toomey, I actually thought of myself as a pretty darn good songwriter. Maybe I still am, but I don't compare to Colgan, and people expect stuff from me that matches what he wrote for me on my breakout album. He still emails me songs every now and then, and some of them are damn good, but honestly, I've got all the money and fame I ever wanted now, and it just makes me feel that much worse for not being able to do it myself. I'm sure as hell not going to use one of his songs again.

I guess I should say it's not really Colgan's fault. I was just young and dumb and willing to do anything to make it in the music business. Colgan, on the other hand, despite having bucketfuls of talent that put mine to shame, had no desire to capitalize on that talent. He always seemed kinda restless and jumpy, but from the standpoint of trying to have a musical career, he seemed perfectly content to make the little circuit from Beaumont to Lake Charles and Lafayette.

Colgan and his band, a weirdly philosophical sort of hard-driving rockabilly alt-country outfit called Slutty Fortuna, developed a cult following at McNeese State in the late 90's. Their name came from some book of philosophy that introduced the Wheel of Fortune, calling it "Slutty Fortuna's Wheel." Colgan carried that book around with him. It was written by some ancient Roman dude. Anyway, I say SF was Colgan's band, and he was by far the best musician. Hell, he's probably still one of the top five guitar players I've ever met, and I've met virtually everyone by now. But actually, the lead singer of the band was a kid from the bayou country south of Lafayette named Jordan Delahoussaye (I'm assuming if he ever had a solo career, the record label would make him change that mouthful.)

Colgan always told people he couldn't sing, but it really wasn't true. He wasn't about to go Pavarotti and sing opera, and hell even the national anthem might be a stretch (to tell you the truth, it's a stretch for almost everyone), but his voice was more than capable of carrying the kind of singer-songwriter stuff he wrote for me. He just didn't want the spotlight.

I've honestly never understood why someone who not only excelled at performing but clearly enjoyed it was so adamant about not trying to really succeed in the business. I think Colgan could have been a star, if he had ever wanted to be. Anyone who knows him knows there are clearly things in his past that trouble him, but I never made much of an attempt to figure out what they were. I mean, he was almost 40 and kicking around in college bands when it was clear he was talented enough that he didn't have to be. There had to be something in his past. Also, to be honest, I was always kind of intimidated by Colgan. I think that's part of why I went along with his scheme to get me a record deal.

It all started on a Sunday afternoon in Lake Charles. There was a battle of the bands that night on campus at McNeese. Slutty Fortuna had won the year before and Jordan D. was MC'ing the thing. A folk-country singer with no accompaniment but an acoustic guitar will never win one of these things, but some percentage of the crowd will like you and since they have to actually remember your name to vote, you get fans who will actually look for you later on, not just people who think you're cool for half a second and never remember who you are.

Anyway, like I said they had this thing every year, and I had done it in the past, but skipped the previous year because I had a prior commitment or something. Since I wasn't there the previous year, I hadn't heard Slutty Fortuna play, but everyone in the music scene on our little sliver of the gulf coast had heard something about them in the past year.

So, I was at least a little excited to meet these guys that were causing such a stir. Jordan Delahoussaye was twenty-two, with blond spiky hair and blue eyes, and immediately recognizable as gay. If you have a picture in your head of a gay front-man of a college band, Jordan matches up with it nicely. He was wearing skinny jeans, fancy boots, and a t-shirt from last year's battle of the bands that had been ripped down one side.

On first blush, Colgan couldn't have looked more different. He was at least 8-10 inches taller for one thing, maybe a foot taller. He wore beat up old jeans, a blue denim button-up shirt, and what looked like an Australian bush hat. Coming out of the back of the hat was a red braid that went down to the top of his ass.

It tells you something about the force of personality of these two guys, that I literally don't remember the name of the bass player. I did get to know the drummer, Marc St. Vincent, later on, but I couldn't have told you his name that day.

So anyway, I gave them my name and checked in to the contest. Jordan asked me how many people were in my band. "It's just me and ol' Bessie here," I replied, patting my guitar case.

"Sometimes that's the best way to do it," Colgan said. I felt like there was a touch of sarcasm toward Jordan, but they both laughed. The dynamic between them was pretty interesting. I got the feeling that Jordan was very attracted to Colgan, but the big man didn't swing that way. Anyway, they put me on the schedule and I saw that I was slotted to play next to last, which is actually a really good position to be in.

I had about four hours before I played, so I figured I'd just hang out and see what the competition looked like. This naturally led to long discussions about music with Jordan and Colgan. As the early bands started playing, we even critiqued them some. The best, according to both me and Colgan, was a jazzy alternative five-piece band from New Orleans called Category 5. They probably weren't quite mainstream enough to win the thing though. I remember reading a few years later that they had become something of local celebs in New Orleans by the time Katrina hit, and felt like they had to change their name. The New Yorker or The Atlantic or someone like that did a nice fluff piece on them.

Over the course of the afternoon, we talked about all sorts of musical stuff. I didn't see Colgan or Jordan after I played my set, but I finished fourth out of twelve, which was the best I had ever done. I figured I'd probably run into those guys on the circuit, but I was excited enough about where I had finished that I didn't give the earlier part of the evening much thought.

This was before most people had cell phones. I think I remember Jordan having one, but Colgan definitely didn't, and neither did I. But we had exchanged e-mail addresses before I played that night. Of course, I didn't check my email but about once a week when I stopped off at my brother's apartment in Beaumont. Anyway, it was probably three weeks after I'd met Colgan that he sent me an email that just said he'd like me to see a couple songs he'd written.

I wrote back to say of course I'd take a look and told him the next few places I was playing. Two nights later, we were both going to be in Port Arthur in little venues down on the waterfront. We decided to meet for lunch at one-thirty in the afternoon at the fish market. When I walked in, Colgan sat a table with two notebooks and his guitar leaning against a table.

When I sat down, he told me that he could make me a star. I just chuckled at him, but he looked up, and said, "I'm serious dude. I've got you an in."

"Wait? What? You've got an in somewhere and you want to give it to some guy you met a month ago?"

"Look, I've been trying to find someone like you for a couple years now. I'm too damn old and can't sing worth a lick. But I promise you, I know people that will give you a recording shot if you come with my recommendation and the right material."

"Well, okay. I'm not trying to look a gift horse in the mouth, man."

"Good." He flipped open the notebook somewhere in the middle and said, "This is the song that's gonna make you rich."

I chuckled again, but then I started reading it. It was full sheet music, but the words are what blew me away…

An Angel's Blood

Daddy was a bricklayer from Boston,
never learned to read nor write too well,
never knew what Mama's love would cost him,
he'd have followed her to hell.
They moved down south in fifty-four
with a head full of plans and dreams,
never knew what they were headed toward;
they thought love was all they'd need.

CHORUS:
It was a sad day in the Southland,
when kindness got him killed.
Hate was on the menu,
and they had to have their fill.
They said the law was served;
they said it was God's will,
but the rain was heaven weepin'
'cause an Angel's blood was spilled.

Mama was a teacher in Macon;
Daddy started a garage.
It was a hard road they were takin',
both willin' to work hard.
For seven years they saved up,
on a little country house.
It was a place where you could see for miles,
nights as quiet as a mouse.
And the neighbors called him Yankee,
but it seemed to be in fun.
Any harm that came from jokin'
could surely be undone.

CHORUS

Joseph Jones was a hired hand,
who worked hard all his life,
never took a sideways look
at Sheriff Dalton's wife.
But she said that he forced her,
on a sultry August night,
and the law was on her side,
'cause Joe was black,
and she was white.

The law found Ol' Joe hidin'
in my Daddy's new tool shed.
By the time Dad crossed the backyard,
Joseph Jones was dead.
They all saw Daddy cryin';

they said we knew you just weren't right.
You know what that nigger done,
and you hid him here all night.

CHORUS

It rained the first day of September;
they hanged my dad at dawn's first light.
It was a time I can't remember,
for I was born that night.
I could have lived so long in hatred,
at the way my Daddy died,
but all my life I've felt the love
of an angel by my side.

CHORUS.

"Damn, that's pretty good." I looked up at Colgan. "Who wrote this?"

"You did, officially."

"I wish, man. Come on, did you write this?"

"Yeah, I wrote it, but it's yours."

"Okaaayy... I mean I get you say you can't sing or whatever, but why don't you want the writing credit?"

"I'm just not interested in the spotlight. Don't look a gift horse in the mouth, eh?"

I had to laugh at that. He showed me a couple more songs, handed me the notebook, and told me to take a couple weeks and learn to play the ones I liked the best. Then send him an email and he'd set up a meeting in Austin. I've often wondered if he actually had any kind of contact in Austin or if he just sent them the songs as me and told them I was coming. He expressly said not to mention his name and that I would be listed as the writer for every song.

The meeting in Austin happened on June 3, 1999. I was nervous as hell, and probably sounded like shit on the first song I did. I don't even remember which song it was, just that it wasn't Angel's Blood. When I finished it, they still seemed vaguely interested, and one of them looked up and said in a deep Texas drawl, "I want to hear that one about the Yankee that gets lynched." The way he said it made me wonder if he actually got the point of the song, but it also took the nerves off a little bit and I belted it out. When I saw a tear in his eye at the end, I knew I was in. They all clearly thought I wrote it, so I played along.

They had me in studio by the middle of August and we were done in a month. The studio decided that it would be best to hold Angel's Blood for the second song, so we started with one that I've often wondered might be a bit autobiographical about Colgan. It's called "A Song About You."

A Song About You (That Just Leaves Me to Blame)

Two-point-five kids and a white picket fence.
That's the life you chose when you had your pick of men.
Can't say that I blame you, most people wouldn't.
You prob'ly made the right choice, leaving me behind.
Still I wonder are you the same girl,
as you were when you were mine?

And does a drifter in a black hat ever cross your mind?
You ever see my face in your glass of wine?
Or at the bottom of the bottle, at the end of a long hard day
of living with the choice you made.
Does the freedom of the road ever call your name?
If you could do it again, I bet you'd do it the same.
That just leaves me to blame.

Well I was nineteen, a rebel kid,
just tryin' to get comfortable, in my skin.
You were the belle of the ball and the homecoming queen,
but you saw right through that whole fake scene.
Then I found myself with the girl you weren't supposed to be,
so I asked you to run away with me.
We headed out for California and your Mama cried.
One whole year, we lived young and wild.

Now does a drifter in a black hat ever cross your mind?
You ever see my face in your glass of wine?
Or at the bottom of the bottle, at the end of a long hard day
of living with the choice you made.
Does the freedom of the road ever call your name?
If you could do it again, I bet you'd do it the same.
That just leaves me to blame.

Now I've had a few women, in my life,
even talked one into being my wife.
But she couldn't handle this ol' drifter too long,
So I went back to singin' a nomad's song.
I write the words about livin' free,
but it's a song about you, and it always will be.

Yeah, I could write all my life about livin' free,
but it's a song about you, and it always will be.

Was there some woman in Colgan's past that he felt this way about? Had she made him essentially give up on the usual progress of life? He seemed to have abandoned the whole process and now seemed to have no desire for success or a family. Why had he abandoned it? What did he trade it for? Art? I mean yeah he wrote good songs, and he played some kickass guitar solos for Slutty Fortuna, but he didn't seem like the "art is my mission" type. I just really didn't understand him, and I still don't, but I think it had to be something more than a bad experience with a woman that made him the way he was.

The reception to both "A Song About You" and "An Angel's Blood" was huge. I was suddenly caught up in a whirlwind. I know I said at the beginning of this that I hated feeling like a fraud by claiming to have written Colgan's songs. And I really do. But man, it's been a hell of a ride. I can't blame Colgan for the fact that I enjoyed the heck out of that ride for the first few years. The rush that you get when a big crowd actually knows what you're singing and really digs it just can't match up with anything else I've ever experienced. I just can't imagine why Colgan didn't want that, and sometimes I do feel bad about taking his deserved share of it.

My favorite song on that album was one that the studio never released. It's called "Thunderlust," and it's one that he honestly should have kept for Slutty Fortuna – it would have sounded better with a huge electric guitar solo in the middle.

Thunderlust

Most men hide with families underground.
Even big mean dogs don't stick around.
The children scream and the women cry.
But one man looks that twister in the eye.
Ol' Ricky Stiles don't look that tough,

but he's standing there in the swirlin' dust.
His heart beats fast when the wind picks up
'cause he was born with Thunderlust.

Thunderlust, it's in his blood.
He'll chase that storm, through the rain and mud
His heart beats fast when the wind picks up
'cause he was born with Thunderlust.

Now all the folks round Mason City say he's crazy,
but they stay glued to their TVs,
to watch that local boy made good,
and just to see where he might be.

'Cause he's seen typhoons down in China,
Monsoons in Bombay,
hurricanes in the Carolinas,
a Cheyenne blizzard on New Year's Day,
but it's in them Iowa fields where he was raised,
someday he'll meet that twister,
that takes him to his grave.

Thunderlust, it's in his blood,
He'll chase that storm, through the rain and mud.
His heart beats fast when the wind picks up,
'cause he was born with Thunderlust.

Yeah he's seen typhoons down in China,
Monsoons in Bombay,
Hurricanes in the Carolinas,
a Cheyenne blizzard on New Year's Day.
But it's in them Iowa fields where he was raised,
someday he'll meet that twister
that takes him to his grave.

It doesn't say a whole lot, but it's just a fun song to sing, I don't really know why. The one contribution I made to any song from that album is that when I play this live, after the first chorus I replace "his heart beats fast" with "he gets so hard" or sometimes even "his dick gets hard." I figure it goes with the "lust" aspect. Even if I'd thought of it in time, the studio would probably never have let me record it that way, but the crowds love it.

CHAPTER 26

THE BEST FRIEND, ONCE MORE

Once I learned that Colgan had left town, I drove around in the vicinity of Kellyville for a good two hours before I headed back to Tuscaloosa. I had no idea what I thought I would find – a tall, red-headed, dead guy walking down the road I suppose. The idea that Colgan could possibly be alive still made no sense whatsoever.

It had started to sink in as I got closer to Tuscaloosa that night. I was about twenty minutes out when my girlfriend Kim called. (I say girlfriend; at the time we had been on two dates, not counting the one in high school). She said she had driven by P.J.'s and it wasn't open, so she was worried about me. Part of me felt like it was a really bad idea to burden a new relationship with all of this, but I really needed someone to talk to about Colgan.

"Something's come up, hon. I need to talk to you in person. You wanna grab some dinner?"

"What's this about? Is something wrong?"

"Honestly I don't know if it's wrong, it could be really good, I guess."

"You're not making any sense, P.J. What's it about?"

"I don't think I can explain it on the phone. Can you meet me at 15th Street Diner in half an hour?"

"Uh sure, I guess."

"Okay, I promise I'll do my best to explain then."

"Well, okay."

I'm pretty sure Kim hung up the phone thinking I was breaking up with her. It's probably what I would have thought if she had said the exact same things to me. Truth be told, I was thinking she might want to break up with me after I started saying I believed my best friend from high school had come back to life.

Kim beat me to the restaurant and was standing out front smoking a cigarette when I arrived. I knew she was trying to quit and instantly felt terrible about stressing her out this way. I parked and practically ran around the building to see her. I'm not sure I knew it as it was happening, but that night is definitely when I realized the depth of my feelings for her.

I got around to the front of the restaurant and she had just put out her cigarette. I opened my arms to give her a big hug and she looked at me for a second and then buried her face in my shoulder, saying, "Are you okay, P.J."

"I t-think so," I stammered. "Let's get some food."

"Okay."

I wanted to reassure her but I was too shaken right then to do it verbally so I reached for her hand as we walked in. She seemed a little surprised but took it and let me hold on until we got seated at a table.

After the waiter took our drink orders, it just came out. I was looking down at my menu and just blurted "I think Colgan may be alive."

Kim knew Colgan a little bit from when we were in high school and remembered when he died. She dropped her menu on the table. "What? How is that even possible."

"Well, when he, umm died, in 1983, we didn't actually have a body. All we really had was a note from the Salvadoran rebels that their ransom had not been met – if I recall correctly they wanted an end to U.S. military aid to El Salvador and a bunch of money – and that, therefore, Colgan and the other hostage had been killed. The CIA met with Michael Toomey and told him the note was real and came from the Salvadoran rebels. It was good enough for Michael and that was good enough for me. I don't know what to think anymore."

"So, tell me why you think he might be alive."

The waiter interrupted us just then and Kim's final sentence hung in the air for a little while, even after we ordered, as we went to the salad bar and made our plates. As I ate my salad, I looked up a couple of times and almost said something. I really appreciated that Kim just sat there and ate and didn't try to coax anything out of me.

Finally, right after we got our entrees, I said, “There are people in Kellyville who say they’ve seen Colgan. I didn’t want to believe them, but they’re sure, and their story makes sense.” I was trying to talk slow and calm and detach my brain to examine the problem clinically. I probably sounded like some ridiculous TV detective.

Kim took a bite of her chicken pot pie and nodded slowly as if to say, “okay, what’s their story.”

“I went to Kellyville today. Wait, back up. Last night I got a call from a lady I went to high school with. She said that she had been walking her dog with her daughter and they had seen a tall red-headed guy in the cemetery by Colgan’s parents’ graves. Actually, she said she had seen Colgan, but I told her that was impossible. She was certain though, especially when she figured out whose graves he had been kneeling at. He waved at them and just walked off the other way into the woods.”

“Wow, spooky…” Kim almost giggled but suppressed it. “Sorry I just don’t know what else to say.”

“I understand darlin’” (that last word just kinda slipped out, we weren’t really at the pet name stage yet), “I had no clue what to tell Tanya. I kept saying it couldn’t have been Colgan and she kept saying it had to be.”

“Did she know him from high school?”

“Yeah, but that was 20 years ago. What creeped me out wasn’t that she said this guy looked like Colgan, it was that he was beside Colgan’s parents’ graves. Everyone in town knows where Colgan’s monument is in the cemetery. Oh my gosh, I wonder what he thought when he saw that – the monument his Dad built for him after he disappeared.”

“So, you do think he’s alive?”

“I’m not sure, but I’m starting to think it’s possible. I went to Kellyville today. I had no idea where or how to look for him, but Matt Haynes, Tanya’s husband, texted me that he might be at this migrant farm-worker camp outside of town.”

“Oh wow, was he there?”

“No, but the lady that was cooking and cleaning at this place – it really wasn’t a camp, the farmers built a bunkhouse for the migrants – used to be our lunch lady at school.”

Kim laughed there, and I had to insert, “Yeah, Kellyville is a really small town.”

“I understand, I don’t mean to poke fun.”

“Anyway, Miss O, the lunch lady, had recognized Colgan when he showed up two days before. But he worked one day in the fields and then went to see his mom's grave – he didn't know his dad was dead, I don't think – and never came back."

"Damn," Kim said. "Okay, so, assuming all these people are right, he's just out there somewhere wandering around." I had a mouthful of food and nodded and looked up at her. She was playing with her hair in a way I had come to recognize (from trivia nights) as indicative of deep thought. "Or maybe he has an obligation somewhere else and he just had enough time to go see his mom's grave. Or he was planning to stay but learning his Dad had died really tore him up."

"Yeah I thought about that. If he somehow survived but was just now able to get back to the United States, he might start by going to Kellyville and see his mom's grave and plan to go to Tennessee to see his Dad. It probably would tear him up that Michael's dead, because they weren't on great terms when Colgan . . ." I stopped, intending to say "died" here, but realizing that obviously didn't fit, "um, disappeared," I finally finished.

"Let's think about this, P.J. You have two pretty compelling eyewitness accounts saying Colgan is alive. What's the evidence that he was dead? The fact that a note from a bunch of communist rebels said so?"

I was already leaning the same direction, but I couldn't let go completely of what I had believed for almost twenty years. Colgan had been dead for nearly as long as he had been in my life. "Well the CIA said it was credible."

"And did they give you any evidence?"

"I never thought about it like that. They only talked to Michael. I don't know what they told him"

We both focused on our food for a minute, having each come to the conclusion that the rumors of Colgan's demise had been greatly exaggerated. For some reason, probably a selfish one, the question of whether Colgan could actually be alive took a back seat in my mind to the question of why he apparently didn't want to talk to me (or anyone, I suppose, but mostly me—I was his best friend by damn, or at least I had been twenty years ago.)

"But Kim, why now, why like this? Everyone in Kellyville loved Colgan. As soon as he came back, he'd be a freaking town hero again."

"Maybe he's in some kind of trouble and can't risk that kind of public exposure?"

"If he's in trouble, why didn't he come to me?"

Looking back, I still feel like I was being selfish, but Kim could tell that I was hurting. She reached out and took my hand. "Maybe he thought it would harm you to be involved. Maybe he thought you had forgotten about him. I don't know, hon, but I doubt he was trying to do wrong by you."

Her empathy snapped me out of my selfishness. "I know Kim. I just… I mean what do I do now? Colgan is probably out there somewhere, and I don't even know if he wants to be found."

Kim touched my arm again. "I'm pretty sure right now we know he doesn't." I had to admit she was right, but she started playing with her hair again. "But we don't know why," she said slowly.

"True, but I think the only way we are going to figure that out is if we find Colgan, who doesn't want to be found."

She began to push back from the table. "You almost done? I need a cigarette. I'll be back in a minute."

I just nodded, but I think she could see the disappointment on my face, so I quickly smiled and said, "See you soon." She smiled back and headed for the door.

I finished my food and decided to get a box for hers. I had filled her box and the waiter had just come back with the check when she came back in. I paid for the food and put my arm around Kim as we walked out. When we got to her car, I gave her a big hug and thanked her for talking to me about Colgan.

"P.J., I can't imagine what you're going through, but I'm here for you. Get in the car. I can tell you aren't anywhere near done talking this through."

I started to protest, but she cut me off. "Get in." I nodded and worked my way around her car. "Thank you," I said simply when I got in.

She just nodded, rolled down her window and lit another cigarette. What the hell, I thought, asking her if I could bum one. She laughed and obliged, asking me if I'd ever even smoked one before. "I grew up the same time as you did, hon, of course I have. But it's been awhile." Of course, I coughed like crazy even though I barely inhaled.

Before that night I had never even been to Kim's house. She had come up to P.J.'s for our first date and we had walked to a nearby restaurant; the second one I picked her up from her office at the University; and, if that night can be called a date, we had met at the diner. I didn't even know what part of town she lived in.

Kim turned onto 359 and headed north, over the river. She turned left at the top of the hill and guided her Altima to a stop in the driveway of a cute little ranch house on 20th street in Northport. I looked down the street and laughed. "I think I lived in those duplexes down there in undergrad." I said, pointing.

She laughed. "Undergrads always live in those. The cops are over there once a week."

"That's all? The undergrads in Tuscaloosa have gone soft."

Kim opened the door and led me into the living room, gesturing at a nice gray sofa in front of the TV and giving me my marching orders for the evening: "Find us a good old movie while I go pop some popcorn. Any time you want to talk about Colgan, we'll just pause the movie and talk."

"Ok, sounds good to me." I watched her walk into the kitchen somewhat in awe of how she had taken it upon herself to take care of me.

I wasn't sure what Kim meant by "old movie," but I figured I'd go all out and flipped it over to Turner Classic Movies, on which *The Great Ziegfeld* was about to start. Kim came back with the popcorn and snuggled beside me on the couch. I put my arm around her and said the only thing I could think of: "Thank you."

She smiled and nuzzled her face into my neck. It had been a long time since a woman had done that. Kim was the first one I had gotten close to since my divorce five years earlier. I wasn't sure exactly where this was going, but it definitely felt right.

Still, the evening would be dominated by discussions about Colgan. We didn't watch more than about the first half hour of *Ziegfeld*. I mentioned something about Colgan and she paused the movie. We went out on the back deck so she could smoke, and we ended up staying out there talking until about midnight. I remember it was a beautiful night, maybe 65 or 70 degrees and clear enough to see some stars, even in town.

Our discussion eventually centered on the potential legal problems Colgan might have faced trying to get back over the border or trying to get back some semblance of a normal life here. The government had definitely issued a death certificate; I'd seen it when we were preparing for the funeral. I imagine it's pretty hard to get that reversed.

Kim suddenly burst out laughing while we were talking about the Social Security Administration. She had remembered the scene from *With Honors* where the lady at the government office asks Joe Pesci for "proof of birth." Pesci responds "I'm sittin' here ain't I lady? What do you think, I happened by spontaneous combustion?" We imagined Colgan being told that he was dead and saying "I'm sittin' here ain't I." After all this time, though, it had to be assumed that Colgan didn't have any documents to prove that he was alive, or that he was American for that matter.

In the end, despite all the talk, there really was very little we could do to find Colgan if he didn't want to be found. One idea that Kim had was to figure out his status in the Social Security death records. If he had been able to change it, he might not be so hard to track down. Kim said her friend Clyde (real name Clytemnestra Howard – this might be my favorite combination of name and nickname ever), who worked at the law school, would have access to the database.

I remember that we talked very little about ourselves that night. Even though we both remember it as the night we really fell in love. And there wasn't really anything physical about it either, or at least not sexual. When we decided to go to bed, Kim got me some blankets and I laid down on the couch. About twenty minutes later, she came out of the bedroom in a nightgown and said, "I can't make you sleep out here. Come to the bed."

I took her hand and she led me in. I won't say I didn't think about fooling around with her, and I'd almost bet she thought about it too, but it just didn't feel right. We cuddled for a minute, but both fell asleep virtually immediately. I'm happy to report that we've had plenty of opportunities since then that have worked out to our great mutual satisfaction. Oh, and I also will happily report that Kim was able to successfully quit smoking about a month later.

CHAPTER 27

THE COLONEL, AGAIN

I first heard the name Colgan Toomey in 1983. His was one of the stories we used to justify that devil's pit of a school. A nice, all-American kid: smart, handsome, talented, he was the star quarterback on his high school football team. He went to Guatemala to help people, to bring them medicine and healing. And then he got kidnapped and killed by a bunch of God-damned Commie terrorists. I told that story to hundreds of recruits. I should have known it was bullshit.

I never would have known the truth if Colgan Toomey hadn't randomly showed up at my house one day. I never did learn how he figured out where I lived. I remember his visit as vividly as any day of my life, but I couldn't tell you exactly when it was. To be fair though, I was pushing 80 and some days were better than others on the mental front. But that day, that day I remember.

It was about 7:30 in the morning when someone knocked on my door. I lived at the end of a gravel road (more red clay than gravel, to be honest) about twenty minutes south of Fort Benning, Georgia. It was more than a mile to the next house up the road. Needless to say, I didn't have visitors all that often.

It's hard to shake fifty years of habit out of a man, so I still woke up by about 0530 every day. I was sitting in my recliner reading a book when the knock came. It wasn't a particularly memorable book, one of those knockoffs that Tom Clancy had other people write toward the end of his career. I don't think I ever picked it back up after I met Colgan.

The man standing at my door was tall, at least a full head taller than me in my old age. I was about six-two in my prime. Now I tell people I may be under six feet, but I'm not yet six feet under. Anyhow this guy who knocked on my door that morning was definitely over six feet. Way over.

I looked past him into the yard, then turned and looked down the road. Not a car to be seen. I didn't think I'd heard one.

The man followed my gaze and then said stuck out his hand and said, "Good morning, Colonel Lawson, I'm Colgan Toomey."

As you might expect in a career Army man with special forces training, I'm usually pretty damn good at hiding my emotions. Not this day. I said something like "What the hell?" I looked up and down the road again. "Where the hell did you come from?"

"Santa Maria prison, San Salvador, El Salvador," he said calmly.

"But…but…I thought you were dead. You got kidnapped by the FMLN."

He looked at me and chuckled menacingly, "Did you really believe that? Or did you just use it as part of your propaganda?" He leaned over me and stared into my eyes. I've stared down the barrel of more weapons than I care to remember, but I have to admit I was scared at that moment.

I stammered some kind of answer about the FMLN kidnapping and killing him, but he wasn't having it. He just shook his head as if to say that it should be painfully obvious that he had not actually been killed. Then he smiled and said, "Are you going to invite me in, Colonel Lawson?"

I opened the door and tried to make a grand gesture with my hand. "By all means, Mr. Toomey." I was shaken, but I had enough pride left not to show it too badly. That changed by the end of his visit.

I walked Toomey down the hall and asked him to sit down on the couch. "Would you like some tea? You've apparently walked a long way from El Salvador." He politely declined and used my question to launch into the reason he had come.

"I was in El Salvador for ten years. 1983 to 1993. Contrary to what you may have heard, I went there willingly. I went there to fight for a people being brutally oppressed, to fight a government that massacred civilians and tortured political opponents, a government that murdered an archbishop in the middle of giving mass. A government built, armed, and supported by these United States of America, and full of cold-blooded killers and sadists trained by the American military. Trained right here in Georgia. Trained by you, Colonel Lawson. I felt like fighting against these thugs was the least that I could do."

He paused for a moment and I tried to think of something to say. I could not. He went on after a long pause, "I do not know if you realize that you have no defense or if you think I am beneath your expression of one. Frankly, I do not care. When I first decided to come here, I planned to kill you. If I thought your death served any purpose, I would not hesitate to do so now. But no purpose could be served by that. Instead I am going to show you the results of your handiwork."

At the time I had no idea what he meant, but I wasn't going to give him the satisfaction of showing it. Over the next two hours, Toomey described in meticulous detail the torture he had suffered at the hands of the Salvadoran government. I recognized more than half of the techniques they used as things we taught at the school of the Americas. Toomey was tortured using fire, electricity, needles, razor blades, sleep deprivation, constant light or darkness, and anything else his captors could think of. He showed me the god-damned scars.

After he showed me his scars, Toomey sat down and gave a deep sigh. "I believe, Colonel Lawson," he began, "that the least you can do is listen to me." There was a seething anger in his voice, but if it had been concentrated and directed solely at me, I had no doubt that I would have been dead already. I nodded my assent to this proposition and prepared for his diatribe.

There was certainly something in the nature of a rant in what he told me next. It was the whole story of how he ended up in El Salvador and his activities there. I have to admit, the man was a pretty impressive military operative for someone utterly lacking in formal training. Of course, I have no idea how much he embellished the facts or his role in them. With some justification, he kept coming back to the torture and deprivation he suffered at Santa Maria and the complicity of the United States in what was done not just to him, but to El Salvador and its people generally. He was not shy about mentioning my personal complicity, but neither did he dwell on it.

It was an interesting story, and there were aspects of it I found pretty incredible, but I must admit he was beginning to lose me after an hour or so. Then he leaned forward, sitting on the edge of my couch, and stared me in the eye. "But what's the point of all this, Colonel Lawson? Is there a purpose? Have I learned anything?" He seemed to want an answer to what clearly should have been a rhetorical question, so I confessed that I really had no idea.

He laughed at that and said, "the purpose has to be about learning. Someone has to get a lesson out of all this. I submit to you, Colonel Lawson, that the lesson is this: not only the Salvadoran Civil War, but the Cold War itself, like the vast majority of all wars ever fought on this planet, had two wrong sides. Capitalism, fascism, communism, socialism – none of it's remotely perfect and none of it's pure evil. Every system ever devised is based on the fatally flawed premise that human beings are capable of governing their affairs without committing unspeakable horrors against one another. No system of thought, no religion, no government can change that by itself. As long as we continue to believe that any system is better than the others, war and destruction will be our lot."

He spoke with the stillness and seriousness of a man giving a prophecy, even if what he said wasn't all that profound. Man's inhumanity to man has been a central theme of the story of this planet at least since Cain and Abel walked its face. Toomey seemed to recognize that his grand finale had fizzled a bit, and he leaned back against the couch.

"My point is, Colonel Lawson, if you have any influence left in your time, what we need to change is the way that history is taught. Wars don't have winners and losers, not most of the time. Not El Salvador." He shook his head. "Well, it's time for me to find out if Thomas Wolfe was right that you can't go home again." With that, he got up and headed toward the door. I followed him because I wanted to see where the hell he might be going. He hopped down off the porch and started loping diagonally across my yard. He crossed the road like it wasn't there and continued into the woods, heading basically southwestern. There wasn't anything that way for several miles. If he followed that path straight through those woods, he'd end up in the Chattahoochee.

I walked back in the house and got myself a beer. There wasn't shit I could do about any of this and I knew it. About the most I could do was get the guy running the place now to stop using the bullshit story of Colgan Toomey, all-American kid kidnapped by commie rebels. I doubted that's what he had in mind.

But I also knew that Toomey was right about El Salvador and right about the complicity of the U.S. Army, the School of the Americas, and Harlan J. Lawson in the atrocities committed there.

CHAPTER 28

THE SOCIOLOGIST

(Once Known as the Opponent)

If you had told me at any point between 1983 and 2000 that Colgan Toomey might still be alive, I'd have given it about the same chances as the idea that I'd ever go on a second date with P.J. Campbell, which, in my mind, were pretty darn close to zero. I wasn't at Colgan's funeral, and of course I didn't have any firsthand knowledge that he had died, but I had heard about his kidnapping and death. I was as sure of the story as everyone else, including the CIA.

At the time Colgan disappeared, I was completing a master's degree in Social Work at Ohio State and would have rated my chances of ever living in Alabama again close to zero as well. I would go on to get another master's, this one in Public Administration from Georgetown, and then a PhD in Sociology. That was the one that brought me back to the south. I never would have imagined it, but the best program in the country for what I was interested in, the intersection of how health care is administered with the disparity in delivery along race and class lines, was located at the University of Alabama at Birmingham.

After graduation from UAB, I taught at a couple of community colleges in Florida, before I came back to Alabama, first to the University of West Alabama in Livingston for two years. There I got a taste of what P.J. and Colgan must have experienced growing up. I'd never lived in a small town until that point. I grew up in Mobile, went to Tulane in New Orleans for undergrad, and then it was off to Columbus, Washington, D.C., and Birmingham. After my PhD, my first teaching jobs were in Tallahassee, which, at about a hundred thousand, was the smallest town I'd lived in up to that point.

Livingston, Alabama was a different world, even to someone who grew up just a couple hundred miles away in the same state. It had about three thousand people, making it more than twice the size of Kellyville, but less than one percent of the average metro areas I'd lived in. About half the people in town were connected to the University in some way.

Apparently, I should have known that the arrival of a young, unmarried professor would cause a stir on campus. However, because I'm fat, the rumors were never about sexual favors from students or affairs with colleagues. Instead they were about whether I was a lesbian and how many cats my strange spinster self might have.

I hated being the subject of those rumors, so I set out to change my status as quickly as possible. I know I talk about my ex-husband being a jerk, and in a lot of ways he was, but honestly, I put Chuck in a pretty ridiculous position. In the environment that I was in, and given my political bent and the subject of my research, it was perhaps inevitable that I would search out the person who would most piss off the townsfolk.

I met Charles Collins in a navy bar in Meridian, Mississippi. (Yes, Meridian has a naval base, despite being a couple hundred miles from the nearest coast.) He was fifteen years older than me, about to retire as a career naval officer, and black. He was also goofy as all get out, toned and muscular, and had a thing for fat white women. It was the first time in my life someone had hit on me from the moment I walked into a bar. I let him take me home that night, and it was the best sex of my life to that point. Four months later we were married.

I could have predicted what most of the people in Livingston would have thought, privately, about my marriage. But I had no idea the reactions would be so overt. About two weeks after the wedding, for example, we were walking around the little downtown area holding hands and two women coming the other way literally crossed the street rather than sharing the sidewalk with us.

Like I said, Chuck could be a complete jerk, but I'm sure the attitude of our neighbors also played a role. I think it bothered me more than it did him. Although he'd never been married before, he'd always been with white women, and I guess he was used to it.

As it turned out, it was always very clear to me that my husband was generally attracted to fat white women. It was much less clear that he was particularly attracted to me. I think this is true of most of the guys I've been with, to be honest. P.J. is the one exception. I have no idea if he has a "type" for big girls, but I know he thinks I'm beautiful. Take note, guys that claim to like big girls.

Over time, I came to understand that part of Chuck's preference for big girls was that they were easy to control and demean. He was never physically abusive toward me, though he threatened it once or twice, but he became more and more downright mean in what he said. One day he told me that race had nothing to do with why folks in Livingston looked at us funny; they were just trying to figure out why a stud like him would be with a fat whore like me.

That day should have been the end of it. I should have kicked him out of the house and moved on. But, contrary to his own statements and the evidence I should have been paying attention to, I believed that he loved me and that the stress in our relationship was being caused by external forces, namely the racist townspeople of Livingston, Alabama.

So, I stayed in the marriage, and when I got the chance, I took a job at the University of Alabama in Tuscaloosa. T-town was still the second smallest place I had ever lived, but it was at least slightly more progressive than Livingston. Turns out the extra population made it a good place for Chuck to find more fat girls than just me to satisfy his fetish. Eventually I wised up and kicked him to the curb.

Anyway, I know this is supposed to be about Colgan and how me and P.J. looked for him. I still remember that night he told me that Colgan might be alive. It was like a Tuesday or Wednesday and we had gone on our second date (well third, if you count the one in high school) the previous Saturday night. I was really starting to like the guy again, but part of me wondered if it wasn't just nostalgia based on the fact that I had had a crush on him most of my high school years.

That afternoon, when I left the University, I decided to drive by the bar and say hi to P.J. I had first met him again at a trivia night at P.J.'s, and I had showed up almost every Thursday night with my team, which usually consisted of me, Clyde, her girlfriend Danielle, and a law student she knew, for about six months before P.J. asked me out. By that point, I was considering asking him again, though I was hesitant because of what had happened in high school. That night would have been the first time I had been in P.J.'s since we had started dating again. I was kind of excited to surprise him.

It shouldn't have upset me so much that the bar was randomly closed at 4:30 on a weekday afternoon. P.J. basically ran the place by himself in slow times; he could have just been out running errands or something. For whatever reason, though, seeing the bar closed and dark filled me with a sense of dread, like something big had gone wrong.

That's when I called P.J. just to make sure he was ok. He seemed vague and distracted on the phone, didn't really tell me where he was, just that "something had come up." He wanted to meet at Fifteenth Street Diner. I almost didn't go, because I was sure he was planning to break up with me.

I never could have imagined that what he did instead would be what really brought us together. I don't know why P.J. confided in me when the questions around Colgan's death were first raised. I mean, I had met Colgan a couple times in high school, but I didn't really know him, and P.J. and I had only been going out a couple of weeks. P.J. seemed to have lots of friends in Tuscaloosa he could have talked to; I mean he owned a popular bar after all. I just know that it really made me feel good that I was the one he chose to talk to.

P.J. always makes it sound like I was completely calm and collected and knew exactly what to do when he said Colgan might be alive. Nothing could be further from the truth. To be honest, I was in complete shock. But when I stepped outside to smoke a cigarette, I called my friend Clyde, who works at the law school. I didn't tell her the whole story, but I asked how we might check whether someone was considered dead by the government or not. She told me she might be able to look in a database maintained by the social security administration.

So, when I went back in, I fibbed a little bit and said we could call Clyde—her real name is Clytemnestra, that always cracked P.J. up—and ask her to look in the social security database. That was really the one idea I had, and it didn't get us anywhere. But I loved that P.J. was willing to be vulnerable around me, and I responded by deciding I was going to take care of him any way he let me that night. The fact that both of us were too emotionally exhausted to do anything but cuddle once we finally went to bed just cemented the feeling that this was turning into something special.

We took it slow and let our love grow over several years. Clyde remarked that we'd had the longest engagement she'd ever seen, and she said that before we ever even decided to get married. During this entire time, "the Colgan problem" was always there with us. I know that it really did hurt P.J. that his best friend didn't seem to want to be found, so finding him mattered to me because it mattered so much to the man I loved. From an emotional perspective though, I was able to see the problem as simply an interesting mystery that I could approach analytically.

Like I said, though, it really never got us anywhere. Clyde quickly determined that the social security database still listed Colgan as dead. We also searched through court filings and criminal databases, but we came up empty. Then we searched to see if there were any odd hits on his dad's social or his mom's, but they also remained undisturbed in death.

How could a person live in twenty-first century America and not leave any trace or electronic footprint? It didn't seem possible. After a few months, I was super worried that there was no way Colgan was really alive. I finally broached the subject with P.J., but he didn't get upset at all. He said that if Colgan really had been in Kellyville last summer, as all the evidence seemed to indicate, then he had somehow lived for twenty years without triggering any kind of electronic footprint. Why, therefore, should we be worried that he couldn't survive the few months since then?

P.J. had a quiet confidence that his friend was alive and that, eventually, he would come back. As the months dragged into years, I seriously worried that if we ever did find Colgan, he would not be among the living. I could not express this fear to P.J., though. Too much of our lives revolved around getting to the bottom of this mystery and finding Colgan. A couple years after that first night in Tuscaloosa, we even drove to Austin to see if there was anyone who might know him.

P.J. remembered that Colgan's martial arts teacher, whom he knew only as Coach K, was related to the family that owned a restaurant called Casa Japonesa. It was one of these weird, iconic Austin joints that served crazy fusion cuisine in an edifice that might have been designed by Frank Lloyd Wright if he ever worked in metal buildings. And neon, lots of neon.

The food at Casa Japonesa was pretty great, but the news was not. Coach K, whose real name was Kuniko but whom everyone at Casa Japonesa referred to as Uncle Kenny, had passed away after being hit by a car about two months earlier. He was 68, and apparently in perfect health before the accident.

Having struck out at Casa Japonesa, we decided to see if anyone at the medical school remembered Colgan. Everyone had heard of him, of course. There was even a plaque dedicated to him and Antonio Rutledge, the other Texas student who was kidnapped in Guatemala in 1983 and killed by the Salvadoran rebels. We found no one, however, who had actually known Colgan. Nor was there anyone who felt like there might be anything wrong with the official story. None of the people we talked to had any inkling Colgan might be alive or any reason to doubt that he wasn't.

Despite the lack of information about Colgan, that trip to Texas was a lot of fun. After a couple days in Austin, we drove out into the hill country, visiting the LBJ ranch and staying in an adorable little bed and breakfast in Marble Falls.

After we returned to Alabama, our lives developed a happy little routine where P.J. often spent a couple of the slow weeknights when he closed the bar early at my house and I spent virtually every weekend crashing at his loft above the bar. It wasn't the most domestic lifestyle, but it worked for us. I honestly got to the point where I wasn't sure I wanted Colgan to come back and upset the apple cart.

CHAPTER 29

THE BEST FRIEND, TAKE FIVE

After all we went through, Colgan just walked into the bar one afternoon. It was about 3:30 on a Tuesday. The only customers were a couple of sorority girls who had just finished a test and were sharing a pitcher of margaritas. I knew it was Colgan immediately. Part of me wanted to punch him in the face.

Colgan walked in and looked around, like he was trying to decide whether it was worth his time to patronize the establishment. He was wearing jeans and a long cowboy shirt, and had a large backpack on, not a school backpack, but one you would actually take for a trip through the woods. There was a guitar strapped to it. At first, I decided to play it cool. I called out "welcome to P.J.'s," and went to see if the margarita sisters needed anything. I could hear Colgan laughing as I went to their table, so I knew he recognized me too.

I got back to the bar as Colgan was taking off his backpack and guitar. He leaned them against the bar, sat on a stool and said, "How 'bout a beer my friend."

"You'll have to be a little more specific, amigo."

"You got Abita Turbodog, Dawg?" he asked with a mock Cajun drawl that I'd never heard from him when we were kids.

"Sure, cher," I replied, mimicking him.

Colgan laughed and just sort of looked at me with a goofy grin on his face. I drew myself a beer after his and motioned him to a table in the corner.

He took the beer I offered and took a long swig before sitting down. "So this place all yours, huh? Not bad."

"It's pretty dead at the moment, but we do all right on the weekends."

Colgan nodded and took another swig of his beer. The small talk was killing me, so I went for the gut.

"Where the hell have you been, man? We thought you were dead for 20 years, and we've been questioning that for most of the last ten. Ever since Miss O saw you at that migrant camp."

"I didn't think you would find out about that," he said sheepishly. "I told her not to tell anyone."

I almost laughed at the idea of anyone expecting Miss O not to spread any bit of knowledge she had acquired, but I stifled it and just shook my head.

Colgan's face darkened. "You don't want to know where I've been. Assume I've spent the last twenty-six years in hell."

That answer knocked down the dam and the floodwaters of anger and frustration burst out. "Oh come on, Colgan, I'm not asking to interrogate you, to judge whether you're worthy to come back into my life or some shit. I don't even really care what the answers are. You're my best friend and I've loved you my whole life, no matter what you've done. What I've really been wondering is why the hell you can't figure that out, and you think you have to keep hiding. Hide from the world I don't care. Why the fuck do you feel like you have to hide from me? And are you really going to sit there and keep hiding."

For about thirty seconds, I thought he was gonna jump up and storm out of the bar. I'm sure the girls on the other side of the room with their margaritas were at least mildly uncomfortable. Instead he folded his hands in front of him and returned my head-shaking gesture.

"You really don't understand," he said at last.

Up to that point, I had literally never seen Colgan not know what to say or do. It softened my anger immediately. "Colgan, man, I'm not pretending I understand. I mean yeah, it doesn't make any sense that you wouldn't have told somebody in Kellyville who you were or that you wouldn't have come to find me before this. It's not like I'm hard to find – name's on the door ya know. And you were a freakin' town hero. Anybody in K'ville would have helped you. But none of that matters anymore. Just stick around a little while, okay."

He took a deep breath and nodded. "I spent several years in a Salvadoran prison being tortured. It kinda makes it hard to stay in one place … or trust anybody."

I tried to decide whether it was a good idea to get into details, but my curiosity got the better of me. "So, the Salvadorans who kidnapped you threw you in prison and told us you were dead?"

Colgan shook his head. "You probably don't want to hear this …" he paused, beseeching me with his eyes to stop him from going on. Seeing no such resistance from me, he finally continued. "I didn't get kidnapped, Petey. Antonio and I faked our own death and joined the rebels. That's why I wasn't about to try to come back to Kellyville and be a hero. I don't want the adulation of people who would hate me if they knew the truth."

So that was it, huh. Colgan intentionally made us think he was dead. I couldn't even tell if he was sorry for it or not. I wanted to yell at him, to rant and rave about how he let us think he was dead for thirty fucking years, and then throw him out of my bar. I didn't even care about him joining a bunch of commie rebels, that wasn't the point. He had intentionally abandoned everyone in his life, and he had just let us assume he was dead, knowing what it would do to those who loved him. But I had just told him it didn't matter and that I wanted him to stick around. I wasn't sure that was true anymore, but I couldn't go back on my word in two minutes.

Colgan seemed aware of my anger. He started to stand up.

"Wait, Colgan. I said it didn't matter and I meant it. Like I said, I just want you to stick around awhile. You can room with me upstairs if you want."

"I'm not here to be a burden, P.J. I haven't been dependent on anyone since my dad walked out to join the monastery when I was seventeen."

I noticed the jab at his dad, and realized again, as I had talking to Michael, how deep the enmity between them had gotten by the time he went off to Central America. I wondered if they might have made up if Michael had known Colgan was alive.

"No burden at all buddy. Maybe we'll let you pull out the ol' six string some nights. Or you can cook if you want to."

He laughed. "I haven't cooked for anyone but myself in twenty-five years, but I'll try if you want me to. But if you want the music, I think I might be better at that."

I led him upstairs to my little loft over the bar. There was a couch that he could sleep on, though not comfortably, in the living room, as well as plenty of space for an air mattress in the little gallery room where the kitchen would be in an apartment that wasn't built over a restaurant. I told him I had a nice air mattress. I did not tell him that I was getting close to moving in with Kim, at which point my bed would logically become available. I felt kinda crunchy about it, but I had to feel him out first before I just let him live there by himself.

Colgan put his backpack and guitar in the gallery room. We talked for a few minutes about the loft and the bar and Tuscaloosa, but nothing substantive. He said he wanted to put together a band for the bar, that could either play whenever I wanted him to, or even be a house band. I told him that sounded like a great idea to me.

I went downstairs to run the bar, hoping the girls with the margaritas hadn't skipped out on me. They were still there, and they ordered another pitcher. I could hear Colgan running the shower upstairs. I still didn't have a handle on how I felt about all this. I hadn't even told Kim or Clyde or Tanya Haynes, and I knew I needed to, but part of me wanted to figure out how I felt first.

Once I thought about it honestly, I knew that there wasn't anything but time that was going to help me understand what I was feeling. Time spent with Colgan. Time spent learning who he was again. And even if it felt hard to see him as the kid I knew, the best friend whom I had always loved, that had dominated my life even in his absence, I still knew that I wanted to spend that time. I wanted to get to know him again. Don't get me wrong, I was scared as hell about what I might find, but I knew that was the road I had to go down, no matter where it led.

Colgan came downstairs a few minutes later in a different untucked cowboy shirt and the same jeans, with his guitar on his back. His hair remained in the long single braid; I doubted that he had washed it. He flashed me a smile, and said "Wish me luck, I'm gonna find us a band." I laughed and just said, "Good luck."

In that moment, he was definitely the same old Colgan. Irrepressibly confident, sure that he could walk around Tuscaloosa for a few hours with his guitar and round up a band. The thought also occurred to me that Clyde, who had never met him, had been right all along about Colgan – he would be found when he wanted to be and not before.

I looked at my watch. Kim would be in class for another twenty minutes. I seriously considered calling her anyway, but I figured she had left her cell phone in her office. I texted her to call me as soon as she could. I had big news.

It was almost an hour later when she called me, because she had to meet with a student after class. The bar was still pretty much dead, and by that time I was pacing back and forth waiting for her to call and wondering how long Colgan would be gone searching for a band.

When Kim finally called, I asked her to guess who walked into the bar today.

"I don't know," she responded, but after a little teasing to get her to guess, she warmed up to the game.

"Coach Saban," was her first guess, because we had been laughing the other day about how Bear had frequented certain Tuscaloosa establishments and that maybe P.J.'s would become the haunt of Tuscaloosa's new favorite resident.

"Nope, bigger news."

Her next guess was Shemar Moore, who was the one person she was allowed to cheat on me with. That gave me a good laugh, but I told her it was even bigger news than her potential for sanctioned infidelity.

After a couple more guesses, I gave a hint about it being someone "from the past." Kim drew in a deep breath and said "No way. Oh my God P.J. Really? Colgan is there?"

"He just walked into the bar this afternoon. Just walked right in. I couldn't believe my eyes."

"Oh I'd have just fallen over right then and there. He's still there right. I'm coming now. Let me call Clyde." She was so excited that the words seemed to tumble out of her mouth without any actual effort of speaking.

"He went to try to get together a band for the bar. All he had with him was a backpack and a guitar…"

Kim cut me off. "Oh my God, you let him leave? What were you thinking P.J.?"

"Umm, I couldn't really lock him in, babe" I offered sheepishly.

"Did he leave his stuff at least?"

"Yeah, everything but his guitar. He's gonna be sleeping upstairs in the gallery room on that air mattress."

"If he comes back."

"I really think he will, Hon."

"Ok, I really am gonna call Clyde. I'll be over there in a little while. I love you."

"Love you too, sweetheart."

It took an hour for Kim to extricate Clyde from the law school and get her the four blocks to 15th street. Colgan, of course, had not yet returned.

Kim was bubbling with excitement, but Clyde seemed skeptical. I think she thought we were pranking her.

"I checked again," she said. "No hits on any database. If he really is alive, the government has no clue."

"But you were right, Clyde," I insisted. "You said that he would only be found when he wanted to be. You were right. Doesn't the fact that the government has no knowledge of him just reinforce that?"

She wasn't particularly impressed by either my logic or my flattery, and she headed home before Colgan returned about 6:15. Kim stuck around though, and I heard her squeal from the kitchen when Colgan walked in. By the time I came out from behind the bar, she had sprinted almost to the door and hugged him.

I don't think Colgan had a clue who she was, but he seemed to roll with it, returning the hug and saying "you must be P.J.'s girlfriend. I've heard a lot about you." To her credit, Kim didn't let on if she thought he should have recognized her.

Ten minutes after Colgan got there, two guys called for him, saying they wanted to play drums and bass in his band. By the weekend, he had five guys, including a sax player that I knew used to play sessions at Muscle Shoals. I stopped booking any other bands within the month. Colgan coming back quickly became the best thing that ever happened to P.J.'s. People were showing up to see Colgan's band before it even had a name. I think Colgan and the bass player threw out about three-hundred names before they finally settled on one that Kim proposed: Toomey and the Troublemakers.

At first, I tried to tell myself not to let the new-found income blind me to the very real issues I still had with Colgan faking his own death and letting us believe it for twenty-five years. But soon I realized it had nothing to do with the money, or even how fun the bar was becoming. I just loved having Colgan around. There was a reason this guy had been my best friend my entire childhood, and even without all the dramatic disappearance and return bullshit, he would have been my best friend if he had just, say, moved back to town after a career change or something. Hell, it was possible that even if that day he walked into my bar, that was the first time I'd ever met him, we might have become best friends. We just clicked like that.

At certain moments, though, it did strike me that Colgan was not particularly reticent about using his real name, even in a town where there might be people who remembered it. Hell, he even used his last name in the band name. If he was running or hiding from anything when he avoided us for all those years, it obviously wasn't after him anymore. Maybe he just wasn't psychologically ready to come back.

Even after he settled into life in Tuscaloosa, there were still ways in which Colgan chose to remain in the shadows. He quickly shut down Clyde's suggestion that she could help him change his status with the government. I don't think he had any desire at all for the United States or the State of Alabama to know that his death had been exaggerated. I paid him under the table for leading the band, and not nearly what he was worth, even with the free room and board thrown in. He never had (or wanted) a driver's license or a bank account. The official records still said he died in 1983.

Despite these incongruities, it really was awesome to have my best friend back. He soon became my de facto business partner as well. His band could sometimes fill the place up on a random weeknight, even in summer. Within a month of Colgan's return, I had moved out of the loft and in with Kim, leaving Colgan to watch over the place for me. He was also the best man at my wedding. Life was pretty sweet.

CHAPTER 30

THE LAST GIRLFRIEND

My name is Eliza Duncan. I am an attorney, an advocate for victims of domestic violence, and a recovering drug addict. I have seen a bit of the darkest of what this world has to offer, and at one time I selfishly thought I had some sort of record for that, if not remotely a monopoly. Then I met a man who had seen evils almost beyond my capacity to imagine. Somehow, he had come through them, and, ironically, he himself allowed me to see the light and beauty of the world.

I would like to say that I was the love of Colgan Toomey's life, but I know it isn't true. I am certain that I wasn't the only one whose comfort he sought in the years after he lost Patrycia, but I do believe I was the last, and I take some solace in that, even though I would give him to any woman in the world if he could be alive again.

For a long time, I thought the woman he called Paty (pronounced close enough to "potty" that I did a double-take at first) must be dead. If she is, Colgan didn't know it, but she was dead to him. The Hollywood mythos of love says that it can overcome all differences, but in the real world it just isn't true. Still, Colgan is probably the only person I've ever met that walked away from a person he deeply loved because she held political opinions he found repugnant. I don't think he ever really regretted it, but it still hurt him. It hurt him the rest of his life that someone he loved could be so callous and spoiled… or maybe it hurt him that he had been able to love someone who was that way.

Anyway, long before I knew anything about Paty, I met Colgan Toomey in a bar on Fifteenth Street in Tuscaloosa called P.J.'s. It was like late May, early June of 2008, and I had just gotten my grades from my second semester of law school. Even though I had done surprisingly well (surprising to me anyway), I was feeling like shit about myself because during finals I had made the stupid, but unfortunately effective, decision to use meth to stay awake and study. I'd only done it twice, but I knew I was slipping out of control of myself.

Possibly one of the worst things I could do in that situation was go sit in a bar and drink all evening. And it sure as hell wasn't a good time to be starting a relationship, not that I had any actual intention of doing so. Nonetheless there I was. PJ's was a bit different than most of the bars in Tuscaloosa. There weren't usually a whole lot of students, and thankfully, very few law students, although I did have to duck professors sometimes. Also, the guy that ran the place could actually cook, so while there were just a couple of standard bar food options, there was a special every night that was really good. My favorite was Thursday nights when he made shrimp and grits. He had several options for toppings in them, but the best was the Philly cheesesteak version with peppers, onions, and cheez whiz.

Anyway, it wasn't a Thursday night when I met Colgan. I'm sure of that because Thursday was also trivia night, and the house band, featuring Colgan on guitar, had that night off. That was the other thing different about P.J.'s; it had decent live music almost every night. Every once in awhile, it would be an outside band, but mostly it was just Colgan and some of his buddies, who played for an hour or two almost every evening. It was also the only place in town that there was good music that wasn't overwhelmingly loud. I know I sound like I'm fifty or something, but most of the bands in Tuscaloosa seemed to equate playing as loud as they could with making good music.

Anyway, that first night, which was a weeknight other than a Thursday, I was sitting there by myself drinking Sweetwater 420 pale ale and listening to Colgan's band do covers of guitar songs from the seventies – Free Bird, Stairway, Layla. These, as it turns out were Colgan's favorites, though the guy could play just about anything.

I know for a fact that neither me nor Colgan was looking for any kind of relationship when we stumbled out of P.J.s together that night. He had randomly walked up to my table after the band shut down and given me some lame line about not seeing me before and how he would have remembered such a pretty girl. I thought he was cute, and I was pretty drunk, so I told him I actually had seen him before and that he was a hell of a guitar player (both of which were actually true).

I didn't realize he lived upstairs of P.J.'s until later. We caught a cab to my place that night. I knew my roommate had headed back to New Jersey or Connecticut or wherever it was as soon as finals were over. She was an Ivy League undergrad, and while she was never overtly mean to anyone, she was, to put it mildly, having a hard time connecting with people in Alabama.

The sex was fine, but not earth-shattering, probably because we were both drunk as hell. It did get better later. But that first night, there was nothing particularly magical, no sudden halo of light like a side quest in this video game we call life that told me I was gonna fall in love with this guy.

The weird stuff started in the morning. When I woke up, this random drunk guy that I had brought home was kneeling on the other side of the bed going through the rosary. Now, I've never been particularly religious, in fact at the time, I probably would have said I leaned toward being atheist, but since I try never to be too sure of myself, I guess I'd say agnostic.

I'm mostly, however, a social justice type, interested in the rights of women and minorities and the poor. I was open-minded enough to know that there were plenty of religious people in the world who had the same priorities, even if most of organized American Christianity consisted of a bunch of reactionary blowhards. I guess that's why I didn't write Colgan off immediately, but I didn't really know how to reconcile the guy kneeling on my floor, rocking back and forth, oblivious to the world, with the guy who stumbled into bed with me last night.

Needless to say, however, I was intrigued. Even if I hadn't been blown away (yet), the guy wasn't a jerk, so I might as well be nice and see if I wanted to get to know him. I put on a nightgown and slipped to the kitchen to make us some scrambled eggs and biscuits. He didn't appear to notice.

He probably did actually notice though, because he came into the kitchen a few minutes later and offered to help. I told him I was almost done so he came up behind me and started rubbing my shoulders. His hands were strong, with long, flexible fingers. It was a little awkward because I really wasn't sure where we stood, but damn it felt good.

As his fingers melted away the tension in my neck and shoulders, I slid the finished eggs off the eye and turned around into his arms. He leaned down to kiss my forehead and ran his fingertips up my spine, which made my body tingle all over. Honestly it had been awhile since I felt like this, and I didn't really know why. Like I said, the drunken sex the night before was basically average. Maybe it was just the fact that he wasn't trying to run off.

I put my hands up his shirt to rub his chest. That's when I felt the scars. I pulled back a little and looked up at him. If these scars were from prison knife fights I needed to get out now. I almost pulled completely away then, but something made me give this guy a chance.

As nonchalantly as I could muster, I asked him what all the scars were from. He tried to get out of it, said it was a long story that we could talk about this later. I remember this whole conversation as if it were yesterday.

"Colgan," I said, "if you want to say we had a fun night and leave it at that, I'll have no animosity toward you at all. We can be friends. Look, I'm stepping out on a limb here and admitting I might want it to be more than that. I've got stuff in my past I'd rather not share with someone I hardly know either. But I'll be honest with you if you're honest with me. Part of me can't believe I'm saying all this, but I need to know."

Colgan let out a long sigh and said, "And I can't believe I'm gonna tell you. I really probably shouldn't… but I have to admit there's something about you. It really is a long story though; let's get our breakfast."

I didn't know at the time how much Colgan really was risking by telling me much of anything. I thought I was taking a risk with my heart by inviting him in. He was literally risking everything he had in his life, though admittedly that wasn't a whole lot, on a random girl he picked up in a bar. Once I knew that, the connection we had was instantly sacred.

I grabbed a couple of plates and the skillet of eggs and told him to pull the biscuits out of the oven. Placing them on the bar that divided the kitchen from the living room in my apartment, I poured us each a cup of coffee and, after learning that he took his black, dumped extra sugar and French vanilla coffee-mate in mine to compensate. We sat on the stools by the bar; there was no dining room table, not that I'd ever really missed having one.

Colgan finished a bite of eggs and looked up at me sincerely. "I'm having trouble figuring out where to start."

"The beginning is usually a good place," I offered.

"In the beginning, God created the heavens and the earth. And the earth was without form and void; and darkness was on the face of the deep," he recited.

"Apparently this is a long story," I laughed. "I better make more coffee."

"Actually, I think I'll skip ahead some. You asked about the scars. As I think you suspected, they come from my experience in a prison." I think he could see my face harden and me lean back a little, so he talked faster. "But how I got there and where the prison was, you would never suspect. It was in El Salvador."

"You were in a Salvadoran prison? Why? How is that better than being in American prison?" I was imagining running drugs from Central or South America as the only way one ends up imprisoned in El Salvador.

"Yes, I was tortured in Salvadoran prison by their government during their Civil War."

He explained to me how he had faked his own death and joined the Salvadoran rebels. "I cannot say today that my choice was right or wrong but my motives were pure. I saw the suffering of the Salvadoran people and the callousness of those who ran the place first hand."

He asked me if I had ever heard of Archbishop Oscar Romero. I had a vague recollection of a murdered priest sometime in the 1980's. Colgan said that eventually the Church would recognize Romero as a saint. Colgan still prayed to him every day. He told me about how he was gunned down in the middle of mass for daring to question the government's massacre of its own people and saying that maybe Catholic soldiers should act on their conscience instead of following such orders. He also told me about some nuns who were killed by the Salvadoran government, and how much it tore him up that we (the United States) were supporting these monsters.

At this point, I had to stop him and ask him how old he was. I didn't think I was even born when Oscar Romero was murdered, and I remembered the Salvadoran conflict ending when I was a pre-teen. Turns out the age difference between us was nineteen years. I looked at the man and couldn't believe he was forty-seven. Maybe it should have mattered to me. Maybe with anyone else, it would have. For some reason, even from the first, it never made any difference with Colgan.

He said his primary role with the rebels was as a medic, but he didn't elaborate on what secondary roles he might have had. He admitted that he had killed people, but said he never fired a gun during the war. He was only slightly more forthcoming about his stay in the Santa Maria prison. He said he could describe what his torturers did to him in meticulous detail, but that could not do anything but bring both of us pain. He preferred to speak of the kindness of a man named Señor Amaya.

Amaya was an old man who had been a guard at Santa Maria for a long time when Colgan showed up. The soldiers who had taken over the place basically turned him into a janitor. He was the only one there who treated any of the prisoners as a human being. Colgan seemed to truly love the man, even though he hadn't seen him since he was released from prison.

Colgan was vague about what had happened since he was released. He said he'd never tried to convince the government he wasn't dead. Therefore, he had to sneak back into the country from Mexico. I didn't press him on details about that either. Apparently since then, he had just kinda floated around playing guitar in various places, but eventually he decided to come back to Alabama where he grew up. P.J., the guy that owned the bar, was his best friend growing up. He laughed and said that anything he had told me could be confirmed by P.J.

After we finished breakfast I was still a bit shell-shocked, so we decided to walk back to P.J.'s and get my car. I continued to quiz him on the way, learning that he hadn't had a driver's license since high school. He didn't need one in Austin and, according to the government, he'd been dead since the summer of 1983, when I was about to turn 3. Being dead apparently really slows the aging process, because he didn't look a day over 35.

It wasn't but about ten blocks from my apartment near the stadium to P.J.'s up on 15th street. After the first couple I reached and took Colgan's hand. He squeezed it. It felt good. We held hands the rest of the way and talked about something. I think maybe music, or the weather in Tuscaloosa; I remember he mentioned the book he was reading, but I honestly don't remember what it was.

When we got back to P.J.'s, he gave me an amazing kiss by my car, and, since there wasn't another car in the lot and I knew he didn't drive, I asked him if I needed to drive him home. He smiled, and looked at me like he was thinking. He later told me he wanted to just make up an address to spend more time with me; he could always walk back to the bar. But the truth won out, and he told me he lived upstairs. I laughed and told him I was glad I didn't know that last night, because this morning was special.

If he had asked me, I'd have come upstairs with him right then and maybe stayed there forever. Within a couple of weeks, we were spending the night with each other about half the time.

CHAPTER 31

THE HIGH SCHOOL SWEETHEART, AGAIN

Like everyone else, I never thought I'd see Colgan again. I fully believed that he was dead. Hell, there were times I thought it was totally my fault, like it should have been my job to give him something to live for here, and I failed utterly.

I never saw Colgan again after I left Kellyville and gave the baby up for adoption. Like I said before, it was stupid of me not to give Colgan a chance to at least be there for me as a friend. But I couldn't take the possibility that he would reject me. It was easier for me to just reject myself and never have to face him.

Since then, though, I've often thought about what I would say if I ever did get the chance to see him again. Or more accurately, what I would have said to him if he hadn't died. Because I knew he was dead, I never actually thought about having to face his girlfriend, or what I might say to her.

When I met Eliza Duncan, I was staying in a battered women's shelter in Tuscaloosa, trying to get clean, keep my ass from going back to prison, and hide from my husband Tommy. Yeah, that was the same guy I said had been good to me before – that completely changed once we got married and he decided he owned me. He had put me in the hospital twice, and the second time, I snuck out against medical advice and went to my dealer's house to hide. Ben had taken one look at me, decided he couldn't sell me anything in good conscience, and dropped me off at the women's shelter.

The law school at the University ran what they called a domestic violence clinic. It helped women get what the state called PFA's. That stood for "protection from abuse" order. From what I could tell, it wasn't a very good name. The piece of paper didn't do much of anything to protect the victim from further abuse. That doesn't mean it wasn't useful though—what the order actually did was make it much more likely that the police believed the woman when it happened again, and much more likely to do something about it. In addition to the PFA's, the clinic helped with divorce, alimony, custody stuff, basically just any legal issue that a woman trying to get out of an abusive relationship might face.

Eliza wasn't among the first group of students the Law School sent over while I was at the shelter. The first group all seemed like entitled little snots who were slumming for law school credit before they started their long careers of screwing over the little guy. I didn't pay much attention to what they said at the meeting, and I didn't sign up for their clinic.

Eliza was different, though. I could tell from the beginning that she was genuine. It wasn't that the others thought domestic violence was okay, or that they didn't want to go through the motions of helping us. They just had no concept of where we were coming from. Eliza did. To this day, I don't know whether she had ever been in an abusive relationship, but I do know she's at least been through real problems in her life. Those other girls never had to do anything harder than choosing which sorority to be in.

I had already decided to let Eliza try and help me when she started talking about her recovery journey. I had always had trouble talking about my addiction, even in small group meetings or one-on-one with counselors. Instead I always just wrote it down and gave it to them. I could do that. I couldn't imagine being able to publicly open up about it in a situation where everyone didn't already know it. I mean if you go to a NA meeting or something, there's no question about why you are there, you really can't hide it. But none of us ever would have known that about Eliza if she hadn't said something. Like I said, I couldn't imagine being able to do that.

I also couldn't fathom the idea that an addict like me would be able to become a law student. I'll admit that my concept of law and lawyers was a bit skewed toward the criminal side; I never really thought about civil lawyers. I guess I always felt like lawyers were just part of the law enforcement system, just people that helped process us criminals and work us through the system.

It's probably a lucky thing that I had already had a couple of one-on-one sessions with Eliza and gotten to know her before I heard the name

Colgan. I probably wouldn't have been able to handle it otherwise. Eliza had helped me get a PFA against Tommy and we were working on my divorce. She said it would be an easy one because there were no kids from the marriage. I liked how she didn't just assume that meant I didn't have any kids. I was always very careful about avoiding pregnancy after high school, because I knew I wasn't capable of going through that again.

While Eliza was typing up the divorce complaint, we were sitting next to each other at one of the long tables at the shelter. Her phone was to the right of her laptop, sitting between us. She just ignored it the first time it rang, and I didn't want to be nosy and look at who was calling. When the person called back, I could plainly see the name was "Colgan." My heart skipped a beat and my voice broke a little as I said, "It's okay if you want to answer it."

She flipped one hand toward me as the other one kept typing and said, "Oh it's just Colgan, I can talk to him when we are through."

"Who's Colgan?" I asked as nonchalantly as I could.

She laughed. "He's my boyfriend. I'm probably not supposed to tell you that according to the rules."

I tried to laugh too. "It's a very unusual name. My high school sweetheart's name was Colgan. What a coincidence!"

Eliza smiled, but I could tell she was spooked. Maybe she just caught it from me, because even with just the first name, I was completely freaking out.

Eliza stopped typing and turned completely to face me. "Was his name Colgan Toomey? From a place called Kellyville?"

I nodded slowly, trying to wrap my head around the situation, but I could not. "But I thought Colgan was dead, he got killed in South America someplace."

"Everyone thought he was dead, hon," she said, patting me on the arm.

"But he wasn't?" I breathed, stating the obvious because there was nothing else I could say.

"No, he wasn't, but he did get thrown in a Salvadoran prison for a few years."

"Really?"

She proceeded to tell me the whole story, and I listened with rapt attention despite myself. What I really wanted to ask her at the end was why she was dating a man twice her age. But if Colgan was anything like he had been in high school, I shouldn't have been surprised. Part of me was sad that Colgan had been alive this whole time and I hadn't even looked for him. But hell, I hadn't even been willing to face him when he came home his freshman year. I knew he was alive for three or four more years after that and didn't try to talk to him then, either. In reality, I knew that then, just like most of the time in between, I was so screwed up in my own life that Colgan was the last thing I needed to worry about.

I also knew that seeing Colgan again now could completely derail my recovery and my life. And the last thing I wanted to do was hurt Eliza, one of the few truly genuine people that had ever tried to help me. So even though I wanted to see Colgan with all my heart and soul, that first day, I changed the subject and we went back to working on my divorce.

After we finished it that afternoon, and Eliza got it filed the next day, there was a month or so that we had to wait for Tommy to be served and file his answer. I didn't see Eliza during this time, but I thought about Colgan non-stop. I couldn't help it. I just couldn't believe he was actually out there somewhere in Tuscaloosa, right here in the same town as me. So close, and yet so many worlds away.

I knew that I couldn't be with Colgan for a million reasons, and not wanting to hurt Eliza certainly remained one of them. But I had to talk to him. For one thing, I had to apologize for not telling him about what happened in high school. I also had to make sure that he knew that I was gonna be okay, that nothing that had ever happened to me was his fault. You're probably thinking that's a no-brainer and wondering why I'd ever think he would even say it was his fault. But that's just how Colgan was. He was so good at everything that he believed he had a duty to fix anything that went wrong in the world. It was probably naïve, but I still wondered if he could have fixed my life if I had let him try.

The next time Eliza came to meet with me about the divorce, I was a bundle of nerves, because I wanted to ask her if I might could meet Colgan. I couldn't just come out and ask, but after a few minutes she noticed something was wrong.

"Are you okay, Stef? You seem jumpy. Has Tommy tried to contact you?"

"No, I haven't heard from him at all. I'm ok."

I've told the lie that I was okay at least a million times in my life. Eliza Duncan is one of the few people that ever gave enough of a shit to see through it.

"Stef," she said gently, "you have every right to tell me it's none of my damn business, whatever it is, but I'm not going to let you sit there and tell me nothing's wrong."

Her caring touched me. "Hon, I'm being perfectly honest when I say nothing's wrong with the divorce process and Tommy. I haven't heard from him in months. I have no idea if he's even still in town. Hell, I don't know that what's on my mind is anything 'wrong' at all, but you're right that I'm in a bit of a state this morning. I know that's obvious."

I still didn't say anything about Colgan, because I really didn't want to upset her. I should have known she would see right through it.

"I could tell you were spooked when we talked about Colgan last time. That's a heck of a lot to process at once, especially with everything else you've got going on in your life. This might be a bad idea, but I think it might help you to see Colgan, you know, get a chance to talk to him again."

I had never told Eliza how or when Colgan and I broke up, or what had happened to me after he went to Texas. Maybe Colgan told her about it. Maybe she was just so intuitive that she figured out, without knowing any details, that there was some sort of tragic unfinished business between me and Colgan. A lot of women would take such a discovery with jealousy and make damn sure that the business remained unfinished because this girl never got close to their man. Eliza was doing exactly the opposite.

We were allowed to check out of the shelter during the day in the company of people who signed up and got background checked. Eliza had already gone through that as part of the law clinic, so she said she would take me and Colgan to lunch the following Monday.

I don't think I've ever been as nervous for anything as I was for meeting Colgan again – not for court, parole hearings, two weddings, etc. I was worried that it would be like the meeting in that old Garth Brooks song, "Unanswered Prayers." Maybe that's why Eliza wasn't worried about me meeting Colgan. She knew he'd just see how screwed up I was and that we didn't have anything in common anymore. The song never mentioned the feelings of the "old high school flame." Did she still care about him? Was she trying to rekindle something? Or did she go back to her seat and look at her husband and think the exact same thing Garth did? Did she even give a shit what he thought of her? Who knows?

I knew I wasn't trying to rekindle anything with Colgan, but I cared very much what he thought. Not necessarily what he thought about me now; there was no reason anyone would want to be with me at this particular stage in my life. But it mattered a great deal what he thought of what happened in high school. Like I said above, I didn't want him to blame himself or even think anything was at all his fault. At the same time, I couldn't bear the idea that he would think I had intentionally been unfaithful to him.

Eliza picked me up about eleven, by herself. My hands were shaking in my lap as we drove across town to get Colgan. He apparently lived above a bar called P.J.'s, where he played the guitar in the house band. I remembered when he first bought a guitar in like tenth grade. I think it was originally for a Boy Scout project or something. He learned a couple of songs from a book and drove his dad crazy playing them over and over again. After a couple weeks, Mr. Toomey went and found someone that worked in the plant that was a guitar master and could teach Colgan. Once he had the basics down, Colgan was playing along with the radio like a month later. Just like with everything else, he was awesome at it almost as soon as he touched it.

Colgan was standing out front when we got to P.J.'s. Like I knew he would, he still made my heart skip a beat. At the same time, I could feel the passage of time like another presence in the car with us as he folded his long frame in behind Eliza. He looked a little nervous too, but of course he caught himself quickly.

He reached up and squeezed Eliza's shoulder. "Hey Babe!"

Then he turned to me. "It's great to see you again Steffanny. I really am glad to be able to talk to you after all these years."

I wondered if he was going to get into the serious stuff right off the bat. I wasn't sure I was ready for that. I think Eliza could tell. She jumped in with something about the weather, and we ended up making small talk all the way to the restaurant.

Once we got seated at a table, I decided the serious issues had to be broached. "Eliza," I began, "I really want to thank you for giving me a chance to see Colgan again. I know that a lot of people in your position would want to keep me away from their boyfriend, but I promise you that there's nothing to fear there. I just had to see him again."

"I understand completely, Stef. I think Colgan has a lot of old friends that are kind of in shock he's alive and aren't quite sure what to think of him. Right, babe?" She laughed, but there seemed to be a little nervousness in it. Colgan just nodded. It was clear that Eliza was in charge there.

I smiled at Eliza, but then turned to Colgan. "Yeah, I guess I partly wanted to tell you how glad I am that you're alive. But mostly I just wanted to apologize for not telling you myself what happened to me in high school. I'm really sorry I didn't talk to you about it, and I hope you never felt like any of that was your fault."

Colgan's deep-sea green eyes swelled like they were going to swallow the table. For the first time I'd ever seen, he seemed to have no idea what to say. "Steffie" he said slowly, just letting my name hang in the air. "Steffie,

I almost tried to find you when P.J. told me. I didn't have any way to get to Montgomery, or any idea beyond that where specifically you might have gone. I really do wish I could have tried to make you feel better about it, but I know I probably wouldn't have been able to. I'm just so sorry it happened to you in the first place." He stopped for a second and chose his next words carefully. "I don't mean 'sorry' in the apologetic sense because I think it was my fault, but just sorry in like a sympathy sense."

"I understand." That was mostly the end of our serious conversation. The food came, and we talked about football and how much Tuscaloosa had grown. Just like in the Garth Brooks song, there was almost no talk about the "old days" when Colgan and I were actually together, before he went to Texas and my life got screwed all to hell.

Still, I knew he was the same guy that I had loved so much, even if there wasn't any renewal of spark between us. I recognized the way he looked at Eliza, and the way she looked at him. On the way back to the shelter, after we dropped Colgan off, I could tell Eliza was confused about what we had been talking about at the beginning of the meal. I didn't go into great detail, but I told her that during my senior year in high school, when Colgan had already gone off to college, I got pregnant after being raped. I had moved to Montgomery and given the baby up for adoption.

Eliza said something that still haunts me to this day, though I don't think she meant it to even possibly connote what crossed my mind. She said that she was adopted, and that she understood that sometimes giving a child up was the best thing a young mother could do for the kid. I didn't have the guts to ask her if she had been born in Montgomery.

CHAPTER 32

THE BEST FRIEND, ONE LAST TIME

April 27, 2011 is a day that no one in Tuscaloosa will ever forget. It was certainly a day that changed my life. Much of what I lost could be replaced, and some of it has been. A thriving business, one that I had poured my life into, was turned to rubble in a matter of minutes. My car, a lightly used Mercedes that I had yet to even make a payment on, was upside down balanced on a front window sill of that business. The house that my wife and I had purchased approximately a year before had half the foundation shifted several inches and a tree lying over what was left of the kitchen and laundry room.

None of that matters. It was insured. Kim and I have a place to live while the house is rebuilt. The car dealer rolled over the loan that I hadn't even started repaying into one on an even nicer model. I haven't had the heart yet to start working on reopening P.J.'s. Part of me doesn't even want to, but the outpouring of support from people who've told me how much it meant to them and how much they can't wait for it to reopen ensures that I will.

Maybe this time I will call the bar Colgan Toomey's. I'd like to, but I don't know whether I can handle walking into work every day under a sign that said that. I still can't believe this is how it ends. After everything we'd been through, after him just walking in one day three years ago, the whole ridiculous, messed-up story of the legendary Colgan Toomey and his funny little crippled friend just stops one afternoon in a random act of nature.

But it wasn't really the random act of nature that killed him. It was his own act of selflessness. On the afternoon of April 27th, there were maybe five or six patrons in the bar. I was doing food prep with two employees in the kitchen. Colgan was upstairs reading a book called The Bridge on the Drina, by a Bosnian writer named Ivo Andric. It was the only possession of his that survived the tornado.

Kim was supposed to be coming over after class, like she did almost every day. But just before five she called me and told me that they were sheltering in place in the basement of her building because a tornado was coming. I flipped the TV over the bar to the local news, just in time to see Alabama's patron saint, the weatherman James Spann, telling everyone on 15th street in Tuscaloosa to "get to your safe place, now!"

I ducked my head back in the kitchen and told Trey and Charles to lock the front door and get all the customers into the walk-in cooler, and then I ran upstairs to get Colgan. At the time I thought he might be asleep, since he hadn't come down that afternoon.

Colgan brought his book as he came back down the stairs and helped me finish ushering the customers into the cooler. It was a fairly tight squeeze but everyone fit fine. Colgan was going to be the last one in, but as he was starting to pull the door to, he heard a toilet flush in the bathroom. I literally grabbed for his arm as he ran toward the sound, but he handed me his book and shoved the cooler door shut.

At the time, I had no idea whether Colgan had made it to the restroom to find the other customer, because it felt like just seconds passed after the door was shut before I could hear the tornado bearing down on us. You always hear people on the news saying it sounded like a freight train, but I remember it being much deeper, a sound that you could *feel* rather than hear. And it didn't feel like I imagine a speeding freight train smashing into a house would feel. It felt almost slow—more like if they parked the freight train next to the house and then started it up and slowly pushed everything over.

Even inside the walk-in cooler, we felt like were being pushed from the right side. We could feel the pressure changes as the tornado passed directly through the bar. Right in the middle, for what felt like an eternity but was probably just milliseconds, all the sound stopped. I don't really know if it was my brain panicking or if the pressure dropped so low that sound waves couldn't move through the air. I don't even know if that's possible, but that's the explanation I read online.

It was all over in like five minutes. I was the one nearest the cooler door, so I tried to push it open. It wouldn't budge. A pile of rubble had been pushed up against the outside. I have no idea how long we'd have been stuck in there if it weren't for Trey. He was a fairly recent Alabama football player, and he was able to push the door with enough force to shove the rubble out of the way. After the door was opened I stood back and let the customers get out. We were under an open sky and the rain, which had been pouring cats and dogs right before the tornado came, was little more than a light drizzle.

Everyone just sort of looked around, turning in a circle as we stepped over wood and glass and brick, the remnants of everything I had worked for. I am ashamed to say that I don't know how long I stood there before I remembered that Colgan wasn't in the cooler with us. When I did, I screamed out his name. Everyone just stared at me. I screamed again, and I thought I heard a voice from where the bathrooms would have been.

Trey had clearly heard something too because he started picking his way through the rubble in that direction. I followed him as quickly as I could. The entire two-story bar and studio had been reduced to misshapen piles of wood, brick, and everything else under the sun. I could see the bed frame from upstairs sticking out from one pile, but the mattress had apparently been blown somewhere. Trey and one of the customers who had followed him began heaving aside debris, and after a few seconds, we could clearly hear a woman's voice.

I got over to them just as the debris was cleared out enough for the woman to push Colgan's body partially off her and look up at us.

"He saved my life," she sobbed. "we ran into each other in the doorway and he told me to get down and laid on top of me."

She later explained that he had tried to keep his body rigid in a protective arc above her, and she had been able to see when a beam from the roof hit him directly in the head.

"I don't think anyone could have survived that."

Trey and the customer dug her and Colgan out of the rubble as I frantically tried to get cell service to call 911. It was completely futile. Not just because Colgan was already dead, but because there was absolutely no cell service in Tuscaloosa that night.

We felt Colgan's body already getting cold. I wanted to sit beside him and weep, but there were just too many other crises that had to be addressed. For starters, the lady, whose name turned out to be Elaine McDonald, had almost certainly broken her right leg. Trey solved that problem by literally putting her on his back and carrying her several blocks to the still standing hospital. We could see it from the bar now, because all the buildings in between had been flattened. I remember wondering if they had power. I didn't think about it at the time, but of course they had backup generators.

As I looked around Fifteenth Street, I could see what looked like thousands of people with dazed, shocked looks on their faces, walking like refugees, often carrying some small memento they had saved, sometimes with pets beside them, slowly making their way to the undamaged parts of the city, which, from our vantage point, basically consisted of the University and its immediate surroundings. I saw everyone walking and I decided I may not be able to help Colgan or anyone else who had died or been seriously injured, but I could do something nice for the survivors.

Everything in my cooler was going to go bad anyway, so I pulled out all the beer that had survived and Charles and I carried it to the intersection of Fifteenth and Tenth Avenue and started passing it out. It didn't take long to get rid of it. It was a silly gesture maybe, but it was something that took my mind off Colgan. It has become part of the folklore of April 27th – I've heard people tell the story to me, not even knowing I was the one passing out the beer.

The beer was gone about the time the first emergency personnel came to our block. The city's resources were understandably overwhelmed. The paramedics checked Colgan and officially ruled him dead. They said an ambulance would still come by and take them to the hospital, but they didn't know when that would happen.

Like I said, everyone in the area of the bar was just sort of slowly walking toward the University, because we could see that the buildings there were still standing. I was glad to know that Kim was almost certainly okay. There was still no cell service (I don't even remember how long it was before it came back), so I couldn't call her. I knew that I should probably join the crowd walking that way and find her, but I couldn't leave Colgan. I found a flat place in a pile of rubble and sat down, just staring off into the distance. I don't even think I cried right then, I just sat there in shock.

Kim, Clyde, and Danielle got there before the ambulance did. It was getting dark by then, but I could barely make out two or three people going against the flow of foot traffic well before I realized it was them. I started waving, but I don't think they could see me. Kim called out, "P.J., are you here?"

I stood up, and with as much cheer as I could muster, called out "Over here, babe." I began slowly picking my way across the field of rubble that had been my bar.

It was like a surreal, slow-motion, dystopian version of the stereotypical image of lovers running across the beach and embracing. I took her in my arms and held her against me as tightly as I could.

I think I was still in shock, but Kim's tears came freely. "Oh, P.J.," she said, "I'm so sorry."

I pulled away from her a little and looked at the ground, as my thoughts tumbled out. "Colgan's dead. He saved a lady that was in the bathroom. The paramedics said someone would come get him. I wanted to go to the University to try and find you, but I couldn't leave him."

Kim screamed in shock. "Oh noooo. NO, P.J., Oh my God, I'm so sorry, baby."

I turned around and led her through the rubble, stopping where I had been sitting to pick up Colgan's book. I would end up carrying it around for a couple hours and then giving it to Eliza. I still haven't read it. We got to Colgan's body and Kim just breathed "noooo" again and squeezed my hand.

Clyde and her girlfriend hung back a bit, but when we turned away from the body, Clyde said something that turned out to be prophetic. "How will they know who he is?"

We just all kind of looked at each other and shrugged, presumably thinking we would tell them who he was. Clyde may have had some idea of the ordeal that we were about to face, but Kim and I had no clue.

It felt like hours before the ambulance actually came for Colgan, but I don't honestly know how long it was. When they got there, the paramedics said normally they'd have let me ride along but tonight they already had a couple of bodies in the wagon. The man wrote down Colgan's name when I told him, but he also noted that there was no identification on the body. He said I should come to the hospital when I can and officially identify him.

After the ambulance left we started slowly walking back toward campus. Clyde's car, parked at the law school, would be closer than Kim's, so we headed that way. Danielle mentioned that we would probably also run into Eliza at the law school. I hadn't even thought about her in my own pain. I tried and failed to imagine being able to tell her about Colgan.

By the time we started walking toward the University, the throng of people had cleared out to some extent. I still felt like a refugee in a war zone. We walked down Tenth Avenue, with the stadium still standing in front of us, but almost everything between Fifteenth Street and campus leveled. I clutched Colgan's book and numbly put one foot in front of the other.

There were probably a hundred people in the law school parking lot when we got there. Most of them were trying to figure out whether particular students were okay. Clyde went off to get a roster out of her office and work on finding or contacting everyone, while Danielle gravitated to some students who were friends of her and Clyde. As it turned out, several law students lost their homes (mostly apartments) that day, but none were killed.

Kim and I sort of aimlessly wandered around the law school, trying to figure out what to do next. We had no idea whether our house was habitable or had power. Kim's car was safe on the other side of campus, but we were waiting for Clyde to make sure all the law students were okay. We also wanted to see if Eliza was at the law school.

We finally ran into her as the crowd was beginning to dissipate about ten o'clock. She ran up and gave Kim a big hug and said, "I'm so glad y'all are ok."

Kim hugged her close and held her there until she was uncomfortable, trying to find the words to tell her about Colgan.

"Eliza," I began…

She pulled away from Kim's hug. "What's wrong y'all? Where's Colgan?"

Kim let out a soft, plaintive wail. She said the same thing she had said to me. "I'm so sorry, Eliza."

I squeezed one arm around Kim and reached for Eliza's hand. Neither of them appeared particularly steady on their feet.

"Colgan didn't make it Eliza. The bar was completely destroyed." Not knowing what else to do, I handed her the book Colgan had been reading.

"What happened? Was he still upstairs?"

"He died a hero, Eliza. I had gotten him down and we had everyone we saw in the bar huddled in the walk-in cooler. He was shutting it when we heard someone in the bathrooms. He ran to get them and didn't make it back. The lady lived though. Colgan put his body on top of her."

"Oh my God," Eliza breathed. We just stood there sort of staring at each other. Tears would come later. We were still in shock.

Neither Kim nor I had been to our house yet at that point. We invited Eliza to come home with us, but all of us ended up spending the night at her apartment once we saw the damage at our house. She was kind enough to let us have the bed and sleep on the couch. She told us there was no way she could be alone that night.

About ten o'clock the next morning, I remembered what the paramedics had said about claiming Colgan's body at the hospital. Kim was on the phone with an insurance company (home, auto, I don't remember), and we waited for her to get done before going to the hospital. We had no idea what we were getting ourselves into. I had this vague sense that they would ask me to confirm the identity I gave the paramedics the night before and then we would make the funeral arrangements.

Instead, there was a representative from the Tuscaloosa County Coroner's Office already at the hospital because of the influx in bodies from the tornado. There were several bodies that had been found without identification, and in a few cases, there hadn't even been anyone to tell the authorities who they were. As we waited in a short line, I thought it would help that at least Colgan didn't fall into the latter category.

But when I told the lady I wanted to identify the body of Colgan Toomey, she didn't have that name on her list. Still, figuring out which body was his wasn't exactly difficult. I told her that he was the tall one with long red hair, and the hospital tech led us to him immediately. Kim, Eliza, and I all confirmed that it was him and coroner's representative wrote down his name.

Then the problem started. "Who's his next of kin?"

We looked at each other. Eliza spoke up. "I'm pretty sure he didn't have any family around here."

The lady smiled, "Well we can figure his next of kin through Social Security. It won't take but a couple of days."

We all looked at each other again. I think everyone realized we couldn't tell her that the SS database would show Colgan was dead.

This time Kim talked. "I think I've got his social security number written down somewhere." She fumbled through her purse. I remembered when we got his number from the death database. She had had that card in her wallet for years.

Kim found the little card she had written it on and the lady copied down the number. She then took down my phone number and said that they would call after they verified his identity and talked to the next of kin.

We left the hospital in various states of panic, knowing we had opened a pandora's box that might never close again. The day after the tornado was Thursday. We fretted all day Friday but didn't go up to the hospital, and they didn't call us either. I decided to be there early Monday morning.

Once they found out the social security database showed that Colgan was dead, the hospital said the person they had in their morgue wasn't

Colgan Toomey and they had no reason to talk to us. Eliza had to file a lawsuit to get them not to bury him in an unmarked grave as a John Doe.

After we got a temporary injunction, the Coroner's Office and the Police Department were finally willing to talk to us. Chief Hall treated us like we were idiots the whole time though, assuming we had somehow been duped into believing some random drifter was our long-lost friend. We decided early on we had to tell him the whole damn story, about Colgan faking his death in El Salvador. When the Chief asked if we had any proof, I yelled at him that the proof was lying in the morgue.

Eliza, however, was able to provide a bit of evidence, because she knew that Colgan had confessed to a priest at Holy Spirit, who turned out to be their old quiz bowl coach Father Sean. I have no idea what Father Sean told the cops, other than confirming that Colgan didn't die in El Salvador in 1983, but Chief Hall suddenly became very interested in what Colgan did in Texas before he came back to Alabama. Some county sheriff from South Texas even showed up to talk to Father Sean. Nobody ever told us what Colgan was accused of, but Clyde said she figured it had to do with him sneaking back across the border.

CHAPTER 33

THE PRIEST

I have served as a priest for almost fifty years, mostly at Holy Spirit Church in Tuscaloosa. I knew Michael Toomey when he was a lay leader, before it was general knowledge that he had studied to be a priest, and long before he took up the monk's habit. I first met his son Colgan in the mid-60's, when he was a small child. Of course, they were in Kellyville, and I was in Tuscaloosa, so I did not know them well.

When Holy Spirit opened a school, I became a teacher in addition to my vocation as a priest. Believe me when I tell you this is a much harder job. You would think it would be easier to teach people science and math, in which I could empirically prove that I was right, than to teach them matters moral, metaphysical, and supernatural, where faith is required. Alas, this is not the case. God seems to have given people an innate desire to know Him and understand Him to the best of our meagre ability. He seems to have been much more sparing with the gift of the love of learning more generally. Or maybe people were just more likely to believe a priest about religious matters.

Unlike many of my students, Colgan appeared to have received both gifts in great measure. I had the privilege of coaching the Holy Spirit quiz bowl team for a few years in the late 1970's. We actually weren't that bad; at least a couple times we were the best team in Tuscaloosa. We played Kellyville twice. They absolutely destroyed us both times. I doubt our cumulative score made it over 100. They scored about 500 both times. Colgan was the best player I've ever seen, and P.J. Campbell could probably have beaten our team without him.

Like most of the priests in western and southern Alabama, I attended Colgan's funeral at Kellyville's football stadium in July of 1983. The main thing I remember was that it had to be as hot as we try to tell people the fires of hell are. I grew up right outside Bangor, Maine, and I've always thought that those of the damned who spent their earthly lives in Alabama will feel right at home in the afterlife. I try to keep this opinion to myself, however.

By the time of Colgan's funeral, many of us knew Michael Toomey fairly well. He had been a fixture volunteering at parish events throughout the region before he joined the monastery. I doubt any of the priests in attendance were particularly upset by P.J.'s speech. All he was really saying was that even though Colgan was a great guy, he was human. He made human mistakes. Priests are sort of experts when it comes to the idea that all humans are fallible. And we certainly know that it applies to each of us. A reminder of that point at a funeral that otherwise consisted of hero-worship was not a bad thing.

Anyone who has been a priest for a long time also knows that just about every confession is a surprise. I have heard the meekest little old ladies confess to things that would make a sailor blush with shame as the saying goes. And I've heard big bad biker-type guys contritely confess to things like looking at women the wrong way or breaking the speed limit.

But the surprise I was in for one spring afternoon in 2010 was several orders of magnitude beyond the average confession. The penitent first stated that he had not confessed to a live priest in over twenty years. The "live priest" part confused me, and I almost asked him about it, but I decided to just give my normal spiel about how it's never too late to return to the Church and that he will be forgiven for his doubt if he turns to the Father in faith. He stammered for a second and I got the impression he wanted to argue that he had never lost faith in God, only in the Church. We got that one a lot.

As he continued, I tried to place the voice, which I knew I recognized. I wasn't able to do so until I had heard the whole story, and I nearly fell out of my chair when I realized I was talking to a man I thought had been dead for almost three decades. His confession began mundanely enough. He had met a woman in a bar and fornicated with her, but now he really liked her, so he wanted to be forgiven for that. This was another common refrain. In Tuscaloosa, I heard confessions to drunkenness and sexual activity virtually every day.

The story soon got a lot more interesting, however. The man prefaced the really interesting parts by confessing that he had lied by omission to this woman that he liked. He had told her about his experiences in the Civil War in El Salvador and subsequent imprisonment and torture by the government of that country. At this point I tried to comfort him with the idea that these experiences must be hard to talk about and the idea of leaving something out probably wasn't the end of the world.

But when he started talking about what he had left out, I realized this might have been the most surprising confession I had ever heard, and that was before I knew the person confessing was someone I thought was dead.

There is this public culture myth that people confess horrific crimes in detail to their priests and we actively withhold it from the police. That almost never happens. I'm not saying we don't take the privacy of confession seriously, we absolutely do. However, two true things are ignored by this trope. First, the vast majority of people who commit serious crimes aren't confessing them to their priests, even if they're Catholic, and even if they're going to confession regarding more mundane sins. Second, even those who do mention such crimes do so generally. Nobody is telling us where the bodies are buried. And, admittedly, we don't ask those questions; it's not our job.

Even though Colgan's confession began with the idea that he had withheld information from his lady friend, I'm pretty sure I am the only person he ever told the full story. At various points in the narrative, he went from angry to remorseful to questioning God in just a few sentences. When he came to Tuscaloosa, it had been more than ten years since most of the events he described had ended. But I could tell that Colgan had yet to make sense of them in his own mind.

I got the impression though, that Colgan had always felt justified at the time of his actions. The suffering of the Salvadoran people warranted his doing whatever he could to help them. At the same time, he now realized his actions caused suffering for his family and friends back home, and he felt remorse for that. But where he had thought of the issue beforehand, he continued to find it justified. He expressed no remorse at all for stealing medicine from the Doctors Without Borders mission, for example.

When it came to the taking of human life, however, he said that he always regretted having to do so. If the killing was justified in the course of the war that he had involved himself in, he justified it, but he still confessed to God about it. He told me that every time, he prayed that he would never have to kill another soul.

He said he came out of Santa Maria prison with a vow to never again take up a cause that required him to kill. He probably made that vow honestly at the time. But Colgan Toomey was not a man to sit idly by and suffer injustice to occur around him. In the years after his release, he became involved in a second war. This one was much more personal, a lonely, solitary quest.

This war, too, was justifiable in Colgan's mind. There is no question that he saw the smugglers on the border, and further into Mexico before that, commit unspeakable acts. Colgan's first act of violence against them, in killing two men who were in the process of torturing and killing a young woman, no, in reality a child, was almost certainly justifiable. His heroic actions in carrying that child across the desert to the hospital are commendable. But he came to know that what those men had done had broken that child irrevocably. They took her life from her as surely as if she had been left to bleed out onto the desert sands. Colgan could not accept that his actions in saving her had been for naught.

I tried to reassure him that no such actions of helping fellow human beings go for nothing, that giving her a chance to reclaim her life, even in excruciatingly difficult circumstances, mattered. I was prepared to absolve Colgan totally for killing her two tormentors.

I think the same qualities that made Colgan a great athlete and a great student, and even in some ways a great Catholic, also led him to create for himself grand quests that, while perhaps completely noble in their theoretical inception, led him to the commission of grave sins.

Colgan's personal war against the coyotes, though triggered by his noble defense of a young lady being tortured and brutalized, became one of these quests. The anger that motivated him began as a righteous light but became a fire that consumed both itself and his entire consciousness during the years he fixated on destroying the men who took such disgusting advantage of poor, lost souls trying to get across the border.

Even Colgan's shockingly revelatory confession did not approach the kind you see in movies. He didn't go over the gory details of his killing, and he certainly didn't tell me where any additional bodies might be.

I never got the impression that Colgan was a dangerous person to be in the community. He didn't really explain why he stopped killing and left South Texas. Lord knows there were still plenty of coyotes and drug runners exploiting the people there. But Colgan's role in that fight was done.

If I had felt that Colgan was in the midst of or about to start one of his quests, I probably would have reported him to the authorities in some general way as a person to watch. As it was, when I figured out who he was near the end of his confession, I invited him to return to the Church, and I genuinely hoped he would take me up on the offer.

He wasn't there every weekend after that, but he did come occasionally.

And he and Eliza almost always showed up when we had special events to help the poor. Eliza was especially fond of our immigration clinics, and she organized several other law students to help do the basic forms for people while local lawyers worked with the complicated cases.

All in all, I was confident that the Colgan Toomey I saw in church once a month or so was a decent man, and I had no fears whatsoever that he would commit any violent crimes in Tuscaloosa. To be honest, it never really crossed my mind after his initial confession. I certainly never saw it as my place to judge anyone for their past crimes. If anything, my job was to try to embody, however imperfectly, God's perfect forgiveness.

Since I had no ongoing concerns, I never considered going to the authorities. In the chaos after the tornado, I was responsible for identifying the bodies of several of my parishioners, all of whom had either arrived here illegally or overstayed their visas, and were thus living in the shadows allowing few people to know exactly who they were. A week after I had finished with that, Eliza and P.J. came to me one afternoon and said the authorities were about to bury Colgan in an unmarked grave and they needed everyone that knew who he was to please tell the police about it.

I hadn't even known Colgan had died and was surprised by the wave of grief that swept over me. Once I had dealt with that, it made perfect sense that there were issues surrounding his body, since according to the official records, he had died thirty years ago in Guatemala. Reasoning that the cops were overwhelmed by other duties in the immediate aftermath of the tornado, I helped P.J. petition to the coroner to keep Colgan's body in the morgue until permanent identification could be made. I don't think our petition made any difference though. It was Eliza's lawsuit that made them keep Colgan's body.

It had been about a month since the tornado when the police chief came to talk to me about Colgan. At the time, I don't think he had any inkling that the body in his morgue might have been involved in any criminal activity. He was just trying to tie up loose ends and get everyone who had been killed by the tornado buried. But eventually he decided he needed to interview me as the only "neutral" party that claimed to know who Colgan was.

As soon as Chief Hall began questioning me, I decided I was going to tell the full truth as best I knew it. I had never in my fifty years as a priest felt the need to breach the sanctity of the confessional before, and I was pretty sure I never would again. But there appeared to be no one who would be harmed by explaining the story, and it would get Colgan a good Christian burial and hopefully give his soul a chance to get headed in the right direction. Whatever he had done, the man came to me seeking forgiveness, and my job is to come as close as I possibly can, with all my human failings, to mirroring God's complete and unconditional love and forgiveness. To my way of looking at it, both Colgan and his friends would benefit from me helping to convince the police that he was who they said he was.

I knew that I would not long be able to obfuscate the details of the confession once I started telling it. My conscience would not allow me to simply tell Chief Hall about Colgan faking his own death and fighting in El Salvador and leave out everything that happened thereafter. So, I told him not only that his dead John Doe's real name was Colgan Toomey, but that he might be wanted in connection with one or more serious crimes in Zavala County, Texas. Colgan had told me they took place near Crystal Springs, and I looked up the county name. I convinced the Chief to contact the Sheriff there.

In the back of my mind, I knew I would eventually spill everything, but I really did worry that Chief Hall would try to publicize the case or take credit for finding a serial killer. He was an ambitious man, and he had received accolades for the way the city had handled the aftermath of the tornado. That was why I told him that I needed to talk to the Zavala County Sheriff, and why I was extremely relieved when they sent someone.

I never met the current holder of the office. Instead, he apparently re-deputized his predecessor to handle everything. Jim Burruss was a good man, even if he was a Baptist. He came to visit me not because he wanted any credit for closing his most famous case, but because he needed to know if Colgan really was the man he had called El Diablo Blanco for half his working life. I confirmed it for him in enough detail that he was sure, and I tried to help him get a little understanding of what made Colgan tick. I don't know that I really can answer that myself. Part of me says he was brilliant and caring and thought outside the conventions of society to try and make the world a better place, and he just lost his way when he couldn't do it.

But maybe there was something darker about Colgan's personality all along. Like I said before, there was an obsessiveness about him, a drive that when he was going to do something he was going to do it right, and nobody was going to get in his way. It seemed like sometimes, though, when success in whatever it was ran into a wall of some sort, he just went and found a new quest. When he got hurt at Texas, he quit playing football. He seemed to give up on El Salvador when he was released from prison there. I wondered if there was some similar obstacle that made him end his war with the coyotes.

CHAPTER 34

THE SHERIFF, AGAIN

A couple of years after I retired as Sheriff of Zavala County, Texas, I got an unlikely phone call from the chief of police in Tuscaloosa, Alabama. At first, he wanted me to come see if I could identify a body that was killed in a tornado. The fella said it might have some connection to an open case in my neck of the woods.

I wanted to tell him that I wasn't the gall-darned Sheriff anymore and he needed to call Blake Griggs and leave me the hell alone. But there was really only one significant unsolved case from my time as Sheriff, and I was damned curious to see if this guy had any information on it.

I don't know what made me think he might, though. DB, el Diablo Blanco, the white devil, as we called him, hadn't been heard from for nearly fifteen years, since the mid-1990s, when he killed a bunch of drug-runners and coyotes, mostly from the other side of the border. At the time he was also known as El Colo Loco. We all figured that once the cartels in Mexico had consolidated their power, they got rid of him, but every once in awhile we'd bust some low-level cartel operative and we'd remember to ask him about ol' DB. The guy'd go white as a sheet and say he heard rumors that El Colo Loco was coming back.

He never did though, and that fact squared with the only pieces of solid information I'd ever gotten from a witness in the case; a crack whore from Laredo who told me that Colo was DB's real name, that he fought in the Salvadoran Civil War but came from somewhere else, and that he was going home (wherever that might be – if she knew, she wasn't saying) and wouldn't be around to "do our dirty work" anymore.

This may come as a shock, but despite Texas's "hang 'em high" reputation, we do believe in some level of due process down here, and, at the time, I wasn't exactly thrilled to have a civilian summarily executing criminals in my jurisdiction. But I did wonder what made him tick – I didn't think he was just some sicko who picked people who wouldn't be missed solely in an effort to avoid getting caught. He was clearly seeking revenge on the smugglers on the other side of the border, and I was willing to bet he had a damned interesting story.

So, I took the Alabama fella's phone call and asked him what case that might be. He hemmed and hawed like he expected me to be the one giving information, but I reminded him that he called me, and he needed to spill it if he wanted my help. I eventually teased it out of him that some civilians in Tuscaloosa were claiming that a person killed by a tornado was a man named Colgan Toomey. The problem was that, officially, Mr. Toomey had died thirty years ago.

At first, the chief had chalked it up to a case of mistaken identity, or maybe even identity theft; some petty criminal weaseling his way into people's lives claiming to be their long-lost friend. (I was a bit confused at this point until I learned that Toomey was pronounced dead without a body.) Anyway, the chief was ready to bury this guy in a potter's field, but his friends were extremely insistent.

The friends told a wild tale of Latin American intrigue where this all-American kid from Alabama, who was in his first year of medical school at the University of Texas, orchestrated his own kidnapping and supposed murder by Salvadoran rebels. The mention of UT made me realize I'd heard the dead guy's name somewhere—big quarterback prospect who never really panned out if I remember correctly. Thinking about that almost made me miss the bigger money clue about the Salvadoran rebels.

The girl in Laredo had told me that "Colo" as she called him had chosen to become Salvadoran and fight in the civil war, meaning that he would originally have been from somewhere else. Colo could clearly be a nickname for Colgan. He would probably have had to come through Texas on his way back to Alabama, and if he had to sneak across the border, he likely saw the way the coyotes abused and took advantage of people.

I played my cards close, but I began to think I might actually have a lead on DB. Sheriff Griggs wasn't going to believe this. He had been a young deputy when we first investigated the coyote murders. Blake Griggs was the only one that fully believed the girl who told me that El Colo was leaving town. The rest of us were waiting for more bodies to turn up, but

Griggs just moved on and told us that DB was done killing and we were never solving the case.

I told the guy from Tuscaloosa that I was intrigued by the information and wanted to learn more, but that there was no way I'd be able to identify the body since I'd never seen a suspect in the case. He apparently was very keen on the idea that he had found a long-lost serial killer, and he was even willing to send me a copy of his file on this guy. I began to think the reason that this guy hadn't already been buried in a potter's field had more to do with the Chief's ambition than with his friends' persistence.

But anyhow, I had no reason not to look at the fella's file, so I gave him my address and told him to send it certified. I resisted calling Griggs for about three hours, but finally I couldn't take it anymore.

"Hey Blake, you know how those lowlifes you're always dealing with keep tellin' ya they're afraid ol' DB will be coming back to get 'em.?"

"That's a hell of a way to start a conversation, Jim. You know as well as I do that El Diablo Blanco"-- he emphasized these words with a sing-song Mexican accent-- "ain't been seen in these parts for a decade and a half. I told you a long damn time ago, he was gone for good. But damn, Jim, I'd say I'm a hard one to shock, old man, but if you, of all people, tell me that DB is back, I just might have to listen."

"Naw, Blake, I'm just yankin' your chain. It's looking more and more like you were right all along when you said that girl was telling the truth about DB leaving town."

"'Bout damn time you decided I was right," Blake laughed.

"Actually, it ain't just the passage of time that has lent credence to your theory."

"What the hell are you talkin' about Jim?"

I told him about the dead guy in Alabama. I could hear the wheels grinding in his head as I told the story, and I thought I could make out the sound of him chewing on a straw the same way he did when I told him what the girl from Laredo had said. Finally, he came out with a classic Griggs line.

"Makes about as much damn sense as any of the rest of this case."

I could tell he was about as excited as Blake Griggs ever got, but again in classic fashion, he downplayed the significance.

"I don't have the manpower to send someone to Alabama, but if you want to check it out, be my guest." There is no doubt in my mind that he was absolutely certain I would, in fact, "check it out," and he was right.

The file that I received in the mail didn't tell me much more than the

Chief had already spilled. Nonetheless, my morbid curiosity about DB convinced me I had to go to Tuscaloosa. The drive from Crystal Springs took two fairly solid days of driving. The first day I didn't even make it out of Texas. I hit Houston toward the end of rush hour and it took two hours to get from there to Beaumont. I stopped fifteen miles from the Louisiana border.

On day two, my old truck bucked and pitched across Cajun country on the travesty of a highway that is I-10. I swear the only part of that thing they maintain with any regularity is that damned 20-mile-long bridge between Lafayette and Baton Rouge. Which by the way, Baton Rouge may be the worst-designed city in the country for traffic. After you cross the river, one of the biggest east-west highways in the country has to take a virtual 90-degree curve to accommodate a little spur that runs for about two miles. The east side of town, where Interstate 12 comes off, is almost as bad, and was a virtual parking lot at about 11:00 on a Tuesday morning. I stopped for lunch to let it clear out, but it didn't help much.

When I finally got out of Louisiana, things moved much more quickly. The main struggle was staying awake on that stretch of Mississippi road between Hattiesburg and Meridian. I'm telling you, it was the same 200 feet of pine trees repeated over and over again, ad nauseam. Western Alabama wasn't much better, but I finally made it to Tuscaloosa about 7:00 pm.

I knew that the city had been hit by a tornado; that was how my suspect died, after all. But I wasn't prepared for the devastation I saw. It had been a little over three weeks since the tornado, and there were whole sections of town that hadn't even been cleaned up. The power was still out across much of the city. The storm cut a swath through the city several blocks wide and miles long. Between destroying a bunch of houses on either end of its path, it went right through one of the main business sections of the city, demolishing a bunch of restaurants and bars along Fifteenth Street. I could see most of the path of devastation from my hotel room window.

One of the bars that got demolished was called P.J.'s. It was still basically a pile of rubble, but apparently had once been a considerably larger pile of rubble, since there was a full dumpster waiting to be hauled from the site when we got there. According to Chief Hall, the story went like this. The tornado struck around ten minutes after five on the afternoon of April 27th. There was some warning, and the bar owner at P.J.'s had gathered his staff and patrons in the walk-in wine cellar, which, though not actually a cellar in the sense of being underground, was the safest place in the bar and withstood the tornado damage.

Mr. Toomey, whom I suspected to be El Diablo Blanco, was the leader of the house band at the bar, best friend of the owner, and lived upstairs in some kind of loft. As he helped the owner herd everyone into the cooler, the storm was already pretty intense outside, and he heard something from a restroom. His body was found draped over a woman that was seriously injured but alive. According to the Chief, she was a random patron of the bar and had no idea who the man was who saved her.

It looked like ol' DB had a spark of good in him at least anyhow. I found myself hoping that the way he died, saving someone, might help him in the cosmic scheme of things, perhaps absolving some of his sins. I don't know if it was some sort of sympathy for DB himself, or just for this wrecked city. But looking at the devastation in Tuscaloosa and at P.J.'s in particular, how much these people had been through, and how much there still was to do made me very reticent to start accusing their dead friend of being a serial killer.

I spoke briefly with P.J., the bar owner, who was Mr. Toomey's best friend, and with Toomey's girlfriend, Eliza. I tried, mostly unsuccessfully, to get some details about his time in El Salvador, learning only that he spent several years being tortured in a prison there after joining the rebellion. I learned more about what he had been doing since he returned to Tuscaloosa. Apparently, he was a heck of a musician and his band, the house band at P.J.'s, was fairly well known in the city. The band was called Toomey and the Troublemakers, so despite the fact that no one had any proof of who he was, the guy wasn't exactly trying to hide his identity.

Once I started talking to P.J. and Eliza, I couldn't bring myself to ask them whether they thought this person they loved could be a serial killer. I was pretty convinced that if this guy wasn't DB, we were never finding out who was, and well, if this guy was DB, it's not like we could prosecute a dead man. So, I couldn't see any good that would come out of turning these folks' memories inside out on 'em.

Even though it wasn't worth ruining these people's lives, I still wanted to know whether DB did it. Luckily my dilemma was solved when Chief Hall introduced me to a priest named Sean O'Malley. He had been the one that initially told the Chief that there might be an important unsolved case in Texas connected to this particular unclaimed body. Father O'Malley's primary goal was to see the body that the Tuscaloosa PD had in cold storage get a good Christian burial. He said he knew it was Colgan Toomey, and he was willing to break the sanctity of the confessional to prove it if he had to. For whatever reason, he preferred to talk to me rather than the Chief. I can't imagine why.

Father Sean confirmed to me in astonishing detail that Colgan Toomey was El Diablo Blanco. Toomey had told him a couple of specific locations, as well as certain details of the way DB had set up the murder scenes. He also knew the name Maribel, which sealed the deal for me.

Sean believed that Colgan Toomey was a man always in search of a quest, if not a war. He did what he did because he believed it was right, whether the world agreed with him or not. Somehow, after El Salvador, his war had come to be against the coyotes of my little corner of the borderland. I certainly cannot say that I condone his actions, but I also don't have tears in me for the likes of the Martinez gang.

Father Sean and I somehow convinced Chief Hall to release the body to Toomey's friends without making a big production about the idea that he might have committed a crime or two in another jurisdiction fifteen years ago. Honestly, it was mostly Sean. I told the Chief that I really didn't know anything about Mr. Toomey, but he fit certain biographical details that were shared by my suspect. It probably wouldn't be enough to get a warrant if he were alive. I told him it was more important that what little knowledge I had corroborated what Father O'Malley knew, and made it very likely that, whether he had killed anyone in Zavala County or not, he was who he said he was.

We finally convinced the Chief, P.J. and Eliza got their friend's body, and I drove the two days back to south Texas. It gave me a lot of time to think about ol' DB. I honestly hadn't gotten a lot of answers for the questions I most wanted to ask. I had a name and a face now, but they belonged to a man I'd never meet or be able to interrogate. That will probably always bother me a little bit. Still, I had learned a few things. DB appeared to be a man who was driven by a mission, a cause. He almost certainly wasn't just getting his rocks off killing people who wouldn't be missed. That made me a little sadder that I would never get to talk to him.

EPILOGUE

June 2, 2011, Kellyville, Alabama

After my son Colgan disappeared in Central America, I purchased a monument to him, a weeping angel, and placed it next to the grave of my wife Sarah Anne. I always held out a faint hope that we might recover his body to receive a good Christian burial there. I loved my son very much, though I know I wasn't always particularly good at expressing it, and I had good reason to fear that he didn't believe it. I am glad that, in the end, he was finally buried beneath that monument.

While I lived, I never dreamed that it would turn out that I had passed away before Colgan, though it is, of course, the natural order of things for the father to expire before the son. After I died, I didn't immediately know that Colgan was still alive. The pathway of a soul to eternal rest with the Lord is not a short one, at least not for a miserable sinner like me. There may be some who have a far quicker journey.

I still remember Colgan's first funeral, when we thought he had been murdered by the Salvadoran guerrilla group he turned out to be a member of. P.J. Campbell is right that my opinion of him never faltered an iota. That kid was as special as Colgan. Every physical advantage that Colgan had in spades, P.J. had the corresponding difficulty, but he never complained. Colgan was tall, lithe, and athletic, while P.J. was short, chubby, and had a permanent limp. Colgan had the gift of gab from the moment he started talking, but P.J. stuttered until he was about 15.

They both had the curse of losing a parent young, though P.J. never knew his father. Angie and I worked hard to give the two of them all the same opportunities. I say that like we were married or something. Even though there was never anything romantic between me and Angie, the four of us really did operate like a family, and for the most part, we were a happy one.

Sometimes I think I should have accepted that family, let myself fall in love with Angie, and married her. I won't say that the idea that maybe I already was in love with her never crossed my mind, but I just couldn't get past the notion that it would mean I was being unfaithful to Sarah Anne. It's possible nothing could have worked with Angie because I did still miss Sarah Anne every day. I missed her every day until I died. I think part of why I joined the Church was to make sure I would never let myself move past her.

That's probably not a good reason at all for joining the Church, but you must remember that I had been destined for the priesthood basically from birth. At the time, the youngest son of a big Chicago-Irish family was often given to the Church with or without his consent, but I embraced the idea wholeheartedly. I was never like the other boys my age, if you know what I mean. Sarah Anne is literally the only woman I ever touched intimately, the only one I ever kissed. I always believed she was the only one on the planet that could have made me walk away from Notre Dame.

Maybe it wasn't fair to either Angie or Colgan (or P.J. for that matter) for me to break up the closest thing any of us had to a family. But it wouldn't have been fair to make them compete with either Sarah Anne or God either. It wasn't fair that I lost my wife four years into marriage when she was just 22 or that Colgan lost his mom when he was three. None of it was fair. I didn't know how to make it any better, but I tried hard not to make it worse.

Angie always knew I would be joining the Church when Colgan went to college. She never spoke a word against it. Maybe she didn't even care. Maybe it's self-centered of me to believe that the reason she never dated was because she wanted more than friendship with her son's best friend's dad. It could be that my feeling that we were all one family was never shared by Angie, and she just went along with everything for P.J.'s sake and because I was her landlord and had more money. I hope that's not the case, but I cannot be certain, because I never seriously discussed it with her.

Once she knew I planned to join the Church, Angie probably saw me as a monk already. Whatever love life either of us had, which almost certainly existed only in our heads, was not a subject to be shared with the other. Maybe it's the fact that I never talked about it before that has me rattling on and on now, when the subject is supposed to be Colgan's second funeral.

You may remember P.J.'s vivid description of the heat the first time we celebrated Colgan's life – something about rats making love in a wool sock. It was almost as hot the second time, even though it was early June rather than late July. The funeral home set up a small tent to provide a little shade over the headstones of myself and Sarah Anne, and the newly dug grave of our son.

I believe that close to four thousand people attended my son's funeral in 1983. We held it in a football stadium, for Pete's sake. I was amazed at the outpouring of love for someone most of the people in our little town knew superficially at best. All of them had heard his name, of course, and many had probably shaken his hand or gotten his autograph at some point. But few really knew Colgan, and I don't think that changed between 1983 and 2011.

In this respect, though, Colgan's second ceremony was the opposite of his first. Other than the priest, Father Sean O'Malley from Holy Spirit in Tuscaloosa, four people were present. Though there may be someone in El Salvador or elsewhere that would contest the point, I believe that they were the four people that knew Colgan best. P.J., of course, knew him as well as one straight male can ever know another. Their early friendship and coterminous upbringing made them closer than many brothers.

The other three attendees were all female. One was P.J.'s wife, Kim. I met her at some point when the boys were in high school. All I remember is a polite, nervous girl who didn't make much of an impression on me. I died before she and P.J. got together as adults and never got a chance to know her. From all appearances, she made P.J. very happy, and she seems to have accepted and befriended Colgan as well. She and P.J. got together right before he began to believe that Colgan might still be alive, and she did everything she could to help find him. After he showed up, she welcomed the new presence into their lives with open arms.

The second female was Colgan's girlfriend, Eliza. Colgan never talked to me much about women, and I freely admit that I would have had very little wisdom to offer him if he had. I also never knew Eliza at all, nor did I know Patrycia or anyone Colgan may have been with in-between. But I could tell that day that Eliza clearly cared deeply about my son, and, that is enough for me to say that I am glad that she was able to be there when he was laid to rest.

The final person in Kellyville that hot June day was one of Kim and Eliza's closest friends, who had become close to P.J. and Colgan through them. Her name was Clytemnestra Howard, and she would eventually become the first African-American Dean of Alabama's law school. At the time though, she taught legal writing and ran part of the admissions office.

It may have little significance in the grand scheme of things, but it pleased my heart that a person of color was within Colgan's inner circle of friends. His life itself had resulted from my participation in the civil rights movement, and I had always tried to impart in him a consciousness of the troubled history of race relations in the society where he grew up—where we had made real progress, and where much, much more still needed to be done. I think he learned from me a desire to help those oppressed, even if he took it in a direction I would never have imagined.

There were no grand speeches at Colgan's second funeral, nor were there any gauche moments that would have made the fine folk of Kellyville want to throw P.J. off a stage. Father Sean simply said a few words about Colgan always sincerely wanting to do what God asked of him, and the four friends, none of whom, it turns out, were practicing Catholics, walked up to the coffin, bowed their heads, and put their hands flat on the lid. After a few silent moments, each stepped back one by one, and then P.J. nodded to the waiting funeral home workers. They stepped from outside the tent and took hold of the casket, slowly lowering it into the earth. The four mourners stood respectfully for a few minutes, then turned, seemingly as one, and slowly walked toward their cars waiting at the edge of the cemetery. The story of Colgan Toomey had reached its end.

About the Author

Dargan M. Ware is a poet and attorney who was an over-the-road truck driver until he decided to go to law school at 35. A friend once described him as a "high-functioning drifter," and he has been unable to come up with a better description. He practices consumer protection law, trying to fight the good fight for regular folks against big corporations. He lives in Birmingham, Alabama with his wife Kristi and their 15-year-old triplets, where he enjoys trivia, cooking, and attempting to get a turn on the computer. Mr. Ware expresses thanks to anyone who reads this book, and encourages you to follow him on Twitter (@manerware), Facebook (the only Dargan Ware in the world as of June 13, 2019), or to visit his website at darganware.com. Peace, Love, and Pandas to all of you!

Made in the USA
Columbia, SC
14 September 2021